No Horse Wanted
Shamrock Stable Series, Book 1

by

Shannon Kennedy

F & I
by Melange Books

Published by
Fire and Ice
A Young Adult Imprint of Melange Books, LLC
White Bear Lake, MN 55110
www.fireandiceya.com

ISBN: 978-1-61235-766-9 Print

Cover Art by Lynsee Lauritsen

Dedication

No Horse Wanted is dedicated to the "real" Twaziem and Lucky Lady. Without them, I couldn't have written this book. These two very special horses have since crossed over the "Rainbow Bridge." I rescued Twaziem the way that Robin does in this story and he was my mother's horse for more than 30 years. I lost Lucky Lady to cancer two years ago, but we still ride together in my dreams.

No Horse Wanted
By Shannon Kennedy

The only thing that Robin Gibson wants for her sixteenth birthday is a 1968 Presidential Blue Mustang. Following their family tradition, what her parents promise her is a horse of her own, one with four legs, not four wheels. Mom competes in endurance riding, Dad does calf roping, her older brother games and her older sister loves three-day eventing, but Robin proudly says that she doesn't do horses. She'll teach her controlling family a lesson by bringing home the worst horse she can find, a starved, abused two-year-old named Twaziem.

Robin figures she'll nurse him back to health, sell him, and have the money for her car. Rescuing and rehabilitating the Morab gelding might be a bigger challenge than what she planned. He comes between her and her family. He upsets her friends when she looks after his needs first. Is he just an investment or is he part of her future? And if she lets him into her heart will she win or will she lose?

Chapter One

Wednesday, September 11th, 2:30 p.m.

One more day, I thought, *one more day!*

Then, I'd be sixteen and nobody could tell me I was a kid. Not my parents or my older brother or my college freshman sister, who all thought it was their life mission to order me around, just because I was the youngest in the family. I'd get my driver's license, go wherever I wanted and no one would call me Princess Robin ever again.

Hello, freedom!

All I needed was a car. The one destined to be mine was a classic! A 1968 Mustang hardtop coupe. No convertible for me, not in Western Washington where it rained more than the sun shone. The brilliant blue paint on my dream car shimmered in the sunlight as I approached the Mustang Corral on the main drag in Podunk, USA—otherwise known as Marysville, Washington.

Why had Brenna moved my car out to the premier spot on State Street? Everybody who came into town could see it there and someone else might buy it before I convinced Dad to sign the papers. Brenna knew I wanted that gorgeous car. I'd told her often enough, and of course, I visited my Mustang every day on the way from school to my father's accounting office. I'd get it for my birthday. I knew it, heart and soul.

I'd talked her down from the list price on the car to fifteen thousand dollars, cash. All I had to do was get my father to agree to pay half, and he was almost there. Okay, so I was his baby and sometimes I played it to get what I really wanted. But, I was a good kid. I might not get the greatest grades in the world and I did bring home every stray animal I found, but I never did drugs, or drank booze or hung out with sleaze-balls. I deserved my Mustang. Once he came up with his share of the bucks, I'd use part of my college fund for my portion.

I'd be driving all over the place. My brother might be happy with the beat-up half-ton Dodge pickup he found on *Craig's List* and my sister might swear there was nothing better than her 1991 four-wheel-drive Jeep. One of my dad's clients saw it parked beside a road up in the boonies with a For Sale sign taped to the cracked windshield. My sister still raved about the great deal she'd made.

They could really be satisfied with other people's cast-offs, but not me. Okay, so my Mustang was more than forty years old and it had been driven by someone else, but it didn't look like a used vehicle. The previous owners treated my car like the treasure it was. I circled around it, admiring the sheen of the Presidential blue color. Freshly washed and waxed, not a glimmer of dust marred the finish. When I got it home, Brenna's brother, Harry, wouldn't be around to keep my car in shape for me. I'd have to do it myself.

No problem. What could be better than washing and waxing my own car? Nothing! Nobody better even think about eating fast food in my car when I got it. That was so not happening!

I headed past the other ten Mustangs, candy-apple reds, canary yellows, a night black convertible, and emerald greens. A real rainbow herd, I thought. Brenna kept the rest of the cars on the sides and toward the back of the lot. I spotted Harry washing the puke green fixer-upper '67 model on the far side of the garage. No matter how hard he tried, that particular rig was destined to be what his older sister called the "loss leader." It needed a new tranny and a rebuild on the engine before anyone could drive it. And who would want to?

Looking at Harry Thornton made my day even better, even if he hadn't seen me yet. Sunshine blond hair curled to broad, tanned shoulders. He'd changed to a T-shirt and shorts to work here, but he still looked majorly hot. Of course, he didn't have a clue. He just thought all the girls wanted to sit at his table because I did.

I wasn't that popular even if I ran track and cross-country. I was blonde, brown-eyed, five-foot-six, and made friends easily. I liked people, well most of them, and they liked to hang out with me. And Harry was always willing to talk to me about cars, especially Mustangs, which had to be the best cars ever made by Ford.

Brenna waved to me from the steps at the front of the office trailer. "Hi, Robin. Come on over."

Shifting my backpack, I went to join her. "Hey, Brenna. What's up with my car?"

She smiled, then ran a hand through her shoulder-length red hair. The blue mechanic's coveralls she wore matched her eyes. "It's not yours until the papers are signed. And like I've told you all summer, your dad needs to do that, since you're not eighteen yet."

"He'll do it," I said. "Tomorrow's my birthday and he knows this car is all I want. I've been telling him that for ages."

Brenna nodded and her smile faded. She actually looked her age, almost thirty. "One of the guys I served with in Afghanistan took it out for a test drive today, Robin. I've been straight up with you. I won't hold a car for someone who can't buy it. This place eats almost as much as Harry does."

I knew she was trying to make a joke, but I could also tell that she was being honest with me. If somebody came in with enough bucks, my car would be gone. "Okay, I'll get my dad in here right away."

She nodded, then headed for the garage to do maintenance on a car she'd just taken in, and I jogged toward the sidewalk. The Mustang Corral wasn't that big as far as lots went. It was sandwiched between a vacuum repair place and a small strip mall. The only business left in the mall was a doughnut shop that was open from before school to midnight. I skipped my usual routine of popping in for a coffee and a maple bar. I had to talk to Dad and he had to get serious about the blue Mustang. Or else!

When I walked into the accounting office twenty minutes later, the secretary told me that my father was finishing up with a client. I had to wait almost an hour for him. Then, he rushed me out the door. He wanted to get to the feed store before it closed because his horse needed

3

some kind of special supplement. Finally, we were on the way home and he was a captive audience. He couldn't get away from me.

"Dad, we have to talk about my birthday."

He glanced sideways at me while he waited for the red light to change at the intersection. "Robbie, we already have it planned. Felicia is coming home from school, and she'll be here tomorrow night to celebrate with us. She's taking Friday off from classes and driving back on Sunday morning."

"Wonderful," I said, hoping he didn't catch the sarcasm. "I can't wait to see her. I'm talking about my big present. I want—"

"I know what you want," Dad said, stepping on the gas. "But it doesn't mean you're going to get it. Presents are supposed to be surprises. You'll have to wait until tomorrow night at dinner to see what you get."

I nearly told him I didn't think waiting was a good idea, not when Brenna had a buyer for my car. However, my cell phone vibrated. When I looked at the screen, it was my best friend and I had to talk to her. Not about the car—she just didn't get why I was so hooked on Mustangs— but about her life, which pretty much sucked all of the time now.

* * * *

Thursday, September 12th, 4:00 p.m.

Leaving the department store sacks unopened and uninvestigated, I closed the door to the closet in my parents' bedroom. Snooping there had been a long shot, but I didn't know where else to look for the papers and keys to my Mustang. I just couldn't find anything to do with the car. Mom and Dad hid the information too well, although the '68 classic hadn't been on the lot when I walked by there today.

So, my car had to be here on the farm. I just hadn't found it yet. And I didn't have a lot of time left to look. Mom had to make a quick grocery store run to get Felicia's favorite junk food and Dad went with her. Hello, it was my birthday. Wasn't I supposed to be the special one today?

I'd searched most of the buildings; anywhere a person could drive a car. The only place left to look was the big barn where my family kept their horses. I figured my older brother Jack would totally freak if the car was in the indoor riding arena, not because the horses might trash it, but because they could spook and get hurt.

Horses were weird at the best of times and Jack fussed over the ones in the barn non-stop. He kept their stalls cleaner than Mom did the house. She often said she wished his obsessive neat and tidy fanaticism would carry over to his bedroom. It hadn't in nearly eighteen years, so I figured she should get over it. I started to leave my parents' room, then remembered that Salt escorted me upstairs.

I glanced around the master bedroom. The eight-week-old, black and white Persian kitten was nowhere in sight. I hurried back to the closet and opened the sliding door. Salt sauntered out and wound through my legs, purring. I scooped him up and closed the closet again, heading downstairs.

The house was hopeless. I'd searched my dad's office, my folks' room, and Mom's sewing room where she made quilts and other handmade crafts to sell. No sign of anything to do with my car. Where could the papers be?

Okay, I'd stop looking for those and go back to hunting for the car. I left Salt on the couch in the living room. He promptly jumped to the back and stalked to the cream drapes that covered the huge picture window. An extra black paw stole around the edge of one drape and batted at Salt. Pepper, the other kitten, was in his favorite hiding place on the windowsill. Leaving the kittens to shadowbox, I hurried out into the golden afternoon.

I was on a mission and I'd find my car, no matter what!

In the barn, I looked down the long row of stalls that bordered the indoor riding arena. The stalls opened onto a wide aisle. Off to my right, a wall separated the stalls from the ring, which was about two hundred feet long and seventy-five feet wide. Sometimes Jack and his buddies practiced football plays inside. There were eight stalls, although we only had three horses right now.

Felicia took her Appaloosa gelding with her to Washington State University in Pullman. She'd fussed more about finding the perfect stable to board him than she did about her stuff for the dorm room. I'd done most of the shopping so the place would be livable, or she'd have a sleeping bag on her bed and her clothes in suitcases since she wouldn't have any hangers for the closet. Of course, as long as her horse was happy, she wouldn't have cared. The whole family loved the indoor arena, except me. I'd voted for a swimming pool—not that anyone listened.

The first box stall held Jack's huge, white Thoroughbred, Nitroglycerin. I shuddered and gave him a wide berth when he pinned his ears and gave me that wicked once-over from pale blue eyes. Jack told me that people used to think blue or glass-eyed horses were blind. I wasn't that dumb. I just knew Nitro was evil. I'd been sure of it even before he ran away with me the last time Mom insisted I come riding with her and Felicia.

Next to Nitro was my mother's purebred Arabian mare. She was tiny in comparison to Nitro, fifteen hands to his eighteen. *Ibn Scheherazade* was a dainty chestnut with a long flaxen mane and tail. She answered to Singer at home because she pranced and danced across the finish line at hard endurance contests, just like Mom's sewing machine stitched material.

Singer's head came up, and she listened intently to the soft thuds overhead in the hayloft. I recognized the thumping of little cat feet. Obviously, the two half-grown kittens, Ginger and Cinnamon, were playing tag again. When I found Salt and Pepper abandoned near the train tracks in Marysville, Mom told me that two kittens in the house were enough and my older cats had to go to the barn because the newest ones needed to be bottle-fed every couple hours. Luckily, it was August so I could get up all night long to do it and not have to worry about school the next day.

Singer snorted and jumped to the back of her stall as the noise continued in the loft. She looked like a horse statue come to life, but she wasn't as smart as Mom claimed. Dad's Quarter horse, Buster, took up the third stall. He searched his manger for any crumbs left from lunch. I always found it hard to believe that this was the same horse that exploded into the arena when it was time to rope a calf since he was such a hog-body at home.

Jack came out of the tack room, all cowboyed up in his jeans, western shirt, and boots. "Thought I heard someone. What's going on,

Robin?"

"Not much," I said, eyeing him. Would he tell me where to find my car?

He grinned at me, a tall, dark-haired, younger version of Dad. "So, are you here to help me with chores, Princess?"

I shrugged. "Sure. Why not? I'll do the cats, the chickens, and the rest. You do the horses."

"All right!" He pumped an arm in the air. "It won't do you any good. I'm still not telling you about your big present."

I'd been charming secrets out of him for years, and he always lost this kind of battle. I just smiled up at him. "Want to bet?"

Chapter Two

Thursday, September 12th, 6:20 p.m.

When we finished chores and climbed the stairs to the inside back porch that my mom called the "mud room," I kicked off my shoes while Jack pulled off his boots. It wasn't worth our teenage lives to track barn muck into the house. I looked through the glass window of the door and saw Felicia setting the kitchen table for dinner. Mom stirred something at the stove.

I could already hear Felicia chattering about some class she was taking and what she'd told her teacher and he'd told her. Like anybody cared, I thought. Of course, I wouldn't say so. My older sister honestly believed we couldn't live without the psycho-babble she loved so much.

As soon as I opened the door, she darted across the room to hug me. *Oh, come on!*

The two of us had a huge fight about her hogging the bathroom and using up my tube of mascara the day she left and now we were supposed to be best buds. *Give me a break!*

"I've missed you guys so much." Felicia whirled away from me and flung herself on Jack. He scooped her up in a big hug.

"How's Vinnie?" Jack demanded. "Does he like the barn? His paddock? Did you find somewhere to buy him organic carrots?"

"I knew it," Felicia crowed. "You miss him more than you do me. You're weird, all right."

"Great diagnosis," I said. "Is that what you're going to tell all your

8

patients when you're a shrink?"

"Only the strange ones," Felicia said, with a toss of her strawberry blonde hair.

"Good to know." I headed for the bathroom to wash up.

Dinner was on the table at six thirty exactly, one of my dad's rules. He freaked when one of my track or cross-country meets ran overtime or started late so we had to eat at a different time. Mom claimed his hang-up about appointments was just a personality flaw and nothing to get in a dither about. Of course, she was the one who said no animals, no TV, no iPods, or cell phones at the table. We had to talk to each other like civilized people, or she'd make us wish we had. I lived with two total control freaks for parents and Felicia and Jack were pretty much the same way.

Mom made all my favorites for supper, spaghetti with meat sauce, Caesar salad, and garlic bread. I didn't have to ask about dessert. She'd have ordered in a cake from the local bakery, chocolate with custard filling, and there'd be chocolate ice cream in the freezer. A pile of brightly wrapped presents covered the top of the breakfast bar.

When I'd looked out in the drive before dinner, I didn't see my car anywhere, but it had to be somewhere. Either that or Mom and Dad arranged for me to go with them to pick it up later. It was all I could do to sit still while Felicia talked about her freshman year at college and Jack shared what happened at football practice that afternoon. Mom told us about a sale at the local crafts store and how she'd loaded up on material for a new quilt. Dad had two new clients, so he was all that, too! Could these people eat any slower?

Finally, they finished and I jumped up to clear away the dishes. Mom put away the leftovers. Jack and Dad arranged my gifts on the table, and Felicia hurried off to her room to bring back a couple more. I had a great family, really I did. And I should be more appreciative of them. My best friend's dad had walked out on her birthday last June— some gift. Mine would never do that, not in a million years.

"Leave the dishes for me, Robbie," Dad said. "Come open your presents."

"You don't have to tell me twice." I hustled to the kitchen table, pausing to hug him on the way. "There's nearly as much stuff here as I get for Christmas. You guys rock!"

Laughing, Mom and Felicia leaned against each other at the far end of the table, looking more like sisters than mother and daughter. They both had bright blue eyes, strawberry-blonde hair and wore the same kind of cowgirl clothes, jeans, western shirts, and Ropers. Little wonder that my sister went off to cow college in Pullman. She'd probably bring home some farmer guy for a new boyfriend.

She'd dumped her last one when he suggested she sell Vinnie to pay tuition. Nobody came between her and that purebred, seventeen-hand, buckskin Appaloosa. She'd gotten him for her sixteenth birthday. Well, actually Mom couldn't find 'the perfect horse' for her. So, Mom cut a picture out of a horse magazine, stuck it on a toothpick, and put it in the middle of Felicia's cake.

The two of them shopped for the next month, visiting horse sales, breeders, and shows, rodeos until they found Vinnie and brought him home. My parents did the same thing when Jack turned sixteen, a picture on a toothpick in the middle of his cake. He and Dad bonded on the quest to find Nitro. Personally, I could think of better places to spend money, like the outlet mall over on the reservation by Marysville.

I reached for the large pink envelope on top of the boxes of presents. This one could be the papers for my car. It had to be. I peeled back the flap. It was the spine of a greeting card. Okay, the card could have the car title inside. But, it didn't.

Hand-painted, the front showed a rainbow group of horses, a buckskin Appy, a solid bay, a snow-white one, and a chestnut dashing across a green field. I recognized all of them, Vinnie, Buster, Nitro, and Singer. Behind them, looking down from the clouds was a shadowy pony, a faded strawberry roan. Tears stung at the memory of my first horse, but I didn't let them fall. "This is amazing, Jack."

"I knew you'd love it." He grinned at me. "I've been working on it for the past month."

"It's definitely a keeper." I'd add it to the bulletin board in my room. Even if I didn't much care for horses, I loved my brother's artwork. Jack's poem inside wished me a happy day and sixteenth year, but it wasn't sappy. And the fifty dollar bill—oh yeah, I could go places with it.

I'm not a real touchy-feely person like Felicia, but I hugged Jack, anyway. "This is the best."

Another grin. "And you're just getting started."

My car, my car, my car!

Where was it? When would I find out about it?

I opened one present after another. Dad gave me raingear. What was he thinking? Even when I ran in the rain, I didn't wear heavy vinyl. I'd die of heat prostration. From Mom, I got a new blue jean jacket, two flannel shirts, and three pairs of jeans. *Come on, give me a break.* Okay, so I lived on a farm. It didn't mean that it was my thing and I'd dress like Ellie Mae off the *Beverly Hillbillies.* Of course, nobody listened when I suggested moving into town, a real one, not Marysville.

Next box. This one was from my mom and my sister. I peeled back the paper and found a carton labeled *Ropers.* No way! They hadn't bought me boots like theirs, had they? Yes, icky big brown lace-up ones. I hoped my disgust didn't show. These looked like I'd be in the Army before I graduated. Well, they were expensive. I'd get the receipt from Mom and return them for something I would actually wear.

Two gifts remained. The first was a package of horse books, and I almost groaned. What would it take to get them off my back? I didn't do horses, and I definitely didn't read about them. However, the entire family was so hooked on them they just couldn't let things go. Last summer, I barely got to hang out with my best friend until she agreed to go to horse camp with me. Vicky loved horses, so she had a blast while it was a real endurance contest for me. Well, I'd pass the books onto her. She'd savor every page.

My parents had a thing about me being home alone when they went to work—talk about control freaks. I'd been fifteen, not a baby. And I'd have been okay by myself for a few hours while Felicia was at the counseling center learning what therapists do and Jack did his lifeguard thing at the pool. Instead, I wound up grooming, saddling and feeding horses, and taking little kids back and forth to the restroom. I told Rocky, the instructor and owner of Shamrock Stables, that she should change the name. It shouldn't be called "Pony Camp," but "Pee-Pee Camp." She laughed her butt off and gave me a coffee card for being a good sport.

With the way I avoided Mom's endurance rides, Dad's calf roping,

Jack's gaming and Felicia's three-day eventing, I'd thought they'd get the message that I wasn't into horses. But, no. One of them was always hassling me. *Come ride with me on the Centennial Trail. Buster needs to muscle up. I made an apple crisp for dessert tonight. Come visit the horses with me while I feed them these apple peels. Vinnie needs braids for this weekend. Come talk to me while I sew his mane.*

Nag, nag, nag. I was so sick of it!

The last gift came from Jack and Dad. I opened it up and stared at the leather bridle and green striped saddle blanket. My stomach knotted. "What is this? A mistake?"

"It's a family tradition," Felicia crowed and ran around to hug me. "I thought you'd figured it out when I came home to go with you and Mom."

"Figured out what?" A sinking dread swept over me. "You guys can't be serious."

"And when you came down to help in the barn tonight," Jack gave me a brotherly shove, "I knew that you'd see the stall I fixed up or the remodeling in the tack room."

I hadn't even bothered to look around the barn this afternoon. Jack was always messing around. Who knew or cared what was going on down there? Well, other than the rest of my family that is!

Sobs clogged my throat as Mom stood and headed for the bakery box on the kitchen counter. "I don't believe you people."

Dad chuckled. "What did you expect, Robin? It's a family tradition. You get to choose a purebred horse for your sixteenth birthday."

"But I don't want a stinky, smelly horse!" I jumped up, letting the bridle and blanket fall to the floor. "Don't you ever listen? I showed you the Mustang again and again. I want a car. My car, so I can go places!"

A tear slipped down my cheek before I could stop it. I swiped it away and ran out the back door. Crying in front of them. No way! Not after this! They'd ruined everything. I grabbed my shoes and raced across the porch. I was so outta there.

My car, my car, my car!

Chapter Three

Thursday, September 12th, 8:00 p.m.

I paused halfway across the lawn to pull on my shoes. Then, I cut across the driveway and ran beside it to the road. Back in middle school when I started cross-country, I'd mapped out a six mile route so I could practice at home. After running it for almost five years, it seemed automatic to take it now. I didn't have to think about where I was going, just head south on Whisky Ridge until I reached the trail through the woods.

Wasn't the fact that not one person in my family understood me bad enough? Did they have to destroy my birthday too? And it wasn't like my birthday was supposed to be unlucky. It wasn't Friday, the 13th. It should have been a good day. I barely complained when they expanded the barn so the horses had more room and added a shower stall so Felicia could bathe Vinnie on a regular basis. Well, not much—I still thought a swimming pool would be more fun.

Tears clogged my throat, and I ran faster. Dust puffed around my shoes from the path. Some green leaves still clung to vine maple branches. I wound through a grove of young alders, passed two cedars and came to the crosswalk on Highway 9. I jogged in place while I waited for the light to change. I was mad, but not stupid enough to dart between cars and semi-trucks that used the old main road between Seattle and the Canadian border.

Maybe I was adopted. That would explain why I didn't look or feel like anyone in my family. Where had all these horse-nuts come from? Why couldn't I have normal relatives? Mine would probably sell me before they parted with one of those four-legged wonders down in the stable. Green light and I was across the highway, heading for the Centennial Trail where I did most of my running. I always ran the dirt track, which meant I had to watch out for horse poop, but it was easier than avoiding the bike riders and dog walkers.

When I got home a little over an hour later, Mom and Dad waited in the kitchen, sitting at the table. Felicia and Jack were nowhere in sight. I grabbed a bottle of water from the fridge and chugged half of it.

"Robbie, we need to talk," Dad said.

"Why?" I knew I sounded like a snarky teenager, but I didn't care. "You never listen to me. What's the point?"

Mom heaved a dramatic sigh. "I thought you'd be over your snit when you got back. Come sit down and we'll tell you what we've planned."

"How joyful." That got me a stern look from her. I stomped over to join them, slumping into a chair. "What?"

Another of Mom's fierce blue-eyed glares before she planted her elbows on the table and gave me a steely once-over. "Your dad and I talked. He should have told you flat-out that the Mustang wasn't an option. You can't have a car until your eighteenth birthday, and the way it works in this family is you pay half of the cost."

I took a deep breath. "I told Dad I could do that. I'll borrow it from my college fund."

He immediately shook his head. "No, Robbie. It costs a small fortune for college, and we don't touch that money except for life and death. Believe me, a classic car doesn't count."

"It does to me." I rolled the water bottle in my hands. "It's the most beautiful thing I've ever seen, and I want it."

"Then, get a job and start saving up," Mom said. "We're not saying you can't have it, Roberta Lynn. We're saying that you have to do what your brother and sister did. You have to earn the money for the car to prove you're responsible enough to have it."

"But, mine will be gone. Brenna won't keep it two years for me."

"Then it isn't meant to be," Mom said. "There are other Mustangs."

14

"What?" I almost felt my jaw hit the table. "I don't want a different one. I want this one. Come look at it again. You'll see how gorgeous it is."

Mom rolled her eyes and shook her head. "The answer is no, Roberta. You are not getting a car. This weekend, you and Felicia and I are going out shopping. We're finding you a horse."

"I hate horses. They're big, ugly and they stink, and they're way too much work."

Dad got up. He came around the table and put a hand on my shoulder. "Now, Robbie, you know you don't mean that. It's not as if you really hate horses. You used to ride Cobbie all over the place, and you took care of him yourself."

I jerked away. "Cobbie wasn't a horse. He was part Welsh Cob and part Welsh pony. He is dead. He's been dead since I was twelve. And going out to find another stinky, smelly horse won't bring Cobbie back. He'll still be dead."

"And we'll all still miss him," Mom said softly. "He was my first horse, Roberta. I loved him, too. Just because I have Singer now, doesn't mean I love Cobbie any less. We choose to love creatures that have shorter life spans than we do, and we grieve them when they're gone."

"Not me." I leaped to my feet, knocking the chair over again. "I won't love another horse. Not ever. You can't make me."

I bolted from the kitchen and ran upstairs. I slammed into my room. They'd wrecked my birthday, and I wasn't letting them get away with it. Mom might force me to go with them on Saturday, but I wouldn't let her get me a horse. I wouldn't. I wouldn't. I wouldn't!

* * * *

Friday, September 13th, 7:15 a.m.

I sat in the school cafeteria waiting for Vicky, stirring my mocha with the straw. On the way to Marysville, Dad had tried talking to me about the stupid horse again, but I pretty much ignored him until he bought me a coffee at the espresso stand. Then, it was Jack's turn. I tuned him out and texted my best friend, begging her to meet me. I didn't know if she'd make it or not. Like she said, since her parents' divorce,

15

her mom got the house and a new job. Her dad got the new car and a girlfriend. And Vick got to take care of her two younger brothers and three younger sisters.

Ten minutes before the bell rang, she hustled across the Commons to join me. "Okay, I'm here. What's the disaster?"

"I didn't get my car," I said.

She plunked her backpack on the extra chair and sat down next to me. "Did you really think your folks would cough up fifteen thousand dollars for a Mustang? That's major bucks."

"They're buying me a horse instead—a four-legged hay-burner."

"A horse? A real horse?" Vicky squealed and jumped up to hug me. "You are so lucky. I'd die for a horse. I'd kill for one. When can I come see it? What are you going to call it? Can I ride it?"

"You can have it," I snapped. "You can freaking move in with my family and have it!"

"Oh, get over yourself," Vicky retorted. "You're the lucky one, Rob, even if you won't admit it. You could be sharing a room with my sister, babysitting all the time and changing diapers when you're trying to do algebra. There'd be no cell phone or your own TV or clothes from the mall whenever you want. I wish my biggest problem was getting a horse for my birthday instead of my parents' divorce."

The bell rang before I had to say that she was right. I did have things better than she did, but I still didn't want a horse. I wanted my car, my amazing Presidential blue '68 Mustang with its automatic transmission.

"So, what are you going to do?" Vicky asked, walking beside me toward Homeroom English. "When does your horse arrive?"

"I have to go shopping with my mom and Felicia on Saturday," I said. "And if they actually make me get a horse, I'm bringing home the worst one I find."

* * * *

Saturday, September 14th, 2:45 p.m.

We spent the day touring stables and checking out the horses they had for sale. This plan had obviously been in the works for a while. Jack had hitched up the horse trailer to his pickup so we could bring home the horse when we found it. Mom and Felicia had chosen six horses for me to look at. If Shamrock Stable, the place where I did day camp during the summer, had been on the list, it might have been different, but my family obviously hadn't considered the beginning level, safe horses suitable.

Two of the horses they chose had already been sold. Hurrah. The other four were experienced gaming mounts, so not my thing. I watched the owner gallop a paint around the barrels and shook my head. "No way."

"Don't you want to try him?" Felicia asked. "Jack said that he's a sweetheart."

"He's too fast," I said. "I don't ride fast horses anymore, and you two can't make me."

Mom frowned at me. "If you just developed some confidence, you could be a very good rider, Robin. You have a good seat and good hands. There is no reason for you to refuse to ride when you're obviously very talented. That would be like Felicia refusing to play the piano or your brother throwing away his paints because his work hasn't been in a gallery."

"I don't want a horse, and I'm not getting on one ever again."

That got me twin glares, but luckily we were soon in the truck and headed off to a nearby café for a late lunch. Felicia pulled out her cell phone. I thought she was texting a friend, but it turned out she was checking the classified ads in the local paper. "Hey, Mom. I think I found one."

"Really? Let me see." Mom drew into a parking lot and reached for the phone. "This does sound interesting. It's a trained, registered Morab gelding. Why do they only want $100.00?"

"I'll call and find out," Felicia said.

"Don't," I said. "Let's quit wasting time on this. That price is definitely a mistake."

The two of them ignored me. What else was new?

Mom called the number and talked to somebody. In minutes, we were on the way north to Arlington. I stared out the truck window at the evergreens and alders that marched alongside the highway. Sunshine danced off the glass.

"There it is." Felicia pointed to the next side street.

Mom slowed down for the turn. She went to the third driveway on the left, parking next to another truck, between the house and a large row of kennels.

I looked around. I didn't see a barn or even a shed. "Where is this cheap horse?"

"I don't know," Mom said. "We'll have to ask the owner. She told me someone else was coming to look at it."

"Good. Maybe they'll buy it." I saw a shape in the dusty corral behind the house. Was that a horse? I opened the passenger door of the pickup and slid out. Felicia followed me. I headed for the corral and stopped when I heard a growl. Did they have a dog? I didn't see one. When I scanned the caged runs, I spotted a giant cat. "What is that?"

"A cougar," Felicia said.

We shared a look. What kind of nutcase would have a wild animal like that?

"Lovely," Mom said. "It's lucky we left Jack home. He'd want us to take it, too." Sighing, she shook her head. "I'll go find the owner."

"Okay," I said. "We'll hunt for the horse."

Mom walked away, and we headed off to the corral. My breath caught. Felicia grabbed my arm, nails digging into my skin.

I just stared at the skeleton pretending to be a horse. Red brown hide stretched over the bones, and I counted every rib. He was male, but I didn't know if he was a stud or gelding. I hadn't gotten close enough to see. Hips protruded, sunken sides, and he was absolutely filthy. Dirt covered his legs, up past his knees and hocks. Chunks of hair had fallen out of his mane. Maybe he'd rubbed them out. Half his tail was missing too. When he shifted, I saw yellow patches on his neck, side and one on his rump. So, he must have some paint blood too. Why else would he be a pinto?

"Let's go, Robin." Felicia pulled on my arm. "It's hopeless. He's hopeless."

I almost went with her. Then, the horse lifted his head and looked at me. And I stopped. "No. He's the one."

"What?" Felicia hissed. "I don't believe you."

"Well, you should," I said. "He's the worst horse I've ever seen, and I'm taking him home."

Chapter Four

Felicia gave me one of her older sister dirty looks that she'd practiced over the years. It meant I was being a spoiled brat, but I didn't care. I kept most of my attention on the horse. He flicked his ears and cocked his head my way, flashing a white blaze, but his big brown eyes nailed me. And there was no way I'd leave him here to die of starvation. I turned and scuffed through the dust to the back porch. I carefully climbed the rickety steps and knocked on the door.

I'd concentrate on making him look good, like a horse again, not a skeleton. Later, I'd find him a good home and sell him. And nobody said I actually had to ride him in the meantime. He could just hang out in the barn with the rest of the hay-burners. Once I sold him, I would put the money toward my car. *My car, my car, my beautiful car*—well, if I got Brenna a down-payment, she'd save it for me. I knew she would. In this down economy, she'd take installments if that was the best I could do.

I pushed open the back door and saw my mother sitting at a kitchen table talking to a scrawny, older woman wearing the worst wig I'd ever seen. "Mom, I've found him. I found my horse."

"He's not yours yet," Mom said. "Mrs. Bartlett tells me there's another buyer coming to see him."

"Who else would want him, but me?" I asked. "He's a wreck. Of course, once he's all the way dead, a vet student might take him to study the bones."

"Roberta Lynn, that's enough. Stop being rude. You have better manners. Use them."

I folded my arms and waited. The door opened behind me, and I saw Felicia standing there. "What?"

"A old fat guy just got here with the worst trailer in creation. And he's feeding your want-a-be horse grain. It's gross."

"What's gross about it?" I asked. "At least someone cares enough to feed him."

"He's scarfing it so fast he almost chokes on each mouthful. Every time he spills some on the ground, he eats the dirt and the grain. He's going to colic."

"I don't suppose anyone cares if he dies of that either." I brushed past my sister and returned to the corral. Sure enough, she was right. A guy older than my dad stood with a bucket of feed. "What are you doing?" I asked. "He's not yours yet."

"He will be."

I nodded. "Well, you're feeding him. That's something. He won't be hungry or abused."

"Nope. My partner and I will put some weight on him and run him up to Stanwood. They'll ship him to the slaughter house in Canada."

"You can't!" I watched the horse nudge the guy for more feed like the two of them were best buddies. "He likes you. Come on. All he needs is a stall and regular meals for a while."

"And six months to a year's rest before he could be trained or ridden." The man shook his head. "Nope, he's history even if he's too dumb to know it."

"Then, why waste grain on him?" Mom asked, as she joined us, Mrs. Bartlett limping along behind. "Or are you just trying to win his confidence to make him easy to load?"

That earned a snort of laughter. "Lady, this grain is heavily salted. In a couple hours, he'll be ready to tank up on water. By the time I run him to Stanwood next week, he'll be more than a hundred pounds heavier."

"And since they'll pay by the pound for him, you'll make more money." Mom put an arm around my shoulders. "Sometimes you need to know when to walk away, Robin. This could be one of those times."

"Or not." Felicia walked over to the fence and pushed down the bottom strand of barbed wire with her boot. She lifted the second line and climbed into the pasture. Murmuring reassurances, she walked up next to the horse. "I want to see his teeth."

"I've looked at his papers," Mom said. "He is barely two and a purebred Morab. Half Morgan and half Arabian."

"And nobody's ever faked registration documents," Felicia said.

She sounded almost as snarky as I did when people irritated me. I saw Mom roll her eyes. Okay, so we were all channeling teenagers. What was it about this situation that brought out the immaturity in each of us?

Mrs. Bartlett leaned heavily on her cane. "Two people want Twaziem. That's amazing since I only put the ad in the paper for one day. Mr. Johnson, you've shared your plans for the colt. Young lady, what are yours?"

Her tone reminded me of my track coach's when my times sucked and I needed more practice to be considered for state competition. I straightened up to my full five-feet-six. "I'll put him in a stall, feed him up, and do everything our vet says he needs to look like a horse again. Once he's ready for training, I'll turn him over to Rocky at Shamrock Stables and she'll break him to ride."

Utter silence, which always made me nervous, so I added, "I don't know why they call it 'breaking' because I've never seen Rocky do anything mean to a horse or pony."

The comment led to a lecture from Felicia about the history of horse training, like anyone really cared. Blah, blah, blah. I could turn her on, and since she knew everything about everything, she never shut up. While she blathered, she looked in Twaziem's mouth, then felt around with her fingers.

"What are you doing now?" I cut her off mid-sentence. "He has teeth or he wouldn't be able to chew the horse-killer's grain."

Dirty looks all around. *Hey, I calls it as I sees it.* Most people figured I was charming because I was blonde. A girl has to use what she's got.

New lecture from Felicia. This one was about how horses had two sets of teeth in their lifetimes and how the permanent set came into the mouth in a certain order. Twaziem would get so many as a two-year-old, more as a four-year-old, some kind of hook when he turned five and he'd really groove at seven. Yeah, yeah, yeah. So, what? Who really cared?

I turned to Mrs. Bartlett. "So, who gets him? Me or the guy who thinks *The Godfather* was a great movie?"

She eyed me, then looked at Mom. "Do you really want him?"

"I'll be honest with you," Mom said. "I prefer horses to the teen boys who chase my daughters and most of the girls who constantly call and text my son. This is the first horse we've seen all day that Robin has wanted. She's got a mean mouth and a crappy attitude, but she's the best person I've ever seen with a sick or needy critter."

"She brings home every stray in the world, and then she visits them when she finds places for them to live. None of them ever go to the pound or shelters." Felicia picked up Twaziem's left front foot, inspecting the hoof. "I was really surprised she hadn't found any more puppies or abandoned dogs when I got home from college."

"I probably will before too much longer," I said. "What are you looking for now?"

"Stone bruises, abscesses and chipped or cracked hooves." When she finished with the hooves, Felicia moved onto the horse's legs. He continued to ignore her, hassling the old guy for more grain. "Well, he doesn't have splints."

I dreaded the next lecture, but I really wanted to know. "What are those?"

Mr. Johnson answered before Felicia could. "They're bruises or swellings that become permanent growths on the cannon bones. And they'll limit what he can do."

My sister nodded agreement, but before she could add to what he said, Mr. Johnson hurried on, "I sympathize with your desire to save this horse, but it's not very economical."

"My husband's an accountant," Mom said. "He'd probably agree with you about the cost of saving him."

Felicia and I shared a look. Was she talking about our father—the guy who always quoted Sir Winston Churchill at us? "The outside of a horse is good for the inside of a man…" Before either of us could say anything or argue with her, Mom gave us the evil eye and we shut down.

She turned on Mrs. Bartlett. "I'm sure you'll agree that the horse hasn't done anything to deserve death, and if he did, he'd have a more humane end if you just turned him in with your cougar."

I almost cheered, but I didn't. *Go, Mom!*

"You have a point." Mrs. Bartlett glanced past us to Mr. Johnson. "I appreciate you coming out, but Twaziem should have a chance for a happy life. And Robin will give him one."

"Got that right," I said. "Nobody will ever hurt him again. I swear it."

Chapter Five

Saturday, September 14th, 5:05 p.m.

Mom went off with Mrs. Bartlett to sort out the registration papers. Mr. Johnson handed me the can of grain. "You got yourself a horse, missy. Take good care of him. Don't water him for at least two hours."

That was a weird thing to say. I watched him leave, and then turned back to Twaziem. "What do you think?" I asked Felicia. "Should I give him the rest of this?"

"Sure. It can't hurt him, and he's already had enough that he has to stay away from water anyway."

"I don't get it. Why?"

"Colic, Robin. If he waters up, it'll flush the grain into his gut and cause an impaction. So, we'll feed him when we get him home, but we'll wait to fill his tub." She headed off to the truck and came back with the halter and lead I'd gotten for my birthday. "Okay, he's all yours. Get him ready to go."

She held the barbed wire strands apart so I could climb through them. I walked up next to Twaziem and slid the noseband of the halter over his face, buckling the headstall behind his ears. The whiskers on his nose tickled my hand when I offered more grain. He didn't care who fed him. He kept nuzzling me. Now, I was his best buddy.

Felicia walked away to meet Mom, and while she was gone, I told Twaziem about not particularly liking horses or really wanting one. "I want my car. Well, it's not mine yet, but it will be. I just have to start earning money for it. No offense, Twaz, but I stopped loving horses when Cobbie died. Even if I don't love you, I'll never let somebody kill you or starve you or abuse you. Deal?"

He nosed me for more food, and I figured we understood each other. I scooped out more grain. He wouldn't ask me for a lot of emotional stuff, and I wouldn't let anyone hurt him. He'd been hurt enough. He nickered softly and nudged my arm. I gave him the last of the grain from the coffee can and began talking about the Thunder Kittens, who lived in the hayloft and stomped around on the ceiling above the stalls.

"You just have to remember that to them it is the floor. They like to make noise. If you ignore them, you'll be fine. They love to annoy Singer because she always has conniptions." He didn't care about kittens or my talking. He pushed at me with his head. "There's no more grain, but we have a lot of hay in the trailer. Come on. Let's go find that instead." I led him over to the gate, unlatched it, and gave it a push away from me. The bottom hinge let go and the thing fell partway on the ground. Twaziem looked at it like the gate was some kind of performing clown. He snorted, but he didn't spook. He just stepped around it and followed me to the back of the horse trailer.

Loosening the rope so he could graze beside the driveway, I unlatched the door and opened it. I stepped up into the two-horse trailer and gave him a little tug. "Hey, you. Step up here." He did. He balked at the opening, but I pretended not to notice. I could reach the hay in the net and grabbed a handful. I held out the alfalfa to him. "Want it? Come here and get it."

He stretched out his neck and tried to reach the hay in my hand. When he couldn't quite get it, he hesitated. Slowly, he lifted one foot and cautiously placed his left front hoof up inside, on the trailer floor. He tried again. The hay was still too far out of his reach. He picked up his right front, put it beside his left. Okay, so now he was halfway in the rig. I held out the hay, and he got a taste. He wanted more and I wanted him to come the rest of the way so I backed up. With a sudden scramble of his hindquarters, he followed. I gave him the handful of hay. Crunch, munch, and it was gone. Then, he found the hay net and the rest was history. He started pulling out a mouthful and chewing. If a horse could look blissful, he did. I praised him, ducked under his neck, and tied him securely to the ring on the wall. He not only had the net of alfalfa grass hay, the manger was full too.

How far had Jack thought we'd have to go to find a horse? Canada? Petting Twaziem's neck one more time, I eased past him to the back door of the trailer. Mom waited for me, Felicia beside her with a file folder of papers. "What do you have?" I asked.

"A bill of sale," Felicia said. "I made sure that his poor condition was detailed. We don't want a hassle from the Animal Control people. And his papers are in order. You just have to send them to the registry to transfer him to your ownership. His registered name is actually *Twa Ziemlich Sonne*, which is a bit strange. *Twa* means 'two' in old Scots and *Zeimlich Sonne* is 'pretty sun' in German, but normally you'd say…"

I tuned her out again and locked the trailer door. Hmm. I wanted to make money, but I didn't have to buy a lottery ticket. I could just sign her up for *Jeopardy*. She'd win thousands. Would she give me enough for my car? While she blathered about Twaz's name, I eyed Mom.

"Can we go now? Or do we have to stay forever? And do we have to take her? Maybe, they could feed her to the cougar."

"I don't think so." Mom patted my shoulder. "And I'm proud of her. When she and Mrs. Bartlett got to talking about cancer, Felicia provided some very good resources."

"Who has cancer?" I blinked and looked back at the trailer. I could hear Twaziem chewing away. "Is that why he didn't get fed? Was she in the hospital? Now, I feel really bad for getting on her case."

"That's kind of you," Mom said, "but she could have had someone check up on her grandkids and make sure they were feeding the horse."

"Well, who fed the cougar?" I asked. "And why?"

"He hasn't been here that long," Felicia said. "The animal rescue people brought him when he was injured in the woods. They fed the horse when they came to take care of the cat. It's the only reason Twaziem made it. And can you imagine what would have happened if they hadn't fed the cougar, and he got loose? He'd have gone hunting, and it might not have been your colt that wound up as dinner."

Those were all good points, but I didn't tell Ms. Knows-Everything. Her head was big enough. She didn't need me saying she was smart. She already knew it. In our family, Felicia was the brilliant one, Jack was the brave one, and I was the beautiful one. We all had our roles to play, and they didn't change.

We climbed in the pickup, and Mom started the engine. "I think we found the perfect horse for you to ride, Robin."

"Not until he turns three," Felicia said. "That's next April, a little more than seven months from now."

"Works for me. He has to be old enough and strong enough," I told them. And a lot could happen in that amount of time. By then, I'd convince my parents he was ready to move onto a new home. I'd get him the best one I could find. Maybe Rocky would help with that. She always had people looking for safe, sane mounts for her beginning riders and Twaziem might turn out to be perfect for them. All anyone had to do was feed him and he obviously thought the person was a friend.

It took over an hour for us to get home because of the traffic. Mom always drove carefully, and when she hauled a horse, she took more precautions. She signaled for turns early, slowed down before she braked, stayed five miles under the limit and pretty much ticked off every speed demon in forty miles. It didn't bug me as much as usual, not with Twaziem on board.

We pulled into our drive, and she tapped the horn. "Now your brother and dad will know we're home."

Suddenly, I was nervous. What if Jack made fun of my horse? Twaziem looked awful. And Dad? Would he be disappointed in me? He never complained when I brought home stray cats or their kittens or dogs and puppies. A starving horse was different. He was going to eat more than the other horses, and he'd need a lot more care.

Mom gave me a quick sideways glance before she focused on maneuvering up the driveway, past the house to the barn. "It'll be fine, honey. We know how you are when it comes to animals."

"You always pick the ones who need you most," Felicia said. "It's heroic even if you are obnoxious about it."

"So, sue me." I tossed my head. "They pick me too."

Mom laughed. "Either way, the result is the same. I always have a houseful of your critters. Bottom line, we're all human, Robin, and you could learn to be patient with the rest of us when we don't live up to your expectations."

"What's that mean?" I stared past Felicia at my mother. "What are you getting at?"

"I'm proud of you." Mom stopped in front of the barn. "It took a great deal of courage for you to stand up to your sister, me, and two other adults. You insisted we do what was right, not what was easy. Good job."

I felt warm all over. Mom rarely praised me, or anything I did. As the baby of the family, I came in third-best most of the time. No way I'd tell her that she'd made me feel good for once. Instead, I pushed open my door and slid out of the truck. I hurried around to the back of the trailer and opened the back end. Twaziem cocked his head around and looked at me, but kept eating. Despite the long driving time, he had plenty of hay left.

"Are you getting him out?" Felicia asked.

"I think he wants to finish the hay first," I said.

"He can finish it in the stall. I'll bring it in for him," Felicia told me. "Mom went to get Jack to put a bale of grass hay in the manger."

"You mean a couple of flakes, not a bale."

"No, she meant a bale, all right. She's not going to have him open it, but if Jack stands it on end, your horse can pull it apart and eat twenty-four seven."

"Where did she come up with that? It's a brilliant idea."

"Rocky suggested it when I called her from Mrs. Bartlett's."

"Why did you get to call her?" I glared at my sister. "I wanted to tell her about Twaz."

"You still can," Felicia said. "I wanted to settle Mrs. Bartlett's concerns about the training. She needed to be sure that Rocky understood Twaziem was a good horse so she wouldn't use whips or spurs on him."

"Is she going to be okay?" I asked, referring to Twaz's previous owner, not the stable owner.

"Well, she's in remission, but there aren't any guarantees. I got her email address so you can keep her posted on how Twaziem does. I think she'll do better now that she doesn't have to worry about him."

I eyed my sister. In jeans, a WSU sweatshirt and her never-removed Ropers, she didn't look much like an angel, but she was really kind to people, even the ones I thought were totally stupid. "Thanks, Felicia. I'll send her pictures every week. I'm glad you're on my side."

"Hey, I'm your big sister." She beamed a sunshine grin. "That's what I do."

Chapter Six

Saturday, September 14th, 6:45 p.m.

I eased my way into the trailer next to Twaziem's left side. There was a lot more room beside him than there was by the other horses that belonged to my family. When I reached the front, I untied the rope and tried to back Twaz out, but he didn't budge. He pinned his ears flat against his head and stomped one foot, then kept eating, pulling hay from the manger. I reached around and pushed on his chest. He ignored me.

"Come on, Twaziem. Mom promised a whole bale of hay in your stall."

He still wouldn't move. I pulled on the rope, but he pulled back, and he was a lot bigger than me. When I pushed on his chest again, he simply leaned further toward the hay and continued chewing.

Finally, I gave up. I petted him to show there weren't any hard feelings. If he didn't want to leave the food, it was okay. Sooner or later, he'd figure out that regular meals were part of his life now and starvation was over. I put the rope over his neck. Squishing past him, I went back out of the trailer.

Jack and one of his good buddies, Bill, had joined Mom and Felicia.

"So, where's your new steed?" Bill demanded. He was as tall as my brother, but he had auburn hair and eyes. "We loaded up his stall for him."

"He wants to finish the hay in the trailer," I said. "Then, he'll come out."

Jack laughed. "Robin, you've got to start out the way you mean to go on. You can't let your horse be the boss."

"Why not? Nitro is. You always say that he does all the work when you win at a gaming event and it's your fault when you lose. Twaziem will come out when he's ready."

"Did he tell you that?" Bill asked.

Ever since I was little, Bill liked to pick on me. I always wondered why he and Jack were friends when Bill was such a jerk and my brother wasn't.

"He didn't have to tell me," I said. "I could see that he's hungry. You'd need a big sign with pictures."

Jack laughed even harder and punched Bill in the arm. "She's got your number."

"Not yet." Bill rubbed his arm. "Do you want me to unload him for you?"

Mom and Felicia looked at each other. Then, Mom said, "I will. I think you guys are too rowdy for him." She stepped into the trailer, talking in a low voice so the horse wouldn't be frightened.

"I don't remember seeing a horse named Twaziem," Jack said. "What does he look like?"

"He's a bay paint with a blaze and three white ankle socks," Felicia said. "I found an ad for him in the paper since Robin didn't care for any of the ones that you and Mom selected."

"What was wrong with the ones I liked?" Jack asked me.

"They all went too fast," I said, "and nobody makes me ride a horse without brakes. Not anymore." I saw my dad and Vicky coming from the house and went to meet them. "I did get a horse."

Dad smiled at me. "Is it what you wanted?"

"Is it better than the car?" Vicky asked.

I took the questions in order. "I didn't particularly want *him*, but he was being starved, and then a guy showed up who planned to take him to slaughter so I had to bring Twaziem home. A horse is alive. It has feelings, and Twaz didn't want to be dog food. To be honest, I'd still rather have my car. It'd be a lot more fun."

"I'm sure it would." Dad put his arm around my shoulders and gave me a quick hug. "Remember, it's like what Sir Winston Churchill said,

'We make a living by what we get, but we make a life by what we give.' And I'm proud of you for giving this horse a home. You don't have to worry about a car being butchered. Are you glad or sorry you saved him?"

"Glad, I guess. He needed me. I was the only one who really cared about him."

"You're the one who cared enough to save him," Dad said, and hugged me again. "Let's go see this wonder horse."

I nodded, grateful that he hadn't said a word about what it would cost to bring a horse back from the brink of starvation. I smiled at Vicky. "Wait till you see him. I think he has a lot of potential."

Vicky pushed a strand of walnut-brown hair from her face. "I can't believe you actually went through with it and got a horse after everything you said."

I stopped to think. She was right. I'd complained a lot about getting a horse instead of my beautiful car. Things had looked different when I watched Twaziem eat grain and dirt, then beg a guy who wanted to kill him for more food. "I did gripe a lot, but I was really mad."

"You sure were," Vicky agreed.

I contemplated telling her to shut up, but it wouldn't do any good. Vicky would keep talking until she wore out the topic. We arrived at the trailer, and she paused for breath. I counted my blessings. Mom had obviously succeeded in taking Twaziem away from the hay. He'd backed partway out of the trailer. His left hind foot hit the ground, then the right. Another step and he was half outside and half inside.

Jack stood rock still. Fury filled his face, and I saw his jaw clench when he spotted Twaziem's prominent hipbones. "You've got to be kidding me. Who did this? Why?"

I walked up beside Twaziem, and Mom passed me the rope from inside the trailer. I encouraged him to back a couple more steps until he was totally out of the trailer. "It wasn't his owner's fault. She was in the hospital for cancer treatments and her grandkids stopped feeding him."

"He's a walking skeleton," Bill said. "Didn't the cops do anything?"

"I did something." I petted Twaziem's neck, calming him when he stamped a hoof. "I brought him home. Now, quit acting macho. He doesn't like it."

No Horse Wanted

"I know you said you were getting the worst horse you could find, Robin, but this one is beyond it," Vicky told me. "He's awful."

A dreadful silence descended on everyone after Vicky's comment, and I wished the ground would open up and swallow me, and Twaz. Of course, it didn't. I'd have to save both of us. Why, oh, why, did Vicky choose now to repeat my childish promise? I glanced at Felicia. If she'd ratted me out, I'd have expected it. We'd sniped at each other a lot over the years, but we were sisters and we fought. Vicky was my best friend. She was supposed to stick up for me.

For once, my parents had been proud of me. For once, I hadn't been a washed out copy of Felicia or less than perfect Jack. For once, I'd been part of the family, not an outsider! I knew it wouldn't last. It never did, but I could hope, couldn't I?

"I said it," I admitted, "but I was really ticked off when I didn't get my car and…"

Support came from a surprising corner. Mom sighed as she stepped out of the trailer, shaking her head. "And here I figured Felicia and I were the only ones who vented first and thought later. We'll have to be a lot more careful, Robin. It's amazing how 'boot in mouth' comes back to haunt a person."

"And Grandma always says to keep 'your words short and sweet, since you never know which ones you have to eat.' Smart advice, huh?" Jack was next to Vicky, holding her hand, like she needed his support too.

I forced myself to look past them to Felicia and my dad. She winked at me and he grinned. Tears stung my eyes. The last thing I'd expected was for them to understand why I'd been so mean about my birthday and the present they wanted to give me, the traditional present that Felicia and Jack got when they turned sixteen.

Slowly, I realized the truth. My family was sticking up for me because Vicky and Bill were here. Nobody mentioned Jack's art or poetry when the football guys were around. We didn't talk about Felicia's love for classical music when her rock band wanted to practice in the garage. Of course, they all were mad at me. They just wouldn't tell me how disappointed and angry they were when we had an audience.

I struggled to swallow the lump in my throat, unable to speak.

Shannon Kennedy

Jack let go of Vicky and came up close to my horse, shaking his head. "A lousy bay and he's not setting one hoof in my barn."

"Don't be mean about Twaz," I said. "And if I can put up with Nitro, you can deal with me having a horse."

"I said 'lousy' and I meant it." Jack pointed to Twaziem's right side. "Watch that patch. It's moving. I wouldn't be surprised if he's not a paint. It's not a usual coloration for Morabs. Breeders try real hard for it."

I stepped around to the other side and looked at the spot, a huge yellow stain on Twaziem's barrel. It moved. The whole thing crawled toward his neck and face. And I'd been petting him. My stomach lurched. "Oh, my Gawd!"

"Gross," Bill said, but he sounded awestruck and horrified at the same time. "I so have to video this and put it online. Let me get my phone."

"Don't even think about it," Mom told him. "I'm not having Animal Control out here beating on the door when your video goes viral."

"I can't believe I didn't see that," Felicia said, moving closer to inspect Twaz. "I assumed he was a paint and needed a good grooming or a bath for his patches to be white and the proper color."

"Maybe you should send him to be dog food," Vicky said. "It's not that far to Stanwood, only twenty some miles."

"We're not going there and neither is he," Jack said. "The cows, pigs, and chickens get lice, and we treat for them twice a year. It's a normal part of farm life. We'll just dust him before he goes into the barn."

"Makes sense." Dad came and took the lead from me, ignoring Twaziem's snort, and issuing orders. "Jack, get the powder out of the vet cabinet. Robin, you ladies are headed for the showers. I'll send the halter to be disinfected as soon as we take it off him. Bill, pull the truck around to the other side of the house and start fumigating the trailer."

"Come on, girls," Mom said. "We'll leave the messy business to the menfolk. I'm so up for that."

"I really don't see the necessity." Felicia took on her know-it-all persona, with its irritating, authoritative tone. "Horses normally have a 101.5 degree temperature and healthy humans are at 98.7 degrees, so the

34

likelihood that Twaziem's lice migrated to us is extremely rare—"

"Except that he's debilitated," Dad said. "I'm not taking his temperature now. I'm just treating the symptoms, and you don't want me throwing you into the utility shower, clothes, and all, Felicia Joyce. Move it. And wash your hair too!"

Vicky wrinkled her nose in disgust. "I'll help with the horse trailer. I'm not hanging out while you shower, Robin."

"You don't have to help," I said. "You can watch TV in my room if you want or use my computer to cruise the Internet."

"Later," Vicky told me with a toss of her hair. "It may be yucky around here, but it's a lot better than my sister's diapers. Hey, can we order in pizzas?"

I had to laugh. Only my best friend could jump from lice to junk food in less than a heartbeat. "Sure. You're the greatest, Vick."

I got a funny look from her and another from my sister who waited to walk with me toward the house. "What?"

"She's acting like such a twit," Felicia whispered. "And you're actually being pretty nice to her. What's up?"

"Same old, same old," I said, with a shrug. "Vicky's still picking up all the slack around the house since her parents' divorce. And this is the only place where she's allowed to be a kid and complain. But, if she stays on my case, I will nail her. You don't get to. She's been my best friend forever."

Chapter Seven

Saturday, September 14th, 10:15 p.m.

Showers, doctoring Twaziem and moving him into his stall, then pizzas, sodas, a horror movie—it'd been a good night. I just wanted to check on Twaz one last time before I climbed into my jammies. Then Vicky and I would go watch TV in my room and talk. Okay, I'd tell her all about Harry, and she'd tell me how wonderful my older brother was, but at least we were finally having some real best buddy time. Whenever I called, I had to wait for her to deal with one of her sibs, and that wasn't much fun.

I hurried into the barn, ignoring the thunder of the kittens playing overhead and went straight to Twaziem's stall. Instead of peacefully eating, he was down on his side. For a moment, I thought he wanted to sleep. Then, he tried to roll over.

No, no, no! I grabbed the extra halter Dad hung on the peg in the aisle way and unlatched the door. I skirted the flailing hooves. Once I got to his head, I put on the halter. "No, Twaziem. You need that powder to kill the lice. You can't rub off the medicine."

He stood still for a moment, shaking. Then his knees buckled. Down he went. I tugged hard on the cheek strap. "Get up!"

He did. Now, he kicked at his belly.

Colic, I thought.

Memories of the way that Cobbie died flashed into my mind. He'd had colic, something brought on by a variety of causes. Felicia could list

36

them all, but I knew too. Stress from overwork. No, all Twaziem had done was eat since he arrived. Moldy hay—not here. Water right after grain—no, we'd waited two hours. Rich food—oh my Gawd. Why hadn't I thought? Twaziem had gone from nothing in his stomach to alfalfa/grass hay in the trailer. No wonder his system rebelled.

I backed toward the door, pulled him with me to the hallway. I grabbed a lead rope, snapped it onto the halter. "Come on, bubba. Let's take a walk."

While he stumbled after me toward the indoor arena, I dug out my cell phone. My parents were the best. If I'd been Vicky, I would have a serious problem since they refused to pay for her cell anymore. It was one more casualty in the divorce wars. Now at least, I didn't have to leave him to go for help. I could call the house from the barn.

Felicia answered. Once she heard my diagnosis, she said, "Okay, I'm getting the vet. Colic is the leading cause of death in horses next to old age."

"Thanks a lot. I needed to hear that." I kept walking and talking at the same time. I could multi-task. I was a teenage girl. "How about some help? Muscle relaxants, mineral oil and people to keep him up and moving?"

"Dad's on the way," Felicia said. "Jack's hitting the vet cabinet. Bill's got the fridge, and Mom's making up the drench as we speak."

Twaziem stopped. He sagged in place. He was going down.

"Gotta go." I hung up, pushed the phone in my pocket, and yanked hard on the lead. "Come on. We're walking here. If you tear up your guts, you're dead."

We made another ten steps. He froze. Went down.

I jerked hard. Once. Twice. He didn't roll.

Pull again. It was like tug-of-war with an immovable object.

"Get up, Twaz," I shouted. "Get up!"

I yanked three more times as hard as I could. "On your feet."

He gave up, staggered to stand. He struggled to follow me.

"You're doing a good job, Robbie." Dad jogged toward me, Vicky behind him carrying a stable sheet. "Dr. Tomlinson is on the way. Your mom is mixing up mineral oil, molasses, and hot water. Jack will be here in a few minutes with the gas reliever, and Felicia is bringing muscle relaxants."

A tear slid down my cheek, and I bit my lip. "What if he dies?"

"Not likely." Dad took the rope from me. "Blanket him so he stays warm and doesn't go into shock."

Vicky stepped to the right side, opening the blanket. "Cobbie died from colic."

"I know he did," Dad said, "but he was old. He had an impaction from the grass clippings someone threw over the fence. We didn't find him until it was too late. This horse is young and strong. He's tough. Nobody else could have survived starvation, lice, intestinal worms, and eating half his tail."

A giggle slipped past. I adjusted the stable sheet on Twaziem so it hung halfway down his left side. "He didn't eat his tail, Dad. That's just dumb."

"Yes, he did. At first, I guessed it had been rubbed out because of the lice. Then, Jack pointed out that the bottom half is what's missing and the top is still here."

"I told you he's awful." Vicky passed me the girth. "You should have picked the best horse you could find, not the worst."

"I picked the one who needed me most." I lifted my chin. "And I don't care how many days and nights I walk him. If it takes a week, I'll be here for him. He deserves a real life."

Vicky gasped. "How long are you going to walk him?"

"Colic can last from one to three days," Dad said. "I'd guess we'll be up all night with this fella. We walked Cobbie for two days straight."

"All day and all night," I said. "I remember being so tired that I thought I'd forget how to walk."

"He still died," Vicky pointed out. "How do you know this one won't?"

"We don't." Dad petted Twaziem's neck. "I'm willing to bet that he's a fighter. He'll try and so will we."

I sighed and glanced at Vicky. When she was in a good mood, nobody could be more fun. For the last six months, since her dad moved out on her birthday, Vicky had done more griping than ever about how I treated my family, and it was getting old.

"This is not going to be a fun night." I didn't want to be rude to

Vicky, but there was no way that the family could concentrate on saving the horse and be good company too. "Maybe, you'd better stay over another time. Would next Saturday be better?"

"Why don't I walk Twaziem while you two decide?" Dad asked. "Vicky, if you want to go home because there's too much work to do tonight, I'll have Jack take you."

I passed the lead rope to Dad and waited until he and Twaziem were on the far side of the arena. "Well, what do you want to do?"

"You invited me to spend the night," Vicky said, "and now that you've got a horse, you don't want me." She sounded as if she were going to cry at any moment.

Guilt swamped me. Had I been picking on Vicky? Yes, she was going through some hard times right now. I should be more understanding instead of trying to get rid of her, but the constant carping about Twaz got old in a hurry.

I took a deep breath. "I'm sorry. I didn't mean to hassle you. It's just that I'm worried about Twaz, and I won't be good company tonight. You can stay if you want."

"No thanks. I'm going home. You've chosen that awful, ugly horse over me."

"No, I haven't." I watched as she stormed toward the gate. "Do you want to sleep over next weekend?"

"Why not? Maybe you can make your horse sick again, and then you can send me home again." She slammed the gate to the arena and stalked through the dark toward the house.

I stared after her, sobs clogging my throat. The last thing I wanted to do was lose her, but it seemed impossible to stay on Vicky's good side lately. No matter what I did, Vicky chewed me out. Most of her time she was right, I thought, but it didn't make my life any easier when I was constantly in the wrong.

Heaving a sigh, I went back to Twaziem. I shrugged when Dad glanced at me. "Vicky decided to go home."

"I don't blame her," Dad said. "You weren't making her feel very welcome."

"It's hard." I sounded like a whiner, but I didn't care. "I was tired of listening to her gripe about how awful Twaziem was. It's not his fault that he's been starved. She was acting like the guy who wanted to take Twaz up to the slaughter house just because he looked awful, and she's supposed to be my friend."

Dad kept walking Twaziem around the arena. "Did you ever think she might be jealous? Vicky loves animals as much as you do, but she can't have any pets. She was telling us that she might not get to do her internship at Shamrock Stables, and that's going to hurt her GPA."

I stopped and stared, then hurried to catch up with him. "Dad, she has to do it. Rocky arranged special hours and everything. If Vicky blows off the internship, then she won't be able to complete her Sophomore Project, and it's majorly important."

"Really?" Dad said, sounding stupid and not like himself. "And why is that, Robbie?"

"Because it ties together our community service obligation, and three of our core classes." I stared after him. "Okay, so you're right. She's overloaded, and I wasn't listening. She's not really mad about the horse."

"No, she's not. Why don't you call and apologize?"

"Because she doesn't have a cell."

He gave me a look that said I was acting like a typical blonde, and I caved. I pulled out my cell and called the house. Felicia answered.

"Tell Vicky to come back and help," I said. "I was being mean and I'm sorry."

"More like the other way around," Felicia said, "but you got it."

I tucked away the phone just as Mom came into the arena.

"Sorry, I took so long," Mom said. "Jack found some laxatives, and Bill is bringing the *Banamine*. We'll simply have to walk Twaziem if he starts having cramps and tries to roll."

"He's already been rolling." I took the lead rope from my father and led Twaziem toward Mom at the far end of the arena. "Dad says he thinks Twaz has a better chance than Cobbie did."

"You bet he does." Mom shook the small bottle holding her home remedy. "Cobbie was a goner when we found him, but we didn't want to accept it."

"It was still hard to accept after two days of nursing," Dad said. "Cobbie was a good pony."

"He sure was." Mom took the cap off of the molasses bottle. "I put everything Twaziem needs in here to ease his constipation. I just hope he takes it better than Singer does when she has colic."

"He will." I stopped Twaz in front of her and stepped around to the right side, lifting up his head so she could get the lip of the bottle in the corner of his mouth. "He's into food."

"It sounds to me like you've already remembered how to be a horse owner." Dad smiled at me. "The good ones always think that their horses are the best."

Chapter Eight

Sunday, September 15th, 2:00 a.m.

Although I thought we might have to walk Twaziem all night, the mineral oil, gas reliever tablets, and muscle relaxants took effect shortly after one in the morning. He was pooping up a storm—all of it pretty solid and no diarrhea. As Felicia said, it took very little to make horse people happy, and she spent most of the time counting turds, cheering whenever Twaz pooped again. She so needed to get a life.

Dr. Larry Tomlinson pronounced Twaziem on the road to recovery after the fourth bowel movement. My horse even stopped pawing, and trying to roll and lie down. He was more interested in the scraps of hay he found in the corner of the arena.

"Go ahead and put him back in his stall, Robin," Dr. Larry said. "We'll watch him for a while and make sure he's okay."

Jack stretched and yawned. "Bill and I can camp out in the aisle. Then if Twaziem starts rolling again, we'll pull him out and walk him. I can med with *Banamine* for the cramps."

"We'll stay too," I said, looking at Vicky. She nodded agreement. So did Felicia.

"Why don't you girls go up to the house?" Mom cuddled next to Dad. "Felicia needs to get some rest so she can drive back to Pullman tomorrow. Robin and Vicky can come back at seven and take over. That way we'll share looking after Twaziem."

Dr. Larry began packing up his supplies. "Poor nursing is what

42

causes the most deaths from colic. Splitting up the shifts to look after Twaziem just makes sense."

I considered the schedule while I led my horse back to his stall. I unhooked the lead and left on the halter. Then, whoever was nursing him would be able to catch him if he suffered a relapse. "Actually, that sounds pretty good. Thanks, Jack."

"What about me?" Bill asked. "Aren't you going to thank me, Freckle-face?"

"Not when you call me names," I retorted. "And I haven't had freckles for years."

"Bill only does it to get your attention." Dad chuckled. "Guys, go get your sleeping bags. The rest of us will stay here and watch Twaziem until you return."

"Works for me," Jack said. "Come on, Bill."

Dr. Larry leaned against the wall, continuing to study Twaziem. "He looks like the kind of horse you'd bring home, Robin. I'll never forget the three-legged dog you found or the way you coerced me into helping you find the owners."

I shrugged. No matter how much he teased me about rescuing animals, I knew he liked me because of what I did. He didn't care if I was Felicia and Jack's baby sister. He never judged me. "You were the one vet I could trust to scan him for a microchip and not charge me a million dollars. And Zeke's owners were thrilled when he came home. I still visit them."

"So do I," Dr. Larry said. "Want to go with me next time? You can help me doctor their feral cats for ear mites and fleas."

"You have the wrong kid, Larry." Dad stopped smiling. "Felicia and Jack are the ones who are going for medical careers."

Dr. Larry reached for a package of chewing gum in his pocket and passed a stick to me, one to Felicia, and one to Vicky. "I know that's what you say. They'll both be excellent doctors, and Jack will make a good veterinarian. He's smart and skillful, but Robin is the one I've waited for. She's got the heart and empathy to make a great vet."

"That's news to me." I stared up at the short, paunchy man as I peeled the paper from the gum. "I hate school and vets have to be smart."

"She's got you there, Larry," Dad said. "Her grades are terrible. If she wasn't on cross-country and track, she'd barely pass. You better concentrate on Jack."

My cheeks burned with a painful blush. Maybe my grades weren't as good as my brother's or sister's, but what was the point in trying when I couldn't measure up to either of them? Why didn't Mom say something? She kept looking at the two men as if she'd never seen them before. Did she even hear the discussion?

Dr. Larry eyed me. "Do you have learning disabilities, Robin?"

"Of course not," Mom finally spoke up. "We've had every test done. We thought she'd get more stimulation in a private school, so we enrolled her in the same one Jack attends. Lincoln High is one of the top ranked schools in the state. They hired Robin's track coach to teach there last summer, but she simply does the minimum amount of class assignments, just enough to keep her athletic eligibility."

"Sounds like me," Dr. Larry said. "I didn't start working until I was a junior in high school. Then it was hard to learn all the stuff I'd ignored for so long. You can still be a veterinarian even if you play around, Robin."

"I can? Then, why does everybody keep pushing all this boring stuff at me?"

"Because you'll have to work harder later on," Dr. Larry said. "It's easier if you start studying now, especially if you get good grades in math and science."

"That's how I got scholarships," Felicia told me. "The good thing about those is you don't have to pay them back. Otherwise, you end up with a ton of student loans when you graduate from college."

That made sense, and it explained why Vicky studied so much. She was determined to go to a four year university.

"But our classes are so boring," I said, "even math and science."

"How can math be boring?" Dad asked. "It's challenging, a puzzle that stretches your mind."

"Your books and accounting stuff aren't boring, Dad," I explained. "It's the junk we do over and over in school. That's really dull."

"I have to admit that she's right about that," Vicky agreed.

Jack and Bill came back with armloads of things they felt necessary for spending the night in the barn. They had blankets, pillows, and sleeping bags, not to mention bags of chips, bottles of soda and a package of candy bars.

Dad kept staring at me as if I'd grown two heads. "You're reading my books?"

"You said it was okay," I reminded him. "And Dr. Larry told me that most small businesses fail because of poor bookkeeping practices. Veterinary clinics are considered small businesses, so I read your textbooks and magazines."

"That was last spring." Dad shook his head, obviously baffled. "I don't understand, Robbie. If you can comprehend difficult accounting principles, then why did you almost fail math last June?"

"You just don't get it." Vicky and I started toward the barn door. "School is boring. Accounting is interesting. It's all about money. What could be dull about that? I like money."

"Who doesn't?" Felicia caught up with us. "Anyway, I told you that you should pay her for grades, and Robin would have a four-point."

My car came to mind, and I said, "I could so go for that."

"I'll bet you could," Mom told me. "I just don't see why we should reward you for not working up to your abilities."

* * * *

Sunday, September 15th, 4:00 p.m.

When I hit the barn that afternoon, I brought my brushes so I could groom Twaziem for the first time. Vicky had gone home shortly after Felicia left at noon. I'd promised to email photos to my older sister so she could see how my horse progressed between now and her Thanksgiving break. She might make it home before then, but there weren't any guarantees.

As for Vicky, I'd see her tomorrow at school. I'd promised to help her figure out a way to do her internship so she wouldn't fail her core classes, and next time she was overloaded, she said she'd share her problems, not chew me out. Twaziem turned to look at me, but he refused to step away from the manger of hay. Was it my imagination or had he already gained weight?

"You can't groom him," Jack said, behind me. "You'll brush off the

45

lice powder, and then it won't kill the bugs. Dr. Larry told me to dust him again in three days."

I struggled to hide my disappointment. Why did leaving him alone bother me so much? I was going to sell him when he was healthy and trained. It'd be better not to become attached to him. It was always harder to find homes for stray kittens and puppies when I loved them. It wasn't like I planned to care for Twaziem, anyway. "Delousing him again means I won't be able to brush him for at least a week."

"Yeah, but you can always brush Nitro for me."

"No way. Nitro always tries to bite me. He's mean."

"Spirited. If you didn't squeal and jump around, Miss Wimpy, then he wouldn't pick on you."

"That's Ms. Wimpy to you." I tossed my head and went to put my brushes in the tack room. It was the same size as one of the stalls, with six saddle pegs. Only four of them held western saddles. Tears misted my eyes when I spotted the tiny one that Cobbie used to carry so proudly. On the front of the peg was a hook and his old bridle.

Putting down my tote-box and brushes, I crossed to the peg and picked up the bridle. The leather was soft, and I wondered who had cleaned and oiled it. I remembered the times I struggled to put on Cobbie's bridle by myself. He was so patient. He'd put his head down for me and open his mouth and just wait while I slipped in the bit and fitted the headstall.

I forced back my tears. I'd forgotten the number of times I bawled over Cobbie. None of my tears brought back the Welsh pony mix. Feeling bad didn't change the facts. Cobbie was gone. All I could do was go forward with my life and learn from my mistakes. It would be stupid to care as much about Twaziem as I had my pony. I couldn't handle the emotional investment.

I picked up my tote-box and put the brushes on the shelf with my name. When had Dad painted 'Robin' on the wall in the tack room? When did he know they were getting a horse for my sixteenth birthday? Why didn't he tell me the car wasn't an option?

I had a lot of questions, but no answers. I went back to Twaziem's stall. He kept eating, but he flicked his ears while Jack mucked. I had a pocketful of carrots for Twaz, so I went into the stall, too. He stomped his rear hooves, and I paused. "If you kick Jack, I won't give you any of these. I'll feed them all to that stinky, nasty, smelly Nitro."

"Nitro doesn't smell," Jack said, indignant. "I bathe him all the time."

Twaziem stomped again, aiming a kick at my brother. "I don't think he likes you."

"Grow up, Robin. Horses aren't people. They're animals. They don't like or hate things the way we do."

"Bull." I stepped up beside Twaziem and offered him a long, stringy carrot. "I don't see how you can go places with Dr. Larry when you think animals don't have feelings."

"Just because I'm not sentimental doesn't mean I won't be a good vet. I can take care of sick animals without crying."

"You're just being a macho jerk." I held the carrot closer. "Come on, Twaz. They taste good. They won't hurt your teeth like sugar."

"If you feed him sugar, you're brushing his teeth. I'm not." Jack finished scooping manure and tossed the last pile into the wheelbarrow parked outside. He came back with a plastic wrapped bale of shavings and dumped out half of it into the stall. Then, he spread the bedding.

"Remember when Cobbie got that cavity? Dr. Larry had to pull out the tooth with his forceps. You cried for hours because he didn't use a sedative."

"He hurt Cobbie." I broke off a piece of carrot and eased the tip of it into Twaziem's mouth. He tried a cautious nibble, then crunched down on it. "See, Twaz, I told you they were good. Nobody's hurting him, Jack. I won't let them."

"I think he's been hurt enough." Jack headed out of the stall, making sure he had his fork and rake. "So, are you going to help me with the chores tonight? I'll split the money with you."

"When I came down here, Dad was trying to convince Mom that they should pay me for good grades like they do for you and Felicia."

Jack laughed. "They only pay for A's and the highest you've ever gotten is a C average."

I shrugged and fed Twaziem another piece of carrot. "I could get a four-point if I wanted."

My brother just laughed again and walked away.

"I could," I told Twaz. He nickered and nosed me. He believed in me even if nobody else did. Well, of course. *Who wouldn't believe the person who saved you from certain death?*

Chapter Nine

Jack had moved down the barn to his horse's stall. My brother was a sure thing, and he'd offered to share the chores as well as the money with me. Grades could wait until my parents came to a consensus. I stepped away from Twaziem and leaned on his stall door. "I'll take care of the horses and the pigs and my cats, but I won't do the steers or milk the cow."

"Works for me." Jack whistled as he unloaded his tools and opened Nitro's door. "I'll do the chickens since the hen house is on the way to the cow pasture."

At the louder sound of his voice, Twaziem lifted a hind foot and kicked at the back wall. His hoof missed the wood by inches, and he followed up with another kick, this time with his right hind. It seemed as if he really didn't like my brother, but I wasn't going to say that again, not when Jack laughed at me. What could I do about it?

Maybe if I made friends with Twaz, he'd realize people weren't all bad. Despite all of Jack's macho claims and the way he acted around his football buds, my brother wouldn't starve or abuse any animal. Sometimes I thought his tough exterior was just the way he hid how he truly felt. When Cobbie died, Jack cried with me. So did Dad.

"Why isn't it okay for a guy to admit he has feelings?" I stood next to Twaziem's brown neck and smelled the bitter odor of lice powder. "Jack would never hurt you. Mellow out, Twaz."

This time when I held out a piece of carrot, he took it. His whiskery nose tickled my hand. I giggled when he bobbed his head up and down, tasting the end of the carrot. The greens hung from his mouth like weird spaghetti. Deciding he liked the whole thing, he chewed it up and gulp, it was gone. He nudged me for more. His old owners must have believed that horses shouldn't have treats. Some people said treats made horses mean, that it caused them to bite. I remembered the training video Rocky showed us with a guy who said, "Treats are a bonus, not a requirement."

Well, I wanted Twaziem to trust me, and we had tons of carrots in the garden, so he could have all he'd eat. Over the next half hour I fed carrots to Twaz, one small piece after another. While he munched them, I told him about my car. My beautiful Mustang with its deep Presidential blue exterior and the blue and black interior. "I visit it all the time on my way from school to Dad's office."

He nodded and nudged me for the last piece of carrot. "A person shouldn't love a machine the way they do an animal," I said. "I'll find you the perfect home. You'll have people who love and care about you. It won't be me, but I'll visit. I promise."

He finished the treat, and I looked at the barn clock. It was five. I only had an hour before dinner and lots of chores to do. "It's time to eat, Twaziem. I'll get everybody fed."

Leaving the stall, I carefully latched the door behind me. Then I went down the aisle to get the hose. Water came first before feed, and all of the horses needed their tubs checked and filled. Because horses required so much liquid, Dad put in huge plastic garbage cans, one for each stall. He thought they were safer than automatic water basins that filled on their own.

I started with Twaziem's tub. It was only half full, which meant he'd taken on about ten gallons of water since yesterday. That was a good sign. Another one was the way he ignored me and the hose. He didn't even lift a hind foot, although I stood behind him in the inside back corner of his stall. The bale of hay in his manger took all of his attention. In spite of eating most of the day, he still had about eight flakes left.

When I finished filling his water tub, I turned off the nozzle. I dragged the hose from the stall and headed toward Buster. His tub had hay and grain floating in it. I went for the strainer, brought it back, and scooped stuff off the surface before I ran water. Next, was Singer. As soon as I opened her door, she jumped back. Personally, I found it hard to believe the hose terrified her. I mean she saw it all the time. I was pretty sure she faked it, but there was always the chance that she was truly frightened. "It's okay," I said. "I'm just here to take care of you."

After her, came Nitro. I was glad I didn't actually have to go inside with him. Dad put the water tub in the front corner of the stall because the Thoroughbred had such an intimidating personality. I watched him warily, hoping he wouldn't try to bite me. He pinned his ears back and glared at me, but kept his distance. "You're mean and evil," I told him. "One day, I know you'll prove it to everybody else, and Dad will get rid of you."

Nitro snorted. He tossed his head and narrowed pale blue eyes. When he stomped toward me, I shut off the water and backed away. His tub was only three-quarters full, but it'd have to do. I wasn't taking the risk of being close to him any longer. I coiled the hose and looked at the clock. Five-fifteen.

I hurried toward the hay loft. I had to give the horses their hay and grain, but I could take care of the cats while I was in the loft. That would speed me up. They didn't need more water so I filled the other dish with dry food. I had to pet them for a few minutes and cuddle each one. Then, I opened a can of meat and split it onto the two plates. After that, I could drop a bale of hay into the arena for the horses.

I dropped more hay into Twaziem's manger at five thirty-five. I still had to grain all four horses and feed the pigs. Twenty-five minutes. How did Jack manage to do everything and get to dinner on time? He must be a superhero. This was awful. I knew I'd be late and Mom would demand to know why. Dad would point out that I was too old to keep the entire family waiting. And of course, I couldn't go to the house and leave the animals to wait for the rest of their suppers. That wouldn't be fair.

It wasn't the horses' or the pigs' fault that I wasn't as fast at chores as Jack. Maybe I should have limited myself to the cats and horses, but the steers were the hardest to do. They had to be brought up from the farthest pasture to the closest one. Then, their water troughs had to be filled and so did the hay racks. It took ages to feed them and milk the cow. That was why I asked Jack to do it.

In the grain room, I filled four coffee cans with feed, then picked up the first two. I wasn't Jack and I couldn't carry all the cans at one time, the way he did. It took two trips from the grain room to the stalls. First, I fed Buster and Nitro, pouring feed into the grain boxes in their stalls, then Singer and Twaziem. Back to lock up the grain before leaving the barn, and I headed for the door, switching off the lights on my way. I glanced at the clock.

Ten minutes till dinner. And I had to feed the pigs. I hurried toward the concrete foundation that served as a pen for the Berkshire hogs. I grabbed their bucket and went to the covered barrel that held their mash. Dad always raised four pigs, two for us and two to sell. That meant six trips between the large container of soaked grain and the pen to fill their feed trough. I checked their water. It didn't need to be filled tonight. Hurray!

Finally, I was done. I turned and ran toward the house. I was so late, and I just knew I'd get the lecture. It wasn't like I could wash my hands and go for dinner. Mom would freak if I smelled like the barn, especially on Sunday. No, I totally had to hit the shower first. Nobody had ever been this late for a meal. Would I even get to eat before Dad chewed my ears?

I hated it when people got mad at me. Mom was the worst. Dad talked a lot, but Mom remembered stuff and brought it up later. I still heard stories of all the things I'd done as a three-year-old, like throwing a new doll in the garbage and demanding a puppy instead. There was no way Mom would ever forget the time, ten years ago, that I put Cobbie in the laundry room because he had a cold and I didn't think he'd get better in the barn.

I was only six then. Two years later when my grandparents visited, they refused to come to the barn to see my pony. Granted, Cobbie was half horse, but he was a pony to me. And if they wouldn't bring him a carrot, I'd ride him up to get one. So, I rode him all the way up the steps to the back deck, into the kitchen, through the living room and right up to the couch. He definitely deserved a carrot for being so good about it.

Everybody started talking at once and Grandfather began yelling like he was still in the Marines. All the shouting made Cobbie nervous, and he took a dump on the new carpet. I was sent to my room in disgrace while Jack led my pony back to the barn. I wasn't supposed to have any supper, but Felicia brought me soup and sandwiches. She acted like it was a big joke and promised me Cobbie got lots of carrots in his grain. I never forgot the look on Dad's face before he turned his back on me in disgust, shoulders shaking.

He'd be just as mad tonight. I eased open the door to the back porch and stopped when I saw Jack removing his boots. Were we both late?

He glanced in my direction. "You better hurry. Fifteen minutes till dinner."

I blinked. "What are you talking about? It was ten to six when I left the barn to feed the pigs."

"Barn time," Jack said. "Didn't you realize I set the clock fifteen minutes ahead? Otherwise, I'd always be late. Grandma taught me that trick. Of course, she calls it bar time because she'll be in major trouble if her customers aren't out the door by two a.m. so she can close the tavern and not break the liquor laws."

"You mean I had fifteen extra minutes?" I unlaced one boot and kicked it under the bench. "I almost had a heart attack. I knew I'd be so late. Why didn't you tell me before you left to do the steers?"

"I thought you knew." Jack opened the door to the kitchen. "You'd better hurry, or you'll be late for supper."

"You jerk." I pulled off my other boot. "You clown. You rotten creep."

"Why are you picking on your brother, Robbie?" Dad kept chopping vegetables for the salad. "What's he done now?"

I glared after Jack as he sauntered out of the room, heading for his shower. "He didn't tell me that he set the barn clock ahead. I thought I was really late for dinner and I'd be the first course."

Dad laughed and grabbed a green pepper. He pointed to the kitchen clock with his free hand. "Ten minutes and you will be. Go, girl, go!"

"I am." I hustled through the kitchen and down the hall to my room.

We were all seated at the dining room table and Dad had just started carving the roast chicken when Mom came in from the den. "Felicia made good time. She's safe and sound in Pullman and is on her way to the stable to check Vinnie. She'll call again on Wednesday night."

"That's great," Jack said. "I promised I'd send her a video of Nitro and me at the Games Day next week. And you're going to email pictures of Twaziem, aren't you, Robin?"

"Yes." I filled half my plate with salad, then passed the bowl to Dad. "I want him to gain more weight first. Dr. Larry said I should use the tape and measure his weight every week. Will you show me how to do it, Mom?"

"Sure, honey." She eyed me and kept putting brown rice on her plate. "Don't you want your dad to do it? He's the one who gives the horses their shots."

"Yes, but Twaz doesn't like Jack, and Dad's a guy too. I don't want either of them to get hurt, and Twaziem seems to like me, you and Felicia better."

"Interesting," Mom said. "I hadn't heard of a horse practicing gender bias before. I wonder if Rocky has. You should talk to her about it this week when you start lessons again."

Chapter Ten

Monday, September 16th, 7:20 a.m.

I sat in the Commons with my mocha, stirring it with the straw while I waited for Vicky. Talk about déjà vu—I'd definitely been here before. Riding lessons? Come on. Get serious. I had plenty to do. Mom and Dad had told me at dinner last night that they'd agreed to pay me for A's and B's on my semester grades. Whoopee! But, how was I supposed to study when I had cross-country practice twice a week, a meet every Thursday for the next two months, Twaziem to look after and now riding lessons on Wednesdays and Saturdays?

"Okay, so what's the emergency?" Vicky plopped down in the seat across from me and actually grinned before she saw the peppermint latte I'd brought her. "Wow, you're the best. And I love your parents. They can adopt me anytime."

"Mom signed me up for riding lessons." I groaned. "Like I'm a little kid. She says I need to brush up my skills so I can train Twaz next spring, as if I'll actually keep him. This was a rescue. I'll find him a great home, but I don't want a horse."

Vicky buried her head in her hands. "Here we go again with all your dramas. Did you ever think the world doesn't turn around you, Robin?"

"No." I sucked up some mocha. "I'm blonde and beautiful, so of course it does. Do you ever get tired of always being right, Vick?"

"No." She took the cap off her cup and sipped. She kept smiling. "In this down economy, I wouldn't bet on finding Twaziem a home, and you know your dad will want enough money to pay him back for the rehabilitation. That will be major bucks between the feed, the vet, the training, and your lessons, which you wouldn't have to take if you didn't have him or me."

"You?" I gaped at her. "What do my lessons have to do with you?"

"Your mom called my mom and said that as long as she had to take you to Shamrock for classes, she might as well drop me to do my internship on Wednesdays and Saturdays. After all, both moms want the same thing—for us to pass our sophomore year with flying colors. And if you hang out with me academically, I might be able to get you on the Honor Roll by Christmas."

"No way."

"Yes, way!" Vicky drank more coffee. "I thought the Honor Roll thing was a bit over the top, but my mom totally went for it."

I shook my head. "I don't believe it. My mom is such a bitch. Who knew?"

"Well, you had to suspect it. No offense. I mean, think about Felicia. She had to get it somewhere."

We both cracked up. The warning bell rang and we got up, grabbing our backpacks to head for English class. Winding our way through the cafeteria, I asked, "So, is all right in your world now?"

"Well, my internship is fine for the moment. I just have to figure out cheer practice and the football games on Fridays," Vicky said, finishing her latte. "So far, Ms. Walker is okay with me leaving early to pick up the kids at their school and Chrissy from day care. But, when the squad starts getting ready for regionals, all bets are off."

"We have two months before that happens," I said, draining my mocha. "We'll figure out something. Hey, maybe your mom will hire a nanny."

"Yes and Santa will bring me Clinton Anderson for Christmas. I'd die to train with him and go to his Academy."

"You'd have to move to Texas, and Jack would totally freak."

"It's Clinton Anderson," Vicky said, dropping her cup in the garbage. "Jack would go with me to learn everything the guy knows about horses."

"Sure, but you have to be eighteen," I said, tossing my cup, "and that's two years away."

"Okay, well maybe I'll get the 'Colt Starting Videos' this year. We can use them on Twaziem."

I laughed. "Oh, he'll love that."

She always made me feel better, and I hoped I'd done the same for her. We made it to English class and our seats before the last bell rang. That was good since Mrs. Weaver was a notorious hard grader and had a zero tolerance for life. Gray-haired, gray eyes, she was older than dirt and looked like a stumpy rock in her gray suit.

Silence reigned in the room as soon as the bell pealed. She stood at her desk and waited until everyone looked at her. "Some of you slackers haven't turned in your letters of intent for your Sophomore Project and you should be starting your hours with your mentor this week. When I call your name, tell me who your mentor is or where you're planning to go."

I cringed and ducked down in my seat. It didn't do much good.

She whipped through the first six letters of the alphabet and got to me in what felt like a heartbeat. "Roberta Gibson."

"I'm here," I said.

"And where are you going? Who will be your mentor?"

I nearly said I had absolutely no idea, that I could skate through the class and end up with a C- or D+ and still stay on the cross-country team, but my best friend from hell spoke up. "She's doing it with Dr. Larry Tomlinson at Equine Nation Vet Clinic in Snohomish."

"Interesting," Mrs. Weaver said. "I'll have your letter by end of school today, Roberta, or you'll be here until I do."

"But I have cross-country practice tonight and Coach Norris will lose it if I don't show up," I said.

"It won't be the first time you hear from him if I don't have your letter today. If I were you, I'd spend the period writing the letter. Victoria will be happy to help since she already has her internship lined up."

I shot a glare across the room at Vicky, then looked down at my notebook. "Yes, ma'am."

A few minutes later, we were excused to visit the computer lab so I could do my letter. Halfway there, Vicky pushed me into the restroom.

"Get out your cell and call Dr. Larry."

"What? If I'm caught, I'll get detention."

"And when Weaver checks up with him, you'll be off cross-country for the season and in I.S.S. until Christmas. I'll stand guard. You call."

"Then why did you say I was doing it with him?"

"Hello, weren't you listening Saturday night? He believes you walk on water. You need to use that. Why do you think Rocky agreed to let me do my internship at her barn? She likes me and says I'm a good rider and trainer."

"Plus you can clean fourteen stalls faster than anyone else on the planet." I checked the restroom. It was empty so I pulled out my phone and called Equine Nation. Of course, it wasn't open yet, but I left Dr. Larry a message about doing the internship with him. I'd check back with him during lunch when students were allowed to use their cell phones.

In the lab, Vicky opened her binder. It was totally organized by class. She took out the rubric for the assignment and a copy of her letter. "Okay, here's my flash drive. We'll adjust the wording so it works for you helping the veterinarian on his large animal calls."

When I rolled my eyes, she elbowed me. "Ouch. That hurt," I complained. "What's your problem?"

"Will you get serious? You don't want to spend every day in the clinic shoveling puppy or kitty poop. You want to go places with Dr. Larry and learn what he does in the field."

"When you put it that way, it makes a lot more sense." I logged on to the computer and clicked on the word processing program. Actually, I was lucky to have her on my side even if I hassled her about it.

* * * *

Monday, September 16th, 2:20 p.m.

I finished my letter and turned it into Mrs. Weaver at the end of the school day. She skimmed through it. "All right. I'll give this back to you tomorrow with my corrections, and you can do a final draft."

"Come again?" I stared at her. "I thought this was all you wanted."

"Did you even read the project requirements?" Mrs. Weaver put my paper on her desk. She folded her arms and narrowed her eyes. "I'm still waiting for your brainstorm."

"My what?"

"Your outline for the letter."

"Who outlines a letter? That's the stupidest thing I've ever heard."

She heaved a sigh like I was the dumbest student she'd seen in a long time. "You typed this, so I know you kept a copy on your flash drive. You can amplify the second and third paragraphs. Ask your older brother to help you outline the letter."

"No way. If I ask Jack for help, he'll come up with some rotten chore I have to do in exchange. I might have to muck out his room. I already have to feed the horses and pigs to share the chore money. It sucked last night."

"That sounds like a personal problem." Mrs. Weaver looked at the clock. "You'd better go if you don't want to be late for track practice."

"Cross-country," I corrected. "Track's in the spring."

I headed for the door, then stopped when I heard a weird sound. I glanced back over my shoulder. Was she laughing? Apparently so. Who knew that was even possible? Okay, if I didn't make it to State this year, I could always try to be a comedian.

I was one of the last girls to reach the locker room, but it didn't take long to change to my shorts and T-shirt. I tied my sweatshirt around my waist and jogged out to the track. I started stretching. No cramps for me. I glanced at Gwen and Porter, two of the other girls on the team. "Has he said where we're running yet?"

Gwen shook her head and kept doing side bends. "Something about a park."

"Downtown," Porter said.

I grimaced. Running through Marysville meant lots of sidewalks and maybe a bit in the local park, but that didn't get me ready for the track meet outside of Arlington. Coach Norris waved to us and we headed toward him, along with everyone else.

"Okay, here's the deal." He laid out the route. It was still pretty easy, just four miles around town and only a couple big hills. "Any comments?"

Porter tapped her foot. "Okay if we do it twice or three times?"

"No. You do it once, Porter." Coach Norris ran a hand through his thinning brown hair. He was in good shape for a guy older than my dad. "The rest of you get going. Gwen, Robin, and Porter, stay here. I want to talk to you."

Steve gave us a sympathetic look, then jogged off with a couple of the guys.

Coach waited until everyone was gone. He frowned at us, his tone stern. "I know what you three are thinking. Don't go there. Until I get permission from the principal and school board to increase the duration, the most we do during practice is four miles. Got it?"

Gwen widened big blue eyes and put on her super-innocent look. "But, it is okay if we keep practicing on our own time, isn't it?"

"You'd better if you want to improve your Personal Records at this meet." He winked. "Now, get out of here and try not to get lost. I expect you back in an hour and a half."

"Yes, Coach." I led off and the other two girls followed me. I saw the guys up ahead of us, but I didn't care. We'd gotten a pretty strong hint that if we veered from the route, Coach Norris wouldn't say anything as long as we kept to the same timeframes as the rest of the team. I glanced at Gwen when she caught up with me. "Up Golf Course Hill and then down 88th street or the other way around?"

She laughed. "Golf Course."

Chapter Eleven

Monday, September 16th, 6:45 p.m.

Conversation ebbed and flowed around the dinner table. I waited for one of the pauses, then glanced across the table at Jack. "Can you help me with an English assignment?"

Silence and the three of them stared at me like I'd escaped from a horror movie. Dad was the first one to talk. "Robbie, I thought you weren't that interested in school?"

"I'm not," I said, "but you told me I had to earn half the money for my car and I guess I want to try for some A's. Besides, Mrs. Weaver isn't like the teachers at my old school. She's not going to let this go. If I don't do my work for her, I'll end up on academic probation. Then, I can't do cross-country."

"How will she stop you?" Mom asked, curious. "Cut off your legs?"

"I just told you. Coach Norris warned us that he'll be sending around grade-checks every week before the meets. Anything below a C in any of my classes and I'll be benched."

Mom nodded, satisfied for the moment. "Well, I knew your teacher wouldn't convince you to give up cross-country. You've been running as long as I can remember. I'd take you with me to the Farmer's Market, and you'd race from one end of the street to the other. You were so cute. When you were exhausted, you'd plop down in front of my booth and go to sleep with your blankie and teddy. Customers had to walk around you."

Shannon Kennedy

"It was really embarrassing when she did that last summer," Jack said.

I stuck my tongue out at him before I remembered I needed his help, and he laughed at me. For once, Mom's stories didn't make me feel bad. I must have been really little when I went with her to the open-air, summer market. "I bet Jack did something equally wonderful."

"Oh, yes." Mom was off and running. "He used to help carry things from the car, and Felicia would want to set up my booth. But, Jack would go out and stop people wandering through the market. He'd say, 'You need one of my Mom's quilts. You have to buy it so I can have a new book or new paints or new whatever.' The other gals wanted to know if I'd rent him out so they could make more money at their stalls."

While she chattered about how amazing the three of us were as little kids, Jack scowled at me. "Don't you dare tell Vicky any of this," he whispered.

"If you help me, I won't," I said, in just as soft a voice.

After dinner, I had dish duty. Once the kitchen was clean, I started looking for Jack. He was nowhere in sight. I stopped in the den and printed off the letter. I stuffed it in my three-ring binder. Carrying it, I headed down to the barn with a brief pause in the garden to pull up a few carrots for Twaziem. As soon as I walked into the barn, he lifted his head and nickered at me.

"Hey, you know me." I gave him a carrot. "That's awesome." While he crunched away, I went over to Nitro's stall. "You said you'd help me."

"I will." Jack kept grooming his horse. "But, Nitro and I need to practice for the races on Saturday. What do you want?"

"Weaver says I have to do a brainstorm. What does that mean?"

Jack stopped and Nitro gave him a dirty look. Jack ignored him. He put the currycomb in his tote and walked up to the front of the stall. "Let me see your rough draft."

"Why does everyone keep calling it that? I worked on this letter for hours."

"If it's the first version, it's rough," Jack said. "If you had more time, you could add more details, right?"

"Well, sure. But, why should I spend more time on it?"

62

"Because if you don't, you'll be walking like the rest of us and hearing about the cross-country team at morning announcements. You won't be part of it." Jack held out his hand for my letter. "Do you want that?"

"No way."

While he read through the letter, I went back to Twaziem and gave him another carrot. He sucked it up like a giant vacuum cleaner. Zip. Crunch. Gone. He was definitely getting the hang of treats, so I gave him a third carrot and then a fourth. We were on number six when Jack called me.

"What do you have?" I asked as I headed back over.

He showed me the corrections he'd made to the letter. Jack flipped to a blank page of notebook paper and drew a series of circles with lines that connected them. "You'll want to create a web, and then you can see where your argument needs to be strengthened. You're trying to convince your teacher that you'll learn a lot from Dr. Larry, not just have a good time."

"This looks like so much work."

"Yeah, but if you get in the habit of doing the brainstorms and developing your writing, you'll have an A in English at the end of the semester, and that'll mean fifty bucks toward your car. Add in your other classes, and you're looking at three hundred and fifty, plus the bonus for a four-point GPA."

"Any other words of advice?" I asked sarcastically.

"Considering how hard you work at cross-country, you should ask the folks for a bonus whenever you beat last year's times and improve your P.R."

"That won't happen until this Thursday at our first meet," I said, "if I'm lucky. And there are no guarantees. People fall, get shin splints, twist ankles—it's like your football team. You guys can get hurt."

"So could you," Jack said. "And I play because it's fun, but if the team goes to State again this year, I'll get an extra two hundred bucks for busting my butt all season. I'm just saying that you should take your shot. You won't know if it's a go until you ask Dad."

I nodded. He had a point. I eyed the letter again and closed my notebook. "Okay, I'll get out of your practice and go do my homework.

Do you want me to set up the barrels for you?"

"No. I want to work on stops and starts. If Nitro sees the barrels, he forgets to focus."

I left Jack brushing his horse, just the way he was when I arrived. I stopped by Twaziem's stall and gave him the last carrot before I left the barn and headed up to the house to do homework. I went into my room and turned on the computer. I'd do my English paper first, then move onto Algebra and History. My teachers would probably die of shock when I turned in the assignments, but it'd keep them off Coach Norris's back, and mine. Then, I could concentrate on cross-country, which I loved. And this might help me get my car. *My car, my car, my car*!

Of course, tomorrow I had to go by the car lot and see what I could work out with Brenna after cross-country practice. Maybe she'd let me make payments on my '68 Presidential blue Mustang and not insist on having my parents involved in the deal. I'd been so busy working on my paper today, I didn't get to have lunch with Harry, and that meant I hadn't asked what he thought of the idea. I'd spent my half-hour break in the computer lab rewriting this stupid letter. Had he missed me? Did he even notice I wasn't sitting across the table from him?

* * * * *

Tuesday, September 17th, 7:03 a.m.

All the way to school, I debated silently how to bring up being paid for cross-country, and track in the spring. I loved running. I didn't do it for money. I'd run even if I wasn't on the team. Dad pulled up to our favorite espresso stand. He glanced at me and I nodded. That was the best part about riding to school with him. He bought my coffee.

Okay, so maybe that wasn't the best part. Maybe it was being able to talk to him about life. Jack wasn't with us today. I could still imagine the look he'd give me and the way he'd call me Miss Wimpy. I had to speak up. I had to ask. The worst that could happen was Dad would refuse and I wouldn't be any worse off.

He passed me a mocha and put his in the cup holder. "What's up, Robbie? You're never this quiet. Don't you feel well? I can take you

64

home if you're sick."

"I'm fine," I said. "And I want to go to school. I did my homework so the teachers won't be on my case, and the team is practicing this afternoon."

"Okay, then what is it?"

I took a deep breath and launched into my spiel about getting a bonus if my times improved at the cross-country meets and if I was one of the runners in my division who made State. Dad kept driving and didn't say anything until I finished. He pulled up in front of the school and stopped. I reached down for my backpack. "What do you think?"

"That I need to talk to your mom, and we'll get back to you," Dad said. "I'm sorry, Robbie. I've been unfair to you and that makes me feel like a jerk."

"What? How do you figure? You're great." If I ever doubted it, all I had to do was look around at my friends. Vicky wasn't the only one who had an absentee father. "You may not do everything I want when I want it, but you're my dad, not my buddy. And I gotta go."

"Yes, but next time you're doing an extracurricular sport like cross-country and I'm not treating it with the respect I give Jack and his football, I want you to tell me right away. Deal?"

"Sure, Dad." I opened my door. He still looked worried, so I leaned back in and kissed his cheek. "Hey, don't beat yourself up about this. If I get enough money saved up, I can have my car."

He managed a smile. "That fills a father's heart with joy. His little girl driving around town in a sports car."

"Yeah," I said. "It'll be great." And I hustled for the Commons so I could hang out with my friends before the first bell rang.

The day zoomed by. None of my teachers had heart attacks when I turned in the assignments, so I figured I'd have to try harder if I wanted to hassle them. I really didn't. I just didn't want them on my back and I hated it when classes were boring, but maybe if I made more of an effort, my teachers might be better. It was worth a try.

I was one of the first people to make it to the cafeteria at lunch, but Harry wasn't around. He didn't show up at all, and when I asked one of his buddies, he said that Harry had gone to a classic auto show with his sister. I had to go by the lot today to make sure they hadn't taken my

Mustang to the sale.

That afternoon, Gwen, Porter, and I split off from the group and ran up 64th. It was a longer rise, not quite as steep as Golf Course Hill, but it still added on two miles. Then, we cut north and wound through a development that would eventually link up with the park and the route the rest of our team ran.

Sunshine warmed the pavement and my shoulders as I ran. Occasional puffy clouds floated overhead and a cool breeze dusted my face. We weren't the only high school cross-country teams out. I spotted a few girls and guys from Mount Pilchuck, my old school. As we cut down one block, Phillip Evans caught up with me. A redheaded senior, he had a steady girl and I wasn't it.

"What's up?" I asked, as we jogged down the block. "Are you going to tell us that your team is the best in the county? We already know it. We were part of it last year till our folks moved us with Coach Norris to Lincoln because they wanted us in a private school with better test scores."

"No, I'm only here to tell you to watch your backs up in Arlington this Thursday." He ran beside me. "Wanda and Ashley are out for blood, yours."

"Why?" Porter asked. "We haven't seen them since the meets last spring, and they weren't much back then, so we didn't have any trouble beating their times. And it wasn't our fault we went to State and they didn't."

"It would have been harder to hold back," Gwen said. "They're so slow."

"Not you two." Amusement leaked into Phillip's blue eyes. "They're ticked at Robin for 'stealing' their horse."

"Twaziem?" I asked, jogging in place when a traffic light turned red. "I didn't know he was theirs. Bartlett is a pretty common name. And have you seen him?"

Phillip shook his head. "Nope. Why?"

I fished out my phone and pulled up the photo I'd taken of Twaz, my walking skeleton of a Morab. "That's him. If we hadn't gotten him, he'd be dead by now. The other buyer was taking him up to the slaughter house."

"So, tell them to get over themselves," Gwen finished. "And we're not busy. We'll leave them in the dust come Thursday."

Phillip laughed again. "That won't be hard. Good luck at the meet." He turned and ran the other direction to catch up with the guys from his school.

I tucked away my phone and waited while Porter tightened the band on her ponytail to keep her black hair out of her face. The light changed to green, and we took off across the street.

At the next light, Porter asked, "So, when do we get to come visit your latest rescue?"

I bumped her with my elbow. "How about Friday night after the football game? I'll ask my folks if I can have a sleepover."

"Works for me," Gwen said. "If I were you, I wouldn't worry about Wanda or Ashley. They're all mouth. It's their cousin, Caine, who will get you. He's pure poison."

"Yeah, but I have the two of you to watch my back," I said. "I'm not scared."

Chapter Twelve

Tuesday, September 17th, 4:20 p.m.

After practice, I showered and changed back to regular clothes before I headed toward Dad's office. Okay, I actually was on my way to the Mustang Corral to visit my car. My beautiful Presidential blue Mustang. Relief washed through me as I got nearer to the lot. I saw it. Hurray! Brenna hadn't taken it to the auto show.

However, some of the others in the rainbow herd were missing, the night-black convertible, a candy-apple red fastback, and a canary yellow hardtop sedan. She must have sold them. All right! She was having a good week, and that meant she'd be more likely to listen to my pitch. I walked across the lot and spotted Harry washing one of the sky blue Mustangs. I waved at him and kept going toward the trailer.

He turned off the hose and jogged toward me. "Hi. I haven't seen you for a while. What's up?"

I shrugged like it was no big deal when he talked to me and my heart wasn't racing like it was at a road rally. "I had to finish my letter of intent for Weaver or she'd mess with cross-country."

He laughed, amusement deepening his dark blue eyes to navy. Gawd, he was a hunk. Best of all, he didn't know it.

"Those teachers who think academics come first." He shook his head, still grinning down at me. "It's enough to ruin your life, huh?"

"Yeah," I agreed. He might be joking, but I wasn't.

He walked next to me all the way to the office. "So, your folks didn't come in to buy that Mustang. It's a lot of money."

I heaved a sigh. "They want me to pay half of it."

"How are you going to make that kind of money?"

"I have some saved," I said, "but I'll have to make payments."

"Well, go talk to Bren. She charges more for installments, and if you miss a payment, you lose the car and your money. And you still have to get your folks to do the paperwork because you're under eighteen."

Whistling, he headed off to finish washing the car. Okay, so he hadn't been a hundred-percent supportive, but he'd talked to me first. That made this the best day ever!

Brenna was sitting at her desk, and she actually had a smile on her face too. She must have made some serious bucks at the auto show. "Hi, Robin. How's it going? Sorry, I missed your folks, but we got a last minute opening for the Corral at the Tacoma Dome last weekend, so we ran down a half-dozen cars and sold them all."

"That's great," I said and sat down in the empty chair across from hers. "My folks wouldn't go for the car. It's a family tradition that we get horses on our sixteenth birthdays, and they just didn't want one with four tires instead of four hooves."

Brenna rocked back in her chair. "I have to say that I wish my parents would have let me get a horse when I was your age. I love them. So, what breed did they choose?"

"I had to choose," I said. "And he's a Morab. It was more of a rescue than finding one I can ride. He's on my phone."

"I hope he doesn't call long distance."

"Well, right now he'd be more interested in calling the feed store," I said, "but I don't let him touch it." I passed over the phone so she could see the photo. "His name is Twaziem. Well, it's actually *Twa Ziemlich Sonne*, and my sister came up with a translation. It means two pretty suns, and since he's from Earth, I think it's a dumb thing to call a horse."

I knew I chattered, but she made me nervous, just looking at the picture and not saying anything. "He might not look like much right now, but he's actually gained weight since Saturday, and my brother deloused him. I thought he was part paint because he had these patches on him, but they were lice—"

"Stop, please." She held up her hand. A tear trickled down her cheek, and she wiped it away. "I can't deal with that kind of stuff, Robin. I went to war and I'm supposed to be tough, but people who hurt animals and kids just anger me."

"Me, too." I took the phone from her and put it back in my sweatshirt pocket. "Anyway, I wanted to talk to you about the car. I can't buy it for the cash price you quoted me, but I still want it. Can we set it up so I can make payments? What would that cost?"

"Wow. Do you ever give up, Robin?"

I shook my head. "Coach says that winners never quit and quitters never win. I really want that car. Now, what do I have to do to make it happen?"

"Come to work for me as a sales rep when you graduate." Brenna managed a weak smile. "In this economy, I couldn't afford to hire you now, but things may turn around in a couple years. Okay, let's get out a contract, and we'll talk about it. But, your folks need to come in and discuss this, too. At sixteen, you're not old enough to make this big of a decision."

At least she wasn't outright refusing to make a deal on my car. And somehow, some way, I'd make it work, I thought a short time later. The Mustang was destined to be mine. I patted its hood as I went by it. Soon, I'd be driving it all over town. I almost danced down the sidewalk to Dad's office. Inside, I sang, *My car. My car. My beautiful car*!

* * * *

Tuesday, September 17th, 5:15 p.m.

I was home in time to help Jack do chores. While I mucked Twaziem's stall, I contemplated how to bring up the subject of the Mustang to my folks. Brenna had agreed to carry her own contract, which meant I wouldn't need a bank loan for the car. I couldn't get the money from a bank, anyway because I was only sixteen.

However, she wanted the full price of twenty-one thousand, and I'd need to make a ten-percent down payment to start the contract. At ten-percent interest with five years to pay it off, I'd be looking at more than four hundred dollars each month. Brenna had told me I'd need to keep insurance on the car, plus there'd be taxes and other fees. That didn't include gas or repairs.

"There has to be a way to make this work, Twaz." I scooped the last pile of wet shavings into his muck bucket. "I'll have to figure it out. Maybe, I'd better buy a lotto ticket."

He flicked an ear at me and kept eating. I was lucky that my parents didn't charge me for his food. He ate more hay than the other three horses put together. I put the plastic fork outside the stall and dragged in the bale of shavings. It was easier to spread them by hand than with any of the tools since Twaz stomped his feet and spooked anytime I got too close with the rake or the fork.

I'd bet Caine hit him with a pitchfork or some other wooden handle. I remembered when he picked up a huge stick and went after a stray dog at one of our cross-country meets last year. I'd intended to rat him out to the nearest official, but Caine backed off when I threatened him with Jack. I brought the dog back with me from the trail, and Coach Norris said we were supposed to be running, not rescuing critters. It didn't stop him from taking home the Airedale puppy mix, which made Dad happy. He said he was afraid I would bring it home with us, and since she was at least six months old, he'd be paying Dr. Larry to fix her. Extra expenses weren't something that made my accountant father real happy.

Jack stopped outside the stall. "Halter him up, Robin. We need to delouse him again. After you do that, I'll finish the chores so you can head for the shower."

"Come on. It's gross. You should do it for me."

"If you're planning to help Dr. Larry, you'll be doing a lot more gross things," Jack said, handing me a rope training halter and lead line. "Let's go for it, Ms. Wimpy."

"Why do I have to use this, instead of his flat nylon one?"

"Because I'll be holding him, and I want control, not to get stomped when he has a whiff of the delousing powder."

"This is sounding more and more like fun." I pulled a carrot out of my pocket. After Twaz ate it, I tied the halter into place. "Come on. Like Grandma says, 'sooner to it, sooner through it.' And this is the last time you'll have to stink, buddy. Promise."

"Until next spring," Jack said. "When we do all the other critters on the farm, you'll do him again."

"Still sucks to be him." I pulled him away from the hay and led Twaziem outside the barn. Jack already had the shaker can sitting on the lawn, a pair of plastic gloves underneath it. He explained how to sprinkle the delousing powder into Twaz's mane, the dock of his tail, his girth area, inside his back legs, around his ears, and along his spine.

But, that wasn't all. I had to work the thick white powder into my horse's coat. The acrid dust blew into my face, up my nose and tasted bitter. Twaziem snorted and snapped at Jack, almost biting him, but my brother just kept pointing out the spots I missed. I'd barely finished when a green and white sheriff's car pulled into the drive.

"I knew it," I said. "This is against the law. It's sister abuse and I'm so turning you in."

Jack laughed. "Go talk to the cop, Ms. Wimpy. He's probably lost. Stay downwind so he doesn't have to smell you, and I'll put away Jaws. After that, hit the shower."

"Okay," I said. "I'll hurry so I can come back down and help after I clean up."

"Don't stress over it. I do chores all the time and I'll make the dinner table. You'd better, too, or Dad will have a fit and fall in it."

I nodded and started toward the cop car, peeling off the plastic gloves. The big, burly guy in a dark blue uniform climbed out and came toward me, carrying a metal case with papers attached. "Hi," I said. "Are you lost?"

"Not if this is the Gibson place."

"Yes, it is." I stared at him, aware of the white powder on my arms and the smell. So much for looking decent when people came to visit. That wasn't happening. "Why?"

"I'm Officer Yardley." He started to hold out his hand like he wanted to shake hands and be polite. "I'm from Animal Control."

He stopped when I shook my head and didn't take his hand. "No, I stink. What are you looking for?"

"It's more of a who." He smiled, but it was still scary because he didn't look all that friendly and the smile didn't touch his dark eyes. "I think I saw the horse, but I'm looking for Maura Gibson."

"That's my mom," I said and jerked my head toward the house.

"And what do you want with my horse? We just got him last weekend."

"According to his previous owner, Maura Gibson is the person who has him now."

I heaved a sigh. "I hate being sixteen. He's mine, but Mom has her name on his papers until I'm an adult."

"Okay, then let's go talk to your mother. And after that I want to see the horse. What were you doing with him?"

"Can't you smell it? I was delousing him. The vet said he had to have it done again today, and my brother made me do it this time. I majorly stink. And Jack said I couldn't come in the barn until I had a shower."

"But your horse can?" The cop walked beside me toward the house. "Why?"

"Because it's supper time and he has to eat." I eyed him. "Don't you know anything about horses? Jack says if Twaziem doesn't get his food at regular times, he'll colic and that would totally suck. I have a ton of homework, and I don't want to walk him all night."

"I can see where that would be a problem." The cop looked like he was trying to hide a grin.

"Yeah, and you don't even know my teachers. They so need to get lives." I led the way into the back porch. I opened the back door and saw Mom in the kitchen stirring something at the stove. "Mom, this cop is here about Twaziem. Don't let him arrest my horse."

Chapter Thirteen

Tuesday, September 17th, 6:05 p.m.

Mom turned off the burner, then came toward us. "What have you been doing, Robin?" She sniffed and caught a good whiff of the delousing powder. "Never mind. I know. Go hit the shower, and on your way, tell your father to come join us. And after that, put supper on the table for me."

"But, what about Twaz?"

"He'll be fine," Mom said. "Before the county can remove him, they have to serve us with papers and that takes time. Believe me, if your dad has to wait for dinner, that will be worse than anything you've ever seen. Get busy."

"Okay." I headed for the study.

Behind me, the cop called, "It was nice to meet you, Robin."

"Yeah. Me, too," I said, but I was lying. I didn't trust the cop. Actually, when it came down to it, I didn't trust anyone but us to take care of Twaziem. A lot of people would look at him and see death walking. They'd be like the guy who wanted to take him to slaughter, not put the time and energy into saving his life.

When I told Dad about the Animal Control cop coming to see Twaziem, Dad hurried off to help Mom. He paused long enough to pat my shoulder. "It'll be okay, honey. Take your shower and keep your cell with you. I'll call if I want you to get our lawyer. Your horse isn't going anywhere."

74

I nodded and headed for my bathroom. I washed my hands and arms before I got out my cell phone and put it on the vanity. Now, it wouldn't stink like the lice powder. I slid out of my clothes, piling them on the tile floor next to the hamper. I'd take them to the laundry room and dump them in the washer right after my shower.

I hurried through washing my hair and showering away the smell. Then, I toweled off and blew dry my hair. I hustled into clean underwear, a T-shirt and jeans. I didn't bother with makeup, which was totally not like me. I always wore it, even when I did cross-country, but it wasn't true that I had to look perfect to go to the barn, no matter what Jack said.

I bundled my smelly clothes into the towels and went to throw everything in the washer on the hot cycle. Once that was done, I checked the meatloaf. It was ready. So were the potatoes when I poked them with a fork. Same went for the green beans—they'd finished steaming after Mom turned off the heat. I wasn't putting the food on the table to get cold. Dad would hate that.

I checked my cell. He hadn't called. Did we need a lawyer or not? When I looked out the front window, I still saw the green and white sheriff's car. Okay, so Officer Yardley was still here. Didn't he have a home? And why didn't he go there?

I pulled on my running shoes. I didn't need my boots. It wasn't like I'd be in the stall with Twaziem. I was just going back to the barn to save him. There was no way I'd let this guy have him, not when he obviously hadn't done much to make the Bartlett brats step up and look after him.

Dad and Mom came out of the barn with Officer Yardley between them. I went to meet them. "He's mine, right?"

"For now," Officer Yardley said.

"For keeps," I said. "So, what's it going to take to make you go away and not come back? How do I make that happen?"

"By being polite," Mom said.

I shook my head. "No. I don't think so. Mrs. Bartlett was dying of cancer and her snarky, nasty grandkids didn't feed Twaziem." I stared at Officer Yardley. "And he left him there to starve. So, why do I have to be polite?"

"Because if you're not," Dad said, "I'll ground you past forever and you'll lose all your privileges, but none of your responsibilities."

I folded my arms, tapped one foot, and glared at him, even though it wouldn't work. Dad was almost as stubborn as I was. The cop grinned at me, but I didn't smile back. I just waited for a long moment, then another one and a third. "He's mine."

"I can see that you folks are trying to do right by him," Officer Yardley said. "And as long as he keeps gaining weight, I don't have a problem with him living here. I'll talk to Dr. Tomlinson about the prognosis and I'll also be in touch with your farrier."

"And you'll leave Mrs. Bartlett alone," I said. "She has enough to contend with. She doesn't need to be hassled because her family messed up when she was in the hospital with cancer. Harass them. If you want their addresses, I'll get those for you. I have friends who still go to school with them."

He stared at me suspiciously. "Why would you do that?"

"Hello? How do you do your job?" I asked, but I didn't wait for an answer from him. "The three of them are rotten, and they had to learn to be mean to animals from somebody, so you should go after their parents."

Utter silence from the three adults who stared at me, then at each other. I didn't have a problem ratting out the three Bartletts. It wasn't because I was afraid of them. I wasn't. I just didn't like Caine who was overtly cruel or his cousins who were covertly abusive. Either way somebody helpless always suffered whenever the Bartletts were around, and it didn't matter if it was a two-legged or four-legged person.

The cop made a couple more notes then closed up the metal case that held his paperwork. "I really don't see the point in citing you folks for doing something kind. I'll be back to check on Twaziem once a week for the next month. As soon as he has a substantial weight gain, I'll close the case." He eyed me. "And if you're willing to give me names, I'll look into it, Robin. This was the first time I found Mrs. Bartlett at home, and now, I know why."

He was gone in less than five minutes. I walked up with my parents toward the house. Dad hugged me, then said, "Robbie, you need to work on your diplomacy."

"What does that mean?"

"Like your grandmother says, 'Diplomacy is the art of telling

76

someone to go to hell in such a way that he looks forward to the trip,'" Mom said. "And honey, sooner or later, people are going to realize that you're very intelligent. You can't play the blonde dimwit card forever."

"Hey, if they're stupid enough to buy into stereotypes, why should I stop them?"

Both my folks laughed, which was my intent. I didn't need to be on Dad's list and grounded past forever when I wanted to have a sleepover on Saturday. We walked into the kitchen together and found Jack sitting at the table, holding a bag of frozen peas on his upper arm. I felt my stomach lurch. "Oh no. What happened?"

"Jaws of the Baskervilles," Jack said. "In other words, your horse took a bite out of me, and I wasn't even the one who deloused him. He has some issues."

"I already told you that he doesn't like guys," I said, "and now I know why. I ran into Phil at practice today, and he told me that Caine, Wanda, and Ashley Bartlett are whining up a storm because I have their horse."

Jack whistled softly. "When is your first meet? Thursday, right? I'll go with you."

"So will we," Mom said. "Now dish up supper, Robin. Slide out of that shirt, Jack, and let me look at your arm. Did he break the skin?"

* * * *

Wednesday, September 18th, 7:00 a.m.

All the way to school, I kept thinking about Twaziem and Jack. My brother hadn't mentioned the horse bite to the cop and that was a relief. I'd never seen the horse do anything other than stomp his feet and kick at the wall. How was I supposed to know he'd bite Jack? I didn't think it had anything to do with the carrots I fed Twaz. Treats didn't make him bite. For some reason, he connected my older brother to his previous home and the abuse he'd suffered. There had to be a solution because if the Morab was dangerous, Dad wouldn't want us to keep him.

"Are you stressing over anything in particular, Robbie?" Dad asked.

"Just Twaz," I said. "I'm going to talk to Rocky when I have my lesson today. There has to be a way to show him that all guys aren't the same. And at least Rocky admits horses have preferences when it comes to riders. Some trainers don't."

"Well, you're thinking up solutions. Good job."

He seemed pretty receptive, so I asked, "Dad, can we talk about the Mustang tonight? You, me, and Mom."

"Sure," Dad said. "As long as breaking into your college fund isn't one of the options, I'd love to hear what you've come up with. I've always admired your determination." He grinned at me. "You brighten my days."

"I do? How?"

Dad chuckled. "Oh, how about the time you decided your grandparents should visit Cobbie when they didn't want to? I barely managed not to laugh after the pony disgraced himself. I thought I'd choke when I saw the look on my old man's face."

I stared at him. "I thought you were mad at me that day."

"At you?" Dad shook his head, still grinning. "Oh, I won't say you've never annoyed me over the years, Robbie. It wouldn't be true. But, that day? No. You're such a spitfire. It's why my mom says that you're just like my father."

"Wonderful. Well, if you expect me to join the Marines, forget about it. It's so not happening."

"Good. Having you in danger would keep me awake nights."

Coffee in hand, I was at school a few minutes later. Porter, Gwen, and I hung out in the Commons, waiting for Vicky, but she was a no-show. I knew she'd be late when the warning bell rang and we hadn't seen her. I stopped by her locker on the way to English and grabbed her stuff before I headed to class. Her younger brothers and sisters must have been in slow motion today and she had to drop them by the day care a half mile away before she came to school. And they were walking, since her mother had the car.

Vicky rushed in the door three minutes after the final bell rang, and Mrs. Weaver glared at her from the front of the room. "You're late, Victoria. Go get an admit slip from the office."

"Please don't make me. Another tardy and I'm on academic probation, and that means I'm off cheer."

"You should have thought of that when you didn't get to school on time."

"If I get kicked off cheer, it messes with athletic scholarships," Vicky tried again. "Please, Mrs. Weaver. I promise I won't be late anymore."

Somebody had to do something, and I knew she'd be bawling in a minute, especially when Mrs. Weaver just pointed to the door. "Oh, come on, Vicky. We all know the truth. You can't get here any earlier."

"Yeah," Porter jumped in. "You have to get those kids to day care before you come here and some days you can't get the four of them moving."

"There are five of them," I pointed out.

"The baby doesn't count," Porter told me. "All Vick has to do is load up the diaper bag, dress the kid, feed her, grab her and go."

"You should just drop out of school, Vicky." Gwen propped her chin on her fist. "You'll never get out of this town even with a college scholarship. You'll be babysitting for your folks forever. Your dad's too busy for kids with his new girlfriend, and your mom's got that new job working swing or graveyard at the casino."

"I've heard nannies make good money," Steve said. "People are always having babies, so there's job security. You can wipe noses and tushies until you're old and gray."

Mrs. Weaver turned her glare on all of us. "I suppose the cross-country bunch is going to keep this up until I give in. Sit down, Victoria. You and I will meet with the counselor and adjust your schedule after class. Now, all of you open your writing notebooks and do a ten minute write. The topic is, what is a hero? Pick someone in the class who exemplifies those traits and defend your position. I want at least two full pages. Three would be better."

Chapter Fourteen

Wednesday, September 18th, 2:45 p.m.

Rocky met us in the Shamrock Stable office so Mom could do a new lesson application for me. Vicky's paperwork was already on file. I adjusted my pink equestrian helmet in front of the mirror, tightening the chin strap. "Did Mom tell you about the cop coming to see Twaz yesterday?"

"Dave Yardley?" Rocky asked. "He's the local Animal Control guy."

I nodded. "Yeah. Do you know him?"

"Yes," Rocky said. "Whenever someone wants to harass a stable owner, the easiest way is to report animal abuse to Animal Control, and then the officer has to investigate. Dave's a 'by the book' guy, but he's not the worst person I've dealt with in the last thirty years."

"Who would that be?" I asked, insatiably curious.

"The person who runs up a big bill and then turns me into Animal Control when I try to collect it." Rocky glanced at Vicky. "And you want to go into this business? Are you sure?"

"I love the horses," Vicky said, "and you can teach me to deal with the people."

"Keep that in mind when things get tense around here," Rocky said. "Sierra will be the third generation to run the barn, and she still has fits about what she calls people who are a waste of time, space, and oxygen. I save my tantrums for deadbeat horse owners."

There wasn't any gray in Rocky's bright red hair. She didn't look that much older than my mom, but Rocky was tiny, barely five-foot-three in her boots and maybe a hundred pounds sopping wet. I'd seen her handle big horses and she never backed down, not from an unruly colt, or a snarky teenager, or the parents of the tiny tots who came to Pee-Pee Camp and thought their little buckaroos should be galloping all over the place even if they couldn't steer left or right. Sierra was my age, but she didn't go to our school yet. She wanted to, but Rocky said she couldn't afford Lincoln High tuition. And her ex wasn't about to pay for it, since Sierra wasn't his 'real' kid.

Rocky crossed to the file cabinets behind her desk and opened the second drawer. She removed a file. "You ride Summer Time, don't you, Robin?"

"Only when you make me," I said. "I like Prince Charming better."

"He's a total slug, and you never make him work," Vicky told me. "If you stood up to him, he'd do better."

"I like slugs and Charming is sweet. He's dependable, and if I squeeze too hard with my legs, he only walks faster. He never tries to run away with me."

"We're definitely dealing with some big fears there," Rocky said. "Vicky, here's your first lesson. Listen to what your customers say and try to figure out what they mean. Now, what did Robin tell you about riding?"

Mom started to speak, but stopped when Rocky held up a hand like a cop. "I want Vicky's impressions, Maura, not yours. She's my intern and one of her responsibilities includes choosing the right horse for a new student. We'll use Robin as our token new person."

"But, she didn't say anything about riding," Vicky said. "She just said she liked Charming because he's slow and steady, and she doesn't want Summer because he's a goer."

"Now you draw an inference from that," Robin said.

I groaned. "She sounds like Weaver. I hate drawing those, and writing conclusions are even worse."

Vicky giggled. "She was really nice to me today, and she totally helped me with the counselor after you guys let her know what was going on at home."

Catching Rocky's frown, Vicky changed the subject back to horse assignments. "Okay, what if I know that Nitro running away with Robin and dodging cars and trucks on Highway 9 majorly freaked her out? And that isn't something she said today. I just know because she vented to me lots of times. Can I use that to assign her a horse?"

"Believe me, any detail helps," Rocky said. "And sometimes you kids share feelings with each other that you'd never tell an adult. So, now what horse does Robin get?"

"Charming," Vicky said with absolute certainty. "She needs to build her skills and confidence. She trusts him. And if she gets scared and clamps her legs on Summer, he'll think she wants to gallop and that will make it harder for her to relax."

"And when would you switch her to Summer?" Rocky asked, still holding the file.

"When she told me she wanted to get off a slug," Vicky said, avoiding me when I tried to elbow her in the ribs. "Speaking up would make her braver, too."

"Okay, then you both have horses to groom and saddle," Rocky said. "But, first I want you to look at this file and tell me what you see."

"Well, it has Summer's name on it," Vicky said, taking the folder. "Do you have one for Charming?"

"I have one for each horse who lives here." Rocky turned back to the drawer and removed another manila file, passing it to me. "What does it tell you about the horse, Robin?"

I opened the folder and looked inside. Two photos stapled to the inside cover immediately caught my attention. One was of a little bitty brown colt standing next to a big bay mare in the round pen. "Oh wow. It's a baby pic of Charming with his mommy. When did you take this?"

"When he was three days old and could come outside for the first time."

The next photo was of Charming this past summer when he turned seven, all decked out in lesson gear with me holding him for class. He looked exactly like his mom, reddish brown with a black mane, tail, legs—a classic bay. "Okay, so there's a grown-up picture too. Then, there's a description of him on the next page, including his height and weight."

I flipped through the papers, skipping over the copy of his pedigree and registration as a half Morgan, half Quarter-Horse. The next two pages detailed all of his veterinary treatments from the time he was a baby through adulthood. Another sheet listed hoof trims and shoeing. More records of deworming, delousing…everything appeared to be here. Then, I saw records for his training and what he knew how to do from the first halter class all the way up to learning how to do games like barrel racing and pole bending.

"It's like a school report," I said, "only it's everything about Prince Charming."

"And mine's all about Summer," Vicky said, "from the time he was donated three years ago."

"Okay, now if Dave Yardley walked in here and wanted to see either horse, what would be the first thing I'd show him?" Rocky asked.

I stared at her. "The paperwork you keep on the horse. It has the height and weight up through the last time you dewormed two weeks ago, and you even listed the kind of dewormer you used. I so need to do this for Twaziem."

"That's right," Rocky said. "It not only helps you and the veterinarian know what your horse requires, it also shows people who spend most of their time in offices that you can keep records."

"Or as Grandma says, 'if you can't dazzle them with brilliance, baffle them with—'"

"We can figure out what your grandmother says," Mom interrupted me with a smile. "My mother-in-law's been married to a Marine a long time, and as your grandpa says, 'once a Marine, always a Marine.'"

"My files impress lawyers and judges," Rocky went on. "They're sure that if I keep these kinds of records for my horses, I also have detailed ones on my customers."

"Weird. Do I have a file?" I asked, passing back Prince Charming's.

Rocky nodded, pointing to the top drawer of the cabinet. "Yes. It's where I keep your application and what you learn in each lesson. Then when I hire an instructor, she looks up what your skills are and the horses you can ride."

"Only Charming," I said, picking up my bag of carrots. "I won't ride anybody else. He's my fella."

Shannon Kennedy

"Only him," Rocky agreed. "And before you ask, I wouldn't have sold him to you. He's still a mama's boy, and it would break Lady's heart to lose him. So, that's why Dani keeps Lady here instead of taking her home. It was part of the deal I made with her folks when they bought Lady last year."

"That's awesome." I grinned at her. That's why I liked Rocky so much. She put her horses first, and while some trainers might say that a mare wouldn't know her foal after it was grown up, Rocky never would. "Okay, I'm going to saddle up. I'll be ready to ride in about a half hour."

"Me, too," Vicky said.

"Okay, that works. I'll meet you in the indoor arena. Robin, if you need help, Sierra's in the top barn tacking up horses for her beginner lesson. You should be fine. Summer camp was only a month ago."

That made sense. I nodded and headed for the barn and Prince Charming. His stall was next door to his mother's, or dam's. He stuck his head over the door as soon as he saw me and nickered. I handed him a carrot. Lady was quick to put her head over the nearby wall and nudge me for a treat.

Normally, I'd have just given her one, but Dani was in the stall grooming her horse and she could be hypersensitive about stuff like that. "Okay if I feed your horse a carrot?"

Dani came to look and I held up the carrot for inspection. Mom had pulled them out of the garden, but she'd washed off all the dirt, too. Dani narrowed baby blue eyes. "Are those organic?"

"That's all my mom grows," I said.

"Okay." She watched me suspiciously while I fed Lady a carrot, then one to Charming again. Petite, blonde and curvy, Dani looked more like my sister than Felicia did.

"So, what's up with the treat thing? I'd never give a horse something bad for them."

A long stare and then she said, "My last horse died of colic. I guess I'm a bit paranoid."

"I know how that feels. My pony did too. Some jerk threw grass clippings from a lawnmower bag over our fence. We lost him after three days."

"We were at Lake Chelan for a family reunion," Dani said. "The

84

owner of the barn where I had my first horse called and told us she had colic. It was a weekend, so it was like impossible to get one of Dr. Larry's associates, and he was out of town too. And the owner of the stable didn't walk my horse. She was going to a party, so she just went…"

"And left your horse alone?" I opened the stall door and went in with Charming. "That totally sucks. My whole family tried to help save Cobbie, but he was old and we didn't find him in time. Now, my mom only turns the horses out to pasture when she's going to be home to watch them."

"It took us hours to get home and by then it was too late," Dani said, petting Lady's brown neck. "I told my dad I'd never keep another horse there, and when Rocky said Charming couldn't be without his mom, this worked perfectly. I can take Lady to shows, fuss over her and if we go somewhere, I don't have to worry. Rocky and Sierra take awesome care of her."

"They take great care of all the horses." I haltered Charming and attached his lead. Having some kind of handle to make him focus was one of Rocky's rules. Now, I could grab his head if he started to walk off while I groomed him.

Holding my hoof pick in one hand, I ran the other down his left front leg and picked up his foot. He pulled it away. "Oh, come on," I said. "You know the routine."

"Here. Let me help." Dani came out of her horse's stall and into Charming's. "Sierra showed me this really great trick for hoof cleaning. Do you still have a carrot?"

"Sure, but he can't have it when he won't let me do his feet."

"Yes, but he can still smell it." She grabbed the lead rope. "Now, start again. Clean his foot. When you finish, give him a little piece of carrot. Then, do the next hoof. When it's done, he gets another piece…"

"And I keep doing the same thing until all his hooves are cleaned. Great idea, Dani."

"You have to remember that he may be seven, but his brain is still maturing, and even when he's full grown, most experts agree he'll only have the intelligence of a three-year-old human being."

Chapter Fifteen

Wednesday, September 18ᵗʰ, 4:00 p.m.

Dani joined us for our class, which was okay with me, but I saw Vicky roll her eyes. Once Rocky checked our saddles, she had us mount up and then warm up. Stops, starts, turning circles, balance exercises, Charming was his usual calm self. Lady could have cared less, and Summer thought the whole thing was boring so he should dance sideways instead of waiting for the next cue. I was glad Vicky had him, not me.

Mom sat in the bleachers in the far corner of the arena. For once she was quiet at a lesson instead of coaching from the sidelines. That made it easy for me to listen to Rocky and to stay relaxed in the saddle. After warming up, we moved our horses out to the wall. Charming wanted to hang by his mama and follow her around the arena, but I turned a couple circles and that gave us space.

Walking, trotting, patterns and exercises at various gaits kept us and the horses focused on performance. Rocky had me pull Charming into the center when she wanted Dani and Vicky to gallop. It was a very controlled run, what she called a slow, show ring lope, but I was glad we didn't have to participate. Oh sure, I knew that Charming was trained for it, but just the idea was enough to freak me out, much less careening around the ring and trying to do it.

We finished by doing our version of the Shamrock Stable Macarena, standing up in our stirrups, reins on the neck and spelling out the name of the barn while we trotted our horses. It was always fun, and according to Rocky, it helped with our balance. It also boosted my confidence when I rode with no hands, controlling Charming with my seat, legs, and other aids. When we lined up in the center, Rocky told me that on Saturday I'd be doing ground school with my lesson horse. There were several things I needed to teach Twaziem. First I had to become skilled at leading him, backing, long line driving, and longeing him. Since Charming was already an expert, he could train me.

"Bring lots of carrots," Rocky said. "You'll need them."

"If I'm doing ground work on the weekend, then why am I riding during the week?" I asked.

"Because you'll be breaking Twaziem to ride next summer when he turns three," Rocky said. "And you need to have incredible skills to train a young horse. You don't want to teach him things he shouldn't learn, like people can fall off."

"Good point," I said, "but I'd rather have you ride him."

She nodded. "I'll be the first person who rides him. Sierra can take over once I know he's trustworthy. She can handle being bucked off, but I'm still a mom and I hate the idea of her being hurt. I don't want you messing up what we've taught him, so you probably won't be on his back before next summer."

"Okay, as long as I don't have to be on him when I might get hurt," I said. "Jack says I'm wimpy and he's right."

"You're not wimpy," Rocky said. "You're smart. Nobody wants to take flying lessons when they're training a horse, so we'll skip those."

After we unsaddled and groomed our horses, we met Mom at the office. She drove Vicky home first, and once we were alone, I asked her about a sleepover on Friday. Asking for something like a slumber party in front of friends meant a guaranteed *no*, but since I hadn't, she was good with it. Like she said, then she didn't have to get up early to go pick up Vicky. We could go straight to the barn in the morning. Porter and Gwen could go on a trail ride while I had my lesson, then the three of us would leave and let Vicky do her internship.

I arrived home in time to help Jack with chores. While he did the other horses, I mucked Twaziem's stall, watered, and fed him. He flicked his ears at me when I worked around him, but he didn't try to bite or kick me. I remembered that I needed to talk to Rocky about his gender bias and decided to email her as soon as I got in the house. Then, I could ask her if she would be able to send me blank pages for the binder I planned to put together for Twaz. Next week when Officer Yardley showed up, I'd show him what paperwork really looked like.

After dinner, it was Jack's turn for dish duty. Mom, Dad, and I headed for my father's home office. I pulled the contract Brenna had given me from my backpack and passed them each a copy. "I really want this Mustang, and so I talked to Brenna about the installment plan."

Mom stared at me and then looked at the figures on the sheet. "Twenty-one thousand dollars? Are you serious? That's a lot of money."

"Not if you spread out the payments," I said. "And Brenna is willing to finance this herself."

"Have you figured out the full amount you'll be paying over five years?" Dad turned on the calculator on his desk. "Let's do some math and see what the full price will be. How will you make the payments?"

Mom looked at him as if he were crazy. "The answer is no. School comes first, and she's not getting a full-time job so she can pay out close to five hundred dollars a month for a sports car, John."

"When you add in the insurance, taxes, and licenses, it comes closer to six hundred," Dad said.

Relief washed through me. He hadn't said no. He just wanted to talk money. With two of us on the same side, we could convince Mom this was a good idea. I just knew it.

* * * *

Thursday, September 19th, 3:15 p.m.

There were approximately ten schools in our division, and of course, all of them had teams at the first meet. There was lots of competition for the top four runners who would be going to the state competition, two girls, and two guys. Porter, Gwen, and I were three of the long distance runners for Lincoln High. We would be one of the first groups to take off since we had more than three miles to cover. It meant we found an empty spot near a couple picnic tables and started stretching.

I really liked our navy and gold uniforms better than last year's crimson and gray. I looked so much better in blue. Hey, that was important when Harry would see me at assemblies and around school. There hadn't been anything except an announcement this morning at school to promote the first cross-country meet, and I wasn't surprised. It was football season after all. Tomorrow's pep assembly would be to rouse everyone's spirits for the game with Northside Academy in Snohomish, but if I P.R.'d today, it might get mentioned, and did I say Harry would see me? Yes! Another reason to do my best.

Coach Norris gave the team his usual pep talk, then looked at me, Porter and Gwen. "I could say that it goes without saying, but I'm saying it anyway…"

We all laughed and he shook his head at us, but kept smiling. "I expect the *Three Musketeers* to come in first, second and third, and everyone to P.R. today or at least try their hardest."

"How can they even finish when they kept getting lost during practice?" Lew asked.

Coach Norris just eyed him for a long moment. "Don't worry about them, son. Just focus on keeping Steve in sight, so you all finish in the top scorers, and I'll be happy."

"I don't get it," Lew said, as we jogged toward the starting line.

He was a dark-haired, dark-eyed junior who could have been a hunk if he didn't sneer when he talked to girls, so I pretty much ignored him. Steve took pity on him and said, "Last year, Robin and Porter went to State. Gwen missed by two points."

"Not this year," Gwen said. "One of them can stay home."

"If we tie, maybe they'll send three of us from our division," I said.

"It's never happened before," Porter said, "but as Coach says…"

"There's a first time for everything," Gwen and I chimed in with her.

Lew looked at us as if we were nuts. It was time to go. We lined up across the track. We watched the official, 50 meters or more in front of the starting line, wait for attention. Then he fired a pistol and we took off. I didn't try to get out in front. Neither did Porter or Gwen since we could make up time in the woods. We hit the first hill, and I took the lead into the woods, passing Lew with a friendly wave. I saw Steve ahead of me and increased my pace a little.

Sunlight glinted through the trees, dancing on the dirt path. It was the perfect day for a run, not too hot with a cooling breeze. The leaves on the maples and alders had started to turn color from green to gold and red. And the track was dry because the rainy season hadn't started yet. I passed two other runners. They wore red, and I recognized Snohomish's colors. Steve was still ahead of me. He was so going down, even if he didn't know it yet.

This time the course was clearly marked with survey tape, so none of the competitors would make wrong turns and nobody could interfere with the race. The trail wound up hill and down, winding through the trees, and I heard the gurgle of a creek up ahead. It was barely down to a trickle. I leaped over it and kept going. Out of the corner of my eye, I saw Porter right behind me. We were making great time. Up ahead, a log and a couple evergreen branches lay across the path. Steve was the only one in front of us now. He was over the cedar log, past the branches. I was right behind him, then Porter and Gwen.

I heard a faint buzz. Weird. What could it be? We were in the middle of nowhere.

And then somebody started yelling behind us. A guy by the sound of it, but I didn't recognize the voice.

I slowed down and Porter pushed my shoulder. "Get going. Yellow jackets. Move it. Move it! Gwen's allergic."

I sped up, passed Steve, and we raced for the next curve in the trail. Once around it, I slowed down to a jog to check out Gwen. "Did you get stung?"

"No. It was the people behind me who got swarmed." Gwen wasn't even breathing hard, and she looked fine. Her face wasn't swollen, and I didn't see any big spots on her legs or bare arms. "I'm okay. If I was stung, I'd be down on the ground, and you'd be doing CPR. Let's go. I want to P.R. today."

"Okay, but get in front of us," I said. "Then if there are any more wasp nests, we'll be the ones who get the brunt of it."

"Oh, aren't you the fun girl," Porter said, sarcasm in each word.

"Yeah, I am," I said. "And I'm so not giving Gwen the kiss of life. She's not my type."

Giggling, Gwen took off like a rabbit being pursued by a dog, her ash-blonde ponytail bouncing against her shoulders. At this pace, we'd have no problem being the first ones back. For a moment, I wondered what the other distance runners would do about the yellow jackets, then decided I didn't have time to worry about them. I needed to keep up with Gwen, and wow, could she run!

We were the first three runners to finish the five kilometers or just over three miles. Gwen came in first, me second, and Porter was right behind us. It would have been awesome if we could have crossed the line together, but the end was always set up in a funnel or lane to prevent that. We had to come in single file so the scoring would be accurate.

Coach Norris caught up to us a couple minutes later. "All three of you P.R.'d. Great job at your first meet, girls! Now, if the rest of the team hustles, we could win this thing!"

Chapter Sixteen

Thursday, September 19th, 6:10 p.m.

To celebrate Lincoln High winning their first cross-country meet, we swung through *Kentucky Fried* for chicken on the way home. As soon as we arrived, Jack headed for the barn to do chores. I'd just walked in the kitchen when the phone rang. I hurried for the landline. "Hello."

"It's me," Jack said. "Your horse has colic. Tell the folks and I'll start walking him."

"I'll be right there." I turned to Mom. "Twaziem colicked again. I'm changing and going to the barn."

"Okay, I'll mix up a mineral oil cocktail," Mom said.

"I'll get the drugs." Dad headed for the refrigerator and the drawer where we kept horse medications. "We'll save him this time, Robbie. No problem."

"I wonder why he's sick. He was fine when I fed lunch," Mom said.

I left the two of them talking as they worked and hustled to my room. It only took five minutes to switch from my track suit to jeans, a T-shirt, and sweatshirt. I pushed my cell into the back pocket of my jeans so I could call Dr. Larry if we needed him. Then, after a pause in the back porch for my boots, I was off to the barn.

When I arrived, Jack already had Twaziem in the indoor arena. Pinned back ears, evil glares and if a horse could stomp his hooves, mine was about to have a serious meltdown. He snaked his head around and tried to bite at my brother again. I went across the ring and took the lead.

92

Twaz's mood instantly changed. Ears up, he nuzzled me. "Yes, I'm here to save you, baby."

"He's a baby with teeth," Jack told me, rubbing his arm. "I've seen dogs lunge like that with their mouths wide open, but never a horse. This guy has some issues. I'm going to take care of everyone else and then go find the ice."

"He's lucky to have you on his side," I said, towing Twaziem around the arena. "A lot of guys would walk off and let him die because of his crappy attitude."

"I'm destined to be a hero." Whistling, Jack headed off to shovel horse poop.

"You've got to get over yourself." I petted Twaziem's brown neck. "My brother will never hurt you. He's not like that creep, Caine. Okay?"

Another bump with his nose and I kept walking him. "No, you don't get any carrots right now. You have to get over your tummy troubles and I need to hear your gut rumbling first, plus I need to see and count lots of turds. Dad will never let me have the Mustang if he has to pay another vet bill for you, so we better not need Dr. Larry tonight."

* * * *

Friday, September 20th, 7:40 a.m.

I barely got to school on time the next morning, and of course, we were on assembly schedule today. Luckily, I had Mr. Sutcliffe for Algebra instead of eagle eye, rule worshipping Mrs. Weaver. He waited at the door and held my mocha while I yawned my way through my backpack, hunting out my math homework.

"Late party last night after the cross-country team won the meet?" Mr. Sutcliffe asked, his brown eyes crinkling with laughter and a big, warm smile on his face.

"I wish," I said. "My silly horse colicked, probably because supper was late, and I was up with him till three in the morning."

"Oh, no." Dani stopped behind me and unzipped her backpack to do the homework hunt. "Is he okay? What did Dr. Larry say?"

"To get used to colics because it's a problem that a lot of horses have when they're so debilitated." I handed over the paper to Mr. Sutcliffe and took back my coffee. "And then he told me to stop having my nails done and to have the artificial ones removed because they'll rip through the glove when I have to stick my arm up Twaziem's tushie and clean out the poop."

Mr. Sutcliffe held out the page as if it came from the barn, not my backpack. "Please tell me you washed your hands before you did your homework."

Dani laughed and handed over her paper. "Come on, Mr. S. If there was poop on it, you could see it."

"Yes, but a couple weeks ago she gave me a paper with teeth marks," Mr. Sutcliffe said. "I knew the assignment was difficult, but I didn't expect anyone to have to chew their way through it."

"My cat got it," I told Dani, "and I didn't have time to do it over."

"That's her story and she's sticking to it." Mr. Sutcliffe laughed, a deep rumble. "I'm going with the idea that I'm a tough teacher, and it was a hard assignment."

"Keep dreaming," I told him.   Still carrying my coffee cup, I headed for my desk.

There was a student pileup at the door. Mr. Sutcliffe admitted this was his first teaching job and he thought we should all be as excited about Math and Science as he was. I had to admire the guy. At least he wasn't a phony, and he was never mean. Maybe I could talk to him about the installment payments on the Mustang and see if he agreed with my dad about the long-term cost of the car.

I'd barely sat down when Olivia strutted over, flanked by two Native American girls. Olivia was Native, African-American and Asian—absolutely gorgeous and a total witch, only I spelled it with a "b." Even if she could really run, she'd lost me as an admirer last spring when she pitched a fit at one of the last track meets and called the official a racist for restarting the long distance race because there had been too much messing around.

"What's up?" I didn't like looking up at her, so I stood. "You have a problem with me?"

"I don't like losing," Olivia said, "especially to princesses like you and your posse."

"Well, suck it up, buttercup." I met her glare for glare. "We crossed the finish line first. Fair is fair." I had to be honest, even with her, so I added, "If Gwen had been stung by those wasps, we'd have lost because she's hyper allergic."

"And you wouldn't have left her," Cedar sneered.

I let the silence build while I looked at her. She always copied exactly what Olivia wore and tried to act like her, but she didn't have her friend's guts. "No more than Olivia would have left you."

A smile flickered across Olivia's beautiful brown face, then disappeared. "Exactly, so we're running with you and your buds starting next practice."

"But, we hate them," Kanisha whined.

"They win so we're running with them." Olivia's tone made it a statement, not a question. She turned away. "We'll see you Monday at practice."

I knew it was petty, but I didn't care since her friends were already sniveling. Plus, I was mad. My family might call me Princess Robin, but nobody else better. "You've got a problem," I said.

"Really?" She swung back to face me, ready to call me out for being prejudiced. "What?"

"I run at least six miles a day, every day." I smiled sweetly. "Since Gwen and Porter are spending the night at my house, we'll do it tomorrow morning before we go horseback riding. Want to come?"

"No," Kanisha said. "Monday's soon enough."

Olivia shot her a glare that promised retribution later. "When and where?"

Oh, damn. Now, I was stuck with her. Even if I didn't like the way she played the 'race card,' I should have expected her to step up since she had no give-up in her. I tore a sheet of paper out of my binder and wrote down my address and directions. "We have to be at the barn in time for Vicky's internship at eight, so we're running at six."

"In the morning?" Cedar whined. "That sucks."

"Then, don't come," I said.

"We'll be there," Olivia told me and walked away, followed by the other two girls.

The final bell rang and Mr. Sutcliffe began his countdown at the door. "You've got ten seconds, nine, eight, five…"

"Hey, you skipped some numbers," Steve griped as he hustled through the door, followed by Vicky and Dani. "You should start over."

"Not happening." Mr. Sutcliffe shut the door and headed toward his desk to take attendance on the computer. "Entry task is on the board. Let's get started, folks. We have a short period and a lot to cover today."

Vicky plopped down in her chair next to me. "Congratulations on P.R.ing yesterday. That's terrific."

"Yeah, right until we got home and Twaz colicked again. Mom's going to put a new bale of hay in his manger before she leaves next Thursday for the meet." I caught the glance from Mr. Sutcliffe and hastily pulled out the composition book he insisted we use as a math journal. Then, I worked the three problems, finding solutions for each one.

History followed Algebra. We had our usual Friday quiz. This one was all about early explorers in America. I had to trust my memory, and it was shot since I'd barely had four hours sleep the night before. My coffee was rapidly wearing off when the bell rang and we headed for English. I so didn't look forward to listening to one of Mrs. Weaver's lectures.

And of course, today she would decide to talk about sentence structure and how to diagram each part—like I cared what she wanted done with verbs, adverbs, adjectives, nouns, and objects. I had a few suggestions. I felt my head droop and jerked myself awake.

"Robin Gibson, would you repeat the assignment for the class?" Mrs. Weaver asked, coming close to my desk.

I squirmed and wished the chair would swallow me. "I'm sorry. I didn't understand it."

Mrs. Weaver stared down her nose at me as if I were a worm. "Would someone like to rescue Robin?"

Dani was the first to speak up. "We're supposed to write a paragraph of ten sentences, then diagram those sentences. It's due in twenty minutes, before the bell rings." She flashed a quick smile at me. "You should write about saving your horse last night. Vet books always go on for pages about colic. It'd be easy to come up with ten lines."

I so owed her. I nodded and looked at the teacher. "Yeah. I could do what she said."

"All right." Mrs. Weaver turned and headed back for her desk. "You'd better get started. You only have eighteen minutes until the bell."

And she was such a clock-watcher, nobody figured she'd give us an extra minute, much less accept any late work. I opened my binder to a fresh sheet of paper, pulled out a pen and wrote. *My horse almost died again last night...*

Chapter Seventeen

Friday, September 20th, 10:15 a.m.

I had first lunch, and wow, was I ready even if there wasn't any caffeine around. I got a sub sandwich, chips, an apple and a bottle of water. I spotted Harry and headed over to his table. I sat down across from him, struggling not to yawn. "Hey. How are you?"

"I'm good." He grinned at me. "Heard you guys won yesterday. Congrats."

"Thanks." Inside me the butterflies did a little dance. He knew I was a runner and had paid attention to what the team was doing. All right!

I fought to control another yawn as I opened my chips. "Yeah, but things got exciting when we found a nest of yellow jackets the hard way."

"Tell me about it." He reached down in his backpack and pulled out a bottle of Mountain Dew, opening it for me and handing it over. "Here have some caffeine first. I didn't think running wore you out that much."

"It doesn't." I gratefully took a swallow. "I was up all night with my horse. He colicked again."

He looked interested, so between bites of my sandwich and sips of the soda, I brought him up to speed on Twaziem's misadventures, the meet and the cop who planned to visit every week. Harry told me all about how the football team was going to win tonight and how my older brother was the best wide receiver around. That wasn't all bad. If Harry actually asked me out, Jack wouldn't freak, his usual response when one of his friends eyed me.

Halfway through lunch, Vicky arrived. She tossed back her hair and gave me a nasty look. "I knew you'd be here telling Harry about your ugly horse."

"What?" I almost choked on a chip. "Vick, what's wrong?"

"You think you're so hot. You said you were going to bring home the worst horse you could find, and you certainly did. Now, you're acting like some kind of hero."

She stormed away before I could say anything. For a moment, I wanted to cry. What was the matter with my best friend? How could she betray me in front of Harry? This was awful. Half the people in the lunchroom were staring at me. The rest were looking after her. A cheerleader doing drama was always interesting and fun to watch.

"I've got to go find out what her issue is, Harry." I stood and gathered up the remains of my lunch. "And yes, I was mad when my family insisted on four hooves on the horse, not four wheels, so I pitched a fit. I'm not perfect."

"I never thought you were." He leaned back in his chair. "Is it okay if I say that I like you better as a human being, or will you rip me a new one?"

I'd have to think about that. Meanwhile, I tossed my garbage and went Vicky hunting. I didn't actually expect her to answer her cell because she was undoubtedly saving her minutes. I was still surprised when she didn't pick up. She was nowhere to be found, not in the bathrooms or the counseling office or the locker room, or the gym decorating for the pep assembly or even with Mrs. Weaver. I tried calling again right before the warning bell rang.

On the way to Science, I texted her. Then, I put away my phone. I wouldn't push my luck with Mr. Sutcliffe. He might dress down in jeans and a Washington State University sweatshirt on Fridays, but I didn't want to lose my cell when he followed the rule about no electronic devices in his classroom. I'd catch up with Vicky at the assembly.

Only I couldn't. She wasn't there. Pity and concern swamped me. She would be in so much trouble with her coach. The cheerleaders always organized and put on the pep assemblies, so for her to miss one when she wasn't dead jeopardized Vicky's standing with the Varsity squad. We were dismissed to go to the buses at the end of the assembly, but I didn't. I went to Ms. Walker instead. I had to wait until she arranged for the cheerleaders to clean up the gym.

"Ms. Walker, do you know where Vicky is? I'm really worried about her."

"Me, too." Ms. Walker patted my shoulder. "All I can tell you is that I got a message from the office saying she had to leave early. She isn't sick, is she?"

I shook my head. "No, but one of her parents probably pulled her out to babysit the kids."

"That's what I thought, too." Ms. Walker kept her hand on my shoulder and urged me toward the door. "Robin, she has to be at the game tonight or I'll have to suspend her from Varsity for a week. The squad has been great about covering for her, but our routines are set up for nine cheerleaders and without her—"

"I'll get her there if I have to babysit for her," I said.

Outside, I grabbed my phone and checked messages. There actually was one from Vicky begging off from the sleepover. She'd catch up with me later. Well, this was total crap, I thought. What was she going to do about her internship? Cancel on that too? Then, she'd be in trouble for bailing on Rocky, fail three classes and be stuck in Podunk, USA, forever.

I called Dad's office and told the secretary to tell him I was taking the bus. I had things to do at home before my sleepover and Jack's football game. Meantime, I called Vicky. Of course, she still didn't answer. She was into avoidance or else the kids had her jumping through hoops. Well, two could play this game. I left her a message that I'd be there to babysit the brats at five. Jack would drop me off and take her to the school, so she'd better have her cheer act together. Oh, and the next time she fouled things up with Harry, I'd pull each and every strand of golden brown hair out of her head.

So, I'm not perfect. Sue me!

On the way home, I contacted Porter and Gwen. I brought them up to speed on the Vicky drama. They promised to show up at my house and do chores with my mom. Like Porter said, even with all our critters, we didn't have anything compared to Shamrock Stables. Last summer, there were forty stalls to clean every day. Porter told me they'd go to the game with my folks, and we'd meet up there.

Then, we could get my dad to stop for pizza and junk food on the way home. And I didn't know how I'd manage to get Vicky to the sleepover, but I was majorly sick of her parents dumping on her. Hello, she had brothers and sisters, not her own kids, not yet. If the crap-fest didn't stop soon, I'd bet Vicky would never get married, much less have a family of her own. If I had to contend with everything she did, I sure wouldn't.

* * * *

Friday, September 20th, 10:25 p.m.

I was finishing my algebra homework when I heard a key in the front door. I closed my math book and got up from the kitchen table to walk into the hall. I spotted Vicky's mom sliding out of her coat. "Hi."

She stopped and stared. "Robin, what are you doing here?"

"Babysitting," I said. "Vicky can't get kicked off cheer, Mrs. Miller."

Utter silence while she opened and closed her mouth like a fish. I folded my arms and waited. Her mom looked like an old-age version of my best friend, but I'd never catch Vicky in a green tuxedo style shirt and black slacks and shoes. Brown-haired, brown-eyed, five-feet-six, her mother looked old and tired under the cosmetics she wore.

"I got called in to work," Mrs. Miller said, "and I needed Vicky to take care of the kids today until her dad got here."

"Well, guess what? He didn't show up. And Vick missed the assembly at school today so her cheer coach was majorly pissed. If she'd missed the game too, Ms. Walker would have suspended her." I wasn't about to cut this woman any slack. She dumped all the crap on my friend, and Vicky barely had a life anymore.

"So, you came to look after the kids so Vicky could go." Mrs. Miller pasted on a smile and reached into her purse. "That was really nice of you. What do I owe you?"

"Nothing," I said. "Vick owes me. You don't. I did all of Vick's

101

other chores, too. I made dinner, cleaned the kitchen, did four loads of laundry, and put it away. The kids went to bed at eight."

"Their bedtime is ten on Friday nights," Mrs. Miller said.

"I know. They told me, but when they started the pushing, shoving, hitting, and kicking the crap out of each other over the TV remote, I did baths and put them to bed," I said. "Next Friday, it'll be seven. Vick's your maid or slave. I'm not."

More gulping. If she was a fish, I'd have thrown water on her so she didn't die. I dug out my phone to text Jack. We'd already agreed that he was to leave Vicky at our house if he had to tie her up and chuck her in my closet. "Your dinner's in the microwave. You just need to nuke it."

"Where is Vicky? The game must be over by now."

"At my house," I said. "You can pick her up at Shamrock Stable tomorrow after she does her internship hours."

"She can't go to the barn. She was supposed to call and cancel that. Who will take care of the kids?"

I tapped my foot. This woman was seriously annoying me. I didn't care what my parents said about being diplomatic. With some people, it just didn't work. "Really? Do you plan to have Vick fail all three core classes when she screws up her Sophomore Project for you and her father?"

No answer. Had I expected one?

I went back to the little dining area off the kitchen and gathered up my books and backpack. I was going to be a lot nicer to my mother even if she never let me have my Mustang. It didn't matter how many kids she had. If there were six of them instead of three, my mom wouldn't turn one into Cinderella to look after the others.

Mrs. Miller came into the kitchen. "This is hard for all of us, Robin. You may not believe me, but I'm not trying to ruin my daughter's life."

I zipped up my backpack. "I'm not the one you need to tell that. You should tell Vick in front of your other kids how much you appreciate her help. Unless your ex shows up next Friday for visitation, I'll be here to babysit. Oh, and I wouldn't make a habit of pulling Vick out of school, unless you want the counselors, the teachers and the principals on you about her potential for being a dropout instead of a graduate."

Chapter Eighteen

Saturday, September 21st, 12:30 p.m.

I leaned back in the passenger seat of Jack's truck while he drove home from Shamrock Stable. If we lived further away from the barn, I could have a nice snooze.

He glanced sideways at me while he waited for the light to change at the intersection on Highway 9. "Babysitting last night so Vicky made the game was above and beyond. She couldn't believe you would step up like that."

"Yeah, I'm great." I yawned. "But if she messes with me again when I'm chasing Harry, all bets are off. You'll have a bald girlfriend."

Jack was still laughing when we pulled into our drive. "Go catch some zs, little sister. I'll feed horse lunch, and then I'll help you give Twaziem a bath when he finishes eating."

I groaned. That had been my lesson today with Prince Charming. Sierra taught me the ins and outs of bathing a horse from wetting them down to scrubbing every inch, rinsing off all the soap, and finally drying them so they wouldn't catch cold. Plus, I'd had to shampoo Charming's mane and tail, condition them, and then comb out every hair. And now, I was supposed to apply everything I learned to Twaziem. It sounded like so much fun. *Not!*

I walked past my parents' cars and wondered why both of them were around on a Saturday. Didn't they have some riding activity to do? Usually, Mom took Singer out to work on the Centennial Trail and condition her for upcoming endurance rides. Dad would be off with his roping buddies.

I went in the kitchen door. Salt and Pepper, the black and white kittens, raced to meet me. They wound through my legs. I bent and scooped up the pair of small flea-lions as Dad called them. "Shall we find some meat for you?"

Salt mewed at me and Pepper tried to bat at my face with a paw. Mom glanced at me from the counter where she made roast beef sandwiches. "If I told you they were lying and I already fed them, would you believe me?"

"No." I laughed, cuddling the little monsters close. "I can tell starving kitties when I see them."

Dad came in from his office, rubbing his ear. "Hi, sweetie. I just heard all about you from Vicky's mom."

"Yeah," I muttered. When he frowned at me, I mustered up a smile as I put the kittens on the floor. "Did you tell her what it would cost for a housekeeper-cum-caregiver for her brats for five hours, and that the bill is forthcoming?"

Mom winked at me when Dad chuckled. Then he said, "No, but I did tell her that I was very proud of you for helping Vicky stay in school, and I wished you'd clean the cat box the way you cleaned her house."

Mom high-fived me. "When she sniveled at me and said she didn't like the way you did laundry, I told her that I taught you how and asked if there was a better way to fold T-shirts and diapers."

"Anything else?" I opened the cupboard to pull out a can of cat meat. "Did she gripe about me putting the kids to bed when the four of them got into a 'knock-down, drag-out' fight over the remote?"

"Yes," Mom said, "and I said that was the way Felicia handled it with you and Jack. I thought it was a much more effective method than time-outs and spankings when the parents got home."

"It sucked being sent to bed at seven." I spooned meat into the double-sided dish and got out of the way before the kitten attack. "But, we never hassled Felicia again when she took care of us. And I don't remember her ever having to clean the entire house, make dinner, do a day's worth of dishes, run mountains of dirty clothes through the washer, and supervise bath time. No wonder Vick looks exhausted most of the time."

"Well, her father is coming for the kids next Friday immediately after school." Dad filled four glasses with milk, then placed the pitcher in the fridge. "And I told her mother that she was absolutely right about you going to the game next week with your friends, so your mom and I will take care of the little kids if he doesn't show up. I'll pick them up at day care when I get off work."

"You are a very evil daddy and I love you lots." I dropped the empty cat food can in the recycle bin, then hugged Mom. "Are you okay with it?"

"Yes," Mom said. "You'll have to cheer extra loud to make up for us missing Jack's game, but I'm not taking Vicky's brothers and sisters to high school football. We'll talk to him about all of this at lunch."

Later that afternoon, I headed down to the barn with an armload of old towels that Mom said were appropriate for horse bathing and a bucket of long, skinny carrots from the garden. I hoped Twaziem agreed this was a good idea. Charming had been a complete gentleman, but Sierra warned me that young horses might dance around the shower stall the first time they got wet. I was glad Jack promised to help, but figured I couldn't go wrong with bribery too.

I hung the towels in the shower stall, took two carrots, and went after my horse. I didn't use the flat nylon halter this time. I opted for what Sierra had called a training one. The thin rope halter had knots that placed pressure on nerves in a horse's face. This should get Twaziem's attention and keep him from biting my brother. I attached the lead to the bottom loop and led him out of his regular stall.

"I don't think you've had this done before," I said, "but you really need a bath to get rid of those dead lice and that awful smell from the delousing powder. This won't be so bad because we're not doing it the old-fashioned way with cold water from a garden hose the way I did Prince Charming. We have a nice shower with lots of warm water."

Twaziem nuzzled me as I led him into the stall. It had rubber mats on the floor so he couldn't slip and drains so he wouldn't have to stand in water. A lot of horses hated puddles because they couldn't see into them. Jack arrived with bottles of soap and shampoo, and a bucket filled with sponges and scrapers. Twaziem made an ugly face at my brother.

"Okay," I said. "What do you want to do? Be chewed into little Jack bits or scrub?"

He laughed. "I think I'll scrub for a while if you can hold him."

"Let's try and see what happens," I said.

Jack put the bucket with the sponges out of the way. He turned on the faucet and adjusted the temperature, holding the hose away from Twaziem until the water was warm, but not too hot.

Meanwhile, I used the sealant that Sierra recommended on the hooves. I didn't want Twaz to have foot problems because his feet got too wet. Once I finished painting each hoof with the iodine mixture, I stepped back and held his head.

Jack slowly stepped up by Twaziem's neck and began spraying him with warm water, up the front legs to his chest, over his left shoulder and then onto his neck. Twaz snorted, but he didn't move, so my brother kept wetting him down. As Jack soaked the back, then the ribs and finally Twaz's hindquarters, I saw the yellow patches of dead lice slide down the coat and onto the floor.

All right, I thought. This was going to work. My horse would feel and look so much better when the parasites were off his body. Once Twaziem was totally wet, Jack put the sponges out of the way while he filled the bucket with warm water and a couple squirts of dish soap. Then, he grabbed a sponge. "Do you want me to keep going or should I try holding him while you do it?"

I shook my head. "Like Sierra told me this morning, if it's not broke, don't fix it. Right now, he's standing super quiet. Let's get this done. Next time, I'll wash him. He has so many gender issues. Maybe, I can get Vicky here, and she'll be able to hold him."

Twaziem stomped his hooves at the sound of Jack's voice but the bay settled down when we got quiet again. He was a strange one. Most of the other horses I'd known liked listening to people, but not this guy. Somehow, he associated chatter with abuse. I slipped him a couple carrots while Jack scrubbed him down with the sponge until suds covered Twaziem's entire brown coat.

Next came his tail. Jack stayed carefully to the side while he washed it. After he finished with the tail, Jack worked shampoo into Twaz's mane. And finally it was time to rinse off the horse. It took what seemed like a long time to get rid of all the soap and shampoo. More carrot pieces to eat and my bay colt stood like a rock. I praised him while I gave him another treat.

When Twaziem was soap free, Jack passed me a damp sponge. "Wipe off his face. We won't use any shampoo this time. But if you do it, then he can't bite me."

"Okay." I draped the lead over my arm so if my horse jerked, he could get away, and I wouldn't get hurt. Then, I washed off Twaziem's head, around his ears and down the center over his blaze. Jack took the sponge from me a couple of times and wrung it out in clean water. I even cleaned under the forelock and wiped around Twaz's eyes. A couple snorts before he nudged me, looking for carrots, and we were good to go.

I handed back the sponge and adjusted the lead so I could hold the horse while Jack used a scraper to get rid of the excess water. After that we toweled Twaziem dry. I stayed up by the front end of him, and Jack did the rest. We couldn't put him back in his usual stall until he was completely dry or he'd catch cold.

Jack left partway through to go clean Twaziem's stall and reload the manger with a new bale of hay. This was the perfect time for daily maintenance since my horse couldn't kick or bite if he was in the shower. I kept talking to him while I finished drying him and figured out that he didn't mind my voice when it was just the two of us. For some reason, he just didn't like the conversations people shared. They must pose some kind of threat.

So much of this was pure conjecture and detective work. It wasn't as if I could ask the Bartletts what they'd done to Twaziem. I had to figure all of it out on my own. He nosed me and I passed him another carrot piece while I toweled his mane. He seemed to enjoy my company. He never tried to bite or kick me, much less charge at me the way Nitro did. I could tell Twaz my problems and he didn't answer me, but at least he didn't tell me I was stupid for wanting my Mustang.

Was this why my family loved their horses? Did they feel like I did? I didn't have to do or be anything special for Twaziem to accept me. And he didn't criticize me for not being perfect, or call my mom or dad and try to rat me out because I wasn't nice or sweet like my brother or sister.

I turned and picked up a big comb. "You're going to look so

Shannon Kennedy

handsome," I told Twaziem as I started to work on the tangles in his mane. "Singer will think you're really hot. And if the weather's nice tomorrow, I'll let you go out to the paddock with her. Sierra says horses are social animals, and you'd probably like being with a mare for a couple hours. Besides, it doesn't matter if the neighbors see you. They can't report you to Animal Control for being skinny because that cop already has a case file on you."

Chapter Nineteen

Sunday, September 22nd, 1:30 p.m.

While Twaziem pulled hay from the bale in his manger, I groomed him. His brown coat shone, a soft red-gold cast to the color. I was pretty sure he'd be more of a blood bay than a golden one. I heard footsteps in the aisle and glanced toward the hall. I couldn't quite believe it when I saw Olivia in a T-shirt and shorts. "What's up?"

"You said you run every day." Her voice was absolutely calm. "I'm here to go with you."

"Where are your friends?" I asked and kept currying my horse. "I thought they were joining us."

"They wimped out after yesterday." Olivia lifted her chin. "I'm not afraid to work, or build my stamina."

I shrugged. "Okay, well, let me finish up Twaz and put him out in the paddock. Then, we'll go."

"Want some help?"

I hesitated. "He's not real nice. He bites and kicks. I don't want you to get hurt."

Her dark eyes widened and she began to smile. "I'll be careful."

"Okay." I stopped currying Twaziem and took hold of the rope hanging from the training halter. "Get one of those carrots and come on inside. We'll see what he thinks of you, but if he gets obnoxious, then get out of here. Deal?"

"You got it." She picked up two carrots out of the bucket and

109

slipped through the door, closing it behind her. She held up the first one. "Hey, fella. Want a treat?"

Twaziem nickered and flicked his ears. Then, he stretched out his neck and pulled the carrot from her hand. Crunch. Munch and it was gone. He reached for the next treat. She gave it to him.

"So far, so good," I said. "Go ahead and grab a brush. Let's see if he'll let you groom him." I eased up my hold on the lead, and Twaz turned back to the hay once he realized we didn't have any more treats.

He stood and ate while we brushed him. Olivia wasn't real chatty and that worked out great. I didn't want to push my luck with the horse. After we finished with his body, I worked on his mane and she stood by his hip to comb out his tail.

"Why is he so thin?" Olivia finally asked.

"I just rescued him a week ago," I said. "He's actually gained about thirty pounds. He really looked awful last Saturday. He had these moving patches of lice, and he'd eaten like half his tail."

"That's majorly gross." Olivia ran the comb through what remained of Twaz's tail. "If you keep conditioning it every time you groom him, then it will grow back faster."

"Good idea," I said. "I will. How do you know so much about horses?"

"I ride at my grandfather's whenever I get the chance." She glanced over her shoulder at me. "You need to scoop out his stall every time he poops, or he'll eat that too."

"Now, I think that is majorly gross," I teased.

She laughed. "What are you doing with him this afternoon?"

"Putting him out in the field for a couple hours," I said. "After we get back from our run, I'll turn my mom's mare in with him. I need to watch the two of them so Singer doesn't kick him and he doesn't hurt her, either. I don't know how he'll be with another horse, and it's not like I can ask his previous owners."

"Why not?" She shook her head. "Never mind. I was being stupid. If they didn't feed him, you can't trust a word they'd say about him."

"Exactly."

We finished up grooming him. She gathered up the brushes and fed Twaziem another carrot. Then, I led him out to the small field near the house. The grass was about six inches high, and I'd already scrubbed out the water tub in the corner and refilled it. As soon as I turned him loose, he trotted away. He snorted and bucked a couple times. Then, his knees gave out and he was down in the green field, rolling.

"That's just great," I said. "A bath yesterday, a good grooming today, and now I get to start over."

"Everybody's a critic," Olivia said. "He probably figures he can do a better job getting himself clean. Shall we run?"

"Yes." I took my grooming bucket from her. "I'll put this in the back porch and tell my mom where we're headed. She can watch Twaziem for us."

When I came back from the house, Olivia was already stretching out. I joined her. I hated muscle spasms and was grateful that she wasn't so busy being cool that she skipped a proper warm-up. "So, how do Cedar and Kanisha plan to win at the meets if they don't build up their stamina?"

It was Olivia's turn to shrug. "It's up to them, but if they realize I'm going to keep practicing, they'll get over themselves. They want to go to State, too."

"Fair enough." I turned and jogged down the driveway. "Let's do it."

* * * *

Sunday, September 22nd, 8:30 p.m.

That night I returned to the barn just to be sure that Twaziem wasn't suffering any ill effects from his busy weekend. He appeared to be fine, still stuffing himself with hay. I remembered what Olivia said about the possibility of him eating manure so I took a few minutes to clean the stall and add more shavings. With three good sized dumps in the back corner, I knew he didn't have colic. That meant I'd be able to sleep all night in my own bed instead of walking him until super late.

I brought back an empty feed bucket from the grain room and turned it upside down in the corner near the manger. I sat down and proceeded to tell Twaz all about my plans for the week. Sure, cross-country practice was high on the list, but so was seeing Harry and visiting my Mustang. I hadn't heard a word from Mom or Dad about the installment plan. They had to make a decision sometime this week, didn't they?

Twaziem considered the question around a mouthful of hay, but he didn't have any real answers, and since he wasn't a talking horse from TV, I didn't expect any. I just wanted to win his trust so he'd get in the habit of believing in people again. I needed to find him a home next spring or summer when he put his weight on, and if he still had issues with guys, that would be tough.

"Robin, are you down here?" Mom was in the aisle outside the stall.

"In here," I said. "With Twaz. I wanted to make sure he was okay before I called it a night."

"How is he?" Mom leaned on the door and held out a carrot for my horse. "Any colic?"

"Not tonight," I said. "And I'm glad."

"He'll do better after you deworm him," Mom told me. "You can't for another two weeks since you just deloused him, but I think that was a wise decision. You dealt with the external parasites first. You can deal with the internal ones later."

Twaziem obviously thought the parasite discussion was bogus. He reached out for the carrot instead. Three treats later, I collected the bucket and went out to join Mom in the aisle. She'd moved down to feed Singer a carrot, then Buster and Nitro. Once she was finished with all the horses, we strolled toward the house.

"Robin, have we ever talked about how horses see?"

I shook my head. "I don't think so. Why? What's up?"

"I'm glad you're making friends with Twaziem. I think it's important, but you also need to be safe. He has three different blind spots. He can't see below his knees."

I remembered Rocky's lectures about horse vision to the day campers. "Or directly behind him and directly in front of him, so the safest place is next to his shoulder and that's where I was."

"Yes, but I'd rather you leaned on the manger or hitched up on it," Mom said. "If he'd jumped sideways, he could have crashed into you. I know he's thin, but he still outweighs you by several hundred pounds. And horses have the reflexes of one of your cats in hot pursuit of a

112

mouse."

"Good point. I'll be more careful." I tucked my arm through hers. "I'm really glad you're my mother and Vick's isn't."

Mom pulled me closer. "Yes, but she's in a tough situation. Six kids and no help. What would you do? What would I do?"

"You'd kick Dad's butt until he stepped up," I said. "But, I can't imagine him leaving on my birthday or Jack's or Felicia's. That was just plain mean, and I've never seen Dad do a single rotten thing to anyone. How will Vicky ever have a happy birthday again?"

"You're her best friend," Mom said. "I guess you'll have to make it happen for her next year. And she's a smart girl. She knows that just because somebody tries to push your buttons, you don't have to play 'elevator' for him, even if it is one of your parents."

"I haven't talked to her about being so nasty last Friday," I said. "I feel like I should, but I don't want to start things up again."

"Maybe, you could hold off and let her bring it up." Mom led the way into the back porch. "You need to show compassion for her and you did, but you don't have to be a doormat."

Another good point, I thought, as we headed for the living room to join Jack and Dad in front of the TV. I would let Vicky do the talking tomorrow. She knew I was on her side after I babysat for her so she could go to the game and stay on the cheer squad. But, she hadn't said much on Friday night.

Of course, by the time I got here, she was sacked out in my room and I hadn't wanted to wake her. The same went for Saturday morning when Porter, Gwen, and I went running with Olivia and her friends. Vicky was still asleep, and since I knew firsthand how hard she worked at her house, I wasn't about to get her up till breakfast. And I hadn't heard a thing from her for the rest of the weekend.

I pulled my cell phone out of my pocket and checked. Nope. No messages from her. What was up with her, anyway? Was she so busy being a super-nanny that she didn't have time to call me and let me know how the first day of her internship went? Well, the road did run two ways, so I sent her a quick text, although I didn't know how much time she had on her cell. Sometimes, things got tricky since she had to pay for it herself. Then, I plopped down on the couch to watch a trainer break a young horse. Why couldn't I have a normal family who turned on sitcoms?

* * * *

Monday, September 23rd, 7:10 a.m.

Back in the Commons again—I so needed to get a life. I stirred up my mocha with the straw and waited for Vicky. I'd texted and called her about six times. No answer. Finally, she stomped into the school and came over to the table where I sat. "Hey." I pushed a latte at her. "Take a load off and tell me about your internship."

She plopped down in the other chair and reached for her cup. A smile flickered across her face. "My mom says we can't be friends anymore."

"I don't want to be friends with your mom. Drink your coffee."

"How can you not like her when my dad's the one who walked away?"

I shrugged. "I got to wondering how you knew they were getting a divorce. Did he tell you on your birthday or did she? And how long has she been playing the 'pity-me' card?"

"Whoa. I thought you were a blonde dipstick. When did you start analyzing my mom?"

"When she came in on Friday night and wasn't sorry that she'd messed up your status on the cheer squad," I said. "She could have been all 'Oh my Gawd. Poor Vicky. I'm killing her dad.' not 'I had to go to work and I needed a sitter, so Vick had to step up.' And that totally sucked."

Chapter Twenty

I grabbed an empty table in the Commons at lunch time when I didn't see Harry. If he showed up, he might sit with me or he'd find another friend. Where was he? At school, I hoped. I opened up my lunch sack and pulled out a sandwich. I'd barely unwrapped it when I saw Dani winding her way through the cafeteria.

She came over and put her tray on my table. "Okay if I sit here?"

"Sure. What's up?"

"Not much." She sat down. "A lot of people are talking about Vicky Miller's meltdown last week."

"Yeah. Poor Vicky." I took a bite of my sandwich. "When her parents divorced, her dad got the new car and a new girlfriend. Her mom got the house, and Vick has to take care of all her brothers and sisters. On Friday morning, they took her out of school to babysit, and she missed the assembly."

"That sucks." Dani poked at the casserole on her plate. "But, she made the game."

"I know. I wanted to see her cheer and my brother play, but her mom didn't get home until after it was over."

"What does that have to do with football?" Dani stopped testing the casserole with her fork. She gaped at me. "You went and took care of all those kids?"

"Somebody had to step up and help. I'm her best friend."

"I'll say. When you guys were carrying on in front of Weaver, I thought it was just to keep Vicky out of trouble with the principal. I didn't know all of it was real." Dani glanced across the room and waved. "Over here, Vicky."

It was my turn to stare at the blonde Mini-Me. "What are you doing?"

"Well, I thought if you two were fighting, I'd show everyone that you're not a bitch, but now I'm showing this school that I like Vicky."

"You're Ms. Popularity," I said, pointing out the obvious.

"Yes, but I only use my power for good." Dani beamed at Vicky as she joined us. "Hey, Robin was telling me that she babysat for you last week."

"Yeah and my mother may never recover." Vicky sat down on my left side. "She wants us to stop being friends now."

"Not going to happen," I said. "I'd never give up the girl who ate paste with me in kindergarten."

Vicky smiled and Dani laughed. Then, Dani said, "Well, sign me up to babysit this Friday."

"What?" Vicky stared at her. "No way."

"Yes, way," Dani told her. "Football bores me, and this would give me a great reason to skip the game."

I thought she might be overdoing it, but for some reason Vicky bought it. She spent the next ten minutes telling Dani about making dinner and the rest of the chores, but Dani just steamrolled over the objections and the two of them set it up for the game in two weeks. After all, my folks had this Friday covered.

"Is this table reserved for a hen party or can a guy have this chair?" Harry didn't wait. He sat down on the other side of Dani, and a couple minutes later, Jack was there by Vicky. Soon Porter and Gwen showed up. Then, Bill and Steve arrived. I was sorry when the bell rang and ended the best lunch I'd had this year.

Vicky headed off to the gym for P.E. Dani and I ambled toward Science. "Vicky was straight up with you," I said. "Her mom really does expect her to do a ton of household chores and look after the kids, too."

"Don't stress over it," Dani told me. "I'll work the kids. That's how I learned about doing laundry and cleaning. My *au pair* taught me."

116

"Your what?" I asked.

"She's kind of like a nanny, chauffer and tutor all rolled into one," Dani explained. "My folks travel a lot on business, and she'll go with me to Vicky's. With the two of us, we'll whip those kids into shape, no problem."

"I'd say so." I grinned at her as we entered the classroom. "I'll bet you'll be the next one kicked out of Vicky's house."

"Possibly, but if I am, we'll get Porter or Gwen or somebody else responsible enough to cover her chores so Vicky can do what she needs to do." Dani followed me over to my desk. "Anyway, I wondered if you'd like to come with me to a horse show next Saturday. I could use some help with Lady. You won't freak if she starts looking around for Charm and he won't be there this time."

"What would I do?" I asked. "My older sister does three day eventing. Mom does endurance riding and Jack games. Dad ropes. I'm really not into all this speeding around on horses. I like Twaziem. He stands around and eats and lets me brush him and talk to him about life."

Dani laughed. "You'd help my dad groom Lady and change her saddles and keep her area clean if there aren't any stalls available for the entrants. Watch my stuff and make sure nobody steals anything. Things like that."

"I'll have to check with my folks," I said, "and arrange to miss my lesson with Rocky. Since it'd be ground school at a horse show, I think she'll be flexible."

The rest of the day flew by. To my amazement, Olivia was right about Cedar and Kanisha. They ran with us. If this kept up, Gwen, Porter, and I wouldn't be the Three Musketeers anymore. We'd be the six somethings, even if I couldn't figure out what. Practice ran late so all I was able to do was check that my Mustang was still in the lot on my way to Dad's office.

Then, Dad and I were on the way home. When we arrived, he had to park behind the sheriff's car and the vet's truck. I didn't go to the house. I headed straight for the barn. What was wrong with Twaziem? Why was Dr. Larry here? Had Twaz colicked again? And what was up with the cop? Couldn't he look at the calendar?

When I reached the barn, I found Mom in the arena with my horse while Dr. Larry looked him over. "What's wrong?" I demanded.

"Just a checkup, Robin," Dr. Larry told me, tying a string on a thermometer. "I wanted to be here this time when Officer Yardley came to see Twaziem."

I eyed the big, burly cop. "You said a week. That would be tomorrow not today."

"This was the only slot your vet had free." Officer Yardley made another note on the papers in his case. "So, you said he's fifteen hands and he weighs seven hundred and fifty pounds."

"Yes." Dr. Larry avoided Twaziem's kick. "In a minute, I'll have his temp for you." He winked at me. "Want to help? It's not as gross as cleaning out an impaction."

"He looks different. What did you do to him?" The cop looked at me. "Just good grooming?"

"No, my brother and I gave him a bath," I said. "It got all the dead lice off him."

I walked up beside Mom and petted Twaziem's brown neck, then I straightened out his black forelock. He nudged me, but I didn't have any carrots. "I'll bring some later," I promised.

Mom gave me a steady look. "What will you do later?"

"Carrots."

She nodded, then jerked her head toward the bucket at the other end of the arena. "Right there. He couldn't have a lollipop like the doctors used to give you, so when Larry called, I went out to the garden."

I went over to the bucket. Talk about someone going above and beyond. As Jack said, Mom was the greatest. In her jeans, sweatshirt and boots, she looked like she'd spent the day in the barn, not in her crafts room. I wondered if she'd been able to do any of the sewing she wanted to get done. Her busy season started right after Halloween and ran through New Year's when she sold all the quilts, wall hangings and stuffed toy critters she made.

I grabbed two carrots and went back to give them to Twaziem. I hated to say the cop was right about anything, but Twaz's reddish brown coat had started to gleam. It still stretched tightly over his ribs, and his hip bones stuck out and up, but he was a little fatter. The bumps of his spine weren't as prominent.

Crunch. One carrot was slicked up. Ears twitching, he chewed and stomped again when Dr. Larry picked up his tail. "Stop it," I told him. "You have this done every time he comes to see you."

"It doesn't mean he likes it." Mom glanced across the ring as the other door opened and Dad came toward us. He'd taken time to change from his accounting suit to his jeans and western shirt. He held a sheaf of papers in his hand.

He nodded at the cop, then smiled at the vet. "You didn't come get your report on Twaziem, Robbie, so I brought it with me."

"I'll have to write in the facts from today." I went to take Twaziem's tail from the vet. "I'm monitoring how he improves from day to day and what I'm doing with him."

"I'll bet I know who taught you that." Dr. Larry slid the thermometer inside my horse's rear, keeping hold of the string. "In a minute, you can add his temp. Have you dewormed him yet?"

"No, it's too soon. I have to wait another week or he could have a reaction from all the poisons introduced to his system."

"Poisons?" Officer Yardley looked super interested, as if he'd just won the lottery.

I hoped he never played poker. He was so easy to hook. I widened my eyes and tried to appear innocent, like a sappy actress in a late night movie. "Hello. You don't think lice powder is talcum, do you? It couldn't have killed the parasites without toxic elements. And worming paste does, too, or it wouldn't eliminate the internal ones."

The excitement faded from his face and I thought, *Gotcha.*

I turned back to the veterinarian. "When I deworm him, I'm thinking he should just have a light dose. I was reading about colic on the Internet and one of the sites warned that dead worms could cause an impaction."

"You're right." Dr. Larry gently pulled out the thermometer, sidestepping so Twaziem kicked the air. "Lost a horse last year when that happened. And he was healthy, not debilitated like this fellow." Another kick from the horse and another quick step away by the vet. It looked like a strange sort of dance. Frowning, Dr. Larry shook his head. "He really hates me."

"It's not you." I dropped Twaziem's tail and glanced at my folks in time to see Mom tighten her hold on the lead to keep the horse from biting Dad. "Not you in particular, I mean. He has gender issues. I don't know exactly what Caine did to him besides hitting him with a manure fork, but Twaziem has issues with guys."

"How do you know someone hit him?" Dr. Larry asked.

"Because he threatens Jack whenever he tries to clean the stall, but I can use the fork around him and Twaz just eats. I know the girls did something to his grain. He sniffs it and plays with it before he tries just a mouthful. He won't touch any of the supplements that Rocky says he's supposed to have. And he goes berserk if you're in the stall when he has the grain, so I only go in when he eats hay."

"Very observant." Dr. Larry walked over to the bucket and came back with a carrot. When he offered it to Twaziem, my horse pinned his ears back and then snatched it away, chewing the carrot extra quick before the veterinarian could change his mind and take back the treat. "I guess I should count my fingers," Dr. Larry said, "but at least this time he took it from me."

"He's getting better." I went and took the papers from Dad to show them to the vet.

There were three pages. The first was a picture of Twaziem with the date and place where we got him. The second listed his height and weight plus all of the food he'd been fed at his various breakfasts, lunches, and dinners. The last page detailed all of the activities he'd done, including the colics and hours in the pasture with Singer.

Dr. Larry reread the final paragraph. "Good idea, Robin. Grass is a natural laxative. Until you can deworm him, put him out a couple hours each day. Now, about your internship. What do your Sundays look like? That's when I get some of my most interesting cases, and you could learn a lot."

Chapter Twenty-One

Monday, September 23rd, 7:00 p.m.

I waited until everyone was almost finished with supper before I brought up the subject of the horse show. "Dani Wilkerson wants me to go with her this Saturday when she shows Lady. I'd have to miss my ground school class, but I'd learn a lot when I prep her horse."

"Is Dani the girl who rode with you and Vicky last week?" Mom spread butter on her roll. "The one on the big bay mare?"

"That's her," I said. "Lady is Prince Charming's mother."

"Have we met her family?" Dad asked. "Has she ever been here?"

"No. I thought she was kind of snooty, but she's okay when you get to know her."

"Most people are," Dad said. "Is Vicky going with you?"

"I don't think so," I said. "She has her internship hours at the barn that day."

"At least she gets to be around horses then." Jack spooned up the last of the potatoes. "She won't get one of her own now that her parents are divorcing. It's one more piecrust promise."

"Piecrust promise?" It sounded familiar, but I couldn't place the reference. "What does that mean?"

"Promises that are easily made and easily broken, like they say in Disney movies," Jack answered. "Vicky's folks have been telling her that she can have a horse for years. Now, since her dad's moved out, he says he can't afford to buy her one. Her mom wants too much in child support."

"Does her dad know that Vicky's picking up a lot of the slack around the house?" I finished my last bite of salad. "Does he even care?"

"Not much," Jack said. "He isn't actually Vick's biological father, so he told her that she isn't his kid even though he's been in the picture since she was five and he's the closest to a dad that she's ever had."

I wasn't about to say it sucked at the dinner table because then I'd get a lecture on my language and my parents hadn't actually agreed I could go with Dani yet. "That majorly stinks."

"Yeah." Jack winked at me. His mindreading skills must have been working because he definitely knew what I was thinking. "I don't know about letting Robin go to this horse event. Who knows what could happen next? Maybe, she'd actually watch me game or go to an endurance contest or a roping without griping the whole time."

"Stuff it, Jack."

"In your ear, Robin."

"Behave, both of you." Mom smiled at Dad. "You're roping this Saturday. Jack's gaming at that competition, and Singer and I are headed for Ellensberg with Linda and her horse. We leave Friday afternoon, and I'll be home Sunday afternoon."

"Then, it sounds like this would be the perfect time for Robbie to go with her friend," Dad said. "If something goes wrong, you can call me and I'll pick you up on our way back."

"What about Twaziem? He'll be home by himself if all the horses are gone."

"He'll be fine," Jack said. "I'll load up his manger before we leave, and we'll lock the driveway gates."

"And when I'm next door, I'll ask Linda's husband to stop in and feed him lunch," Mom said. "With Zeke keeping an eye on the place, Twaziem will be just fine."

"Then, we have a plan for the weekend." Jack pushed back from the table and stood. He limped toward the counter with his plate.

"What happened to you?" Mom asked. "Did you get hurt at football practice?"

"No, I got kicked when I was doing stalls," Jack said. "No worries."

"Did you put ice on it right away?" Dad asked. "Or were you being stupid and macho?"

"Well, I guess I was macho." A faint grin creased Jack's face. "It didn't hurt that much before, but it does now. I didn't want to come up before I finished chores."

"Go soak that leg, son," Dad said. "Next time, ask for help."

"I've been telling you for years that Nitro is pure mean," I said. "Next time, you'll listen to me."

"Like that's going to happen when you're wrong," Jack told me. "It was your horse who nailed me, not mine. And you can do the dishes for me tonight."

"Unfair," I complained. "I always end up doing them for you. I'll do them tonight because you're hurt, but I'm filing a grievance with the union. I'll bet Felicia will too."

"Twaziem is really quick with his heels." Mom shook her head ruefully. "I'm glad that Larry is such a horseman or he could have been kicked today. The horse certainly tried for him. I wanted the colt to spend most of his time in the stall until he gained more weight, but I think it would be safer if the kids put him in the arena while they muck."

"Makes sense to me." Dad rose and began to clear the table. "Once he learns that we won't abuse him, he'll settle down. He's just nervous."

"He only needed a good home and he has one now." I got up and started stacking dishes. "He's a lot better than he was when he arrived."

"Try explaining to him that kicking the guy who comes to do the room is rude," Jack said. "I'll put him in the arena from now on, but that horse doesn't like me. He wheels and tries for me as soon as I open the door. I don't know if I can get a halter on him."

"I told you before that he had gender issues, and you said horses weren't the same as people." I ferried plates to the kitchen. "You told me horses don't hate or love the way we do."

"Well, I'm beginning to change my mind. Twaziem has done a lot to convince me," Jack said.

"Starting tomorrow, you go put Twaziem in the arena, Robbie. I don't want that horse to hurt your brother again." Dad gestured toward the hall. "Jack, you're not doing that leg any good by standing on it. If you want to play football tomorrow, go soak it."

"And your head," I added sweetly. "I'll handle my mean horse from now on."

When Jack left, Mom asked, "Robin, are you afraid of Twaziem? If you are, I'll take him into the arena or to a paddock."

"Twaz doesn't scare me," I said. "I'll bet Jack moved too fast or swung a tool too quickly or something. Twaziem wouldn't kick him without a good reason."

"What seems like a good reason to a horse isn't always one to a person," Mom said. "I think I'll call Mrs. Bartlett and ask her if there's any reason for Twaziem to go after a teenage boy."

"Hello." I picked up the butter dish and bowl of jam. "I already told you that her grandson is downright mean and nasty. He undoubtedly did something to my horse, and now Twaz is defending himself from Jack even though it's stupid. Jack might have moved too quickly, but he'd never do anything cruel to an animal."

"It would still be nice to know more about the horse's background," Dad said. "Why don't Robbie and I drive over to Mrs. Bartlett's tomorrow on our way home? We can tell her how the horse is doing and see if we learn anything."

"All right." Mom collected the glasses. "I'm probably worrying too much. We don't know what made the horse kick. It could simply be an accident. If we're all careful around him until he relaxes, everything should be fine."

"We'll try that." Dad glanced at me. "I want you to be careful too, Robbie. You're not as big as Jack and I don't want to see you hurt."

That made sense and I decided to use the training halter on Twaziem more often. Sooner or later, he'd have to figure out that the guys around here weren't mean, but it might take a while. Rocky said horses had really long memories and never forgot anything, especially abuse.

As soon as I finished cleaning the kitchen, I headed for my room to do my homework. I was halfway through the first set of algebra problems when I heard limping footsteps in the hall. "What is it, Jack? You'd better go rest that leg or Dad will have kittens."

"It's Vicky." Jack loomed in my doorway. "She wants to talk to you, and you didn't pick up when she called your cell."

I reached into my purse and pulled out my phone. It was dead. "I forgot to charge it. I'll go talk to her on the landline. How is she?"

"Crying," Jack said. "And since I can't slap her folks, I came to get you. I hate it when she's upset and there's nothing I can do."

"She doesn't actually want any solutions," I told him. "She wants you to listen while she vents. It's a girl thing."

"I'd rather solve problems than emote about them," Jack said. "It's a guy thing."

I laughed and headed for the hall, stopping to give him a quick hug. "Sorry my horse is so ornery."

"It's okay." Jack ruffled my hair. "I'm glad you saved him, even if he is a monster."

"Me too." I walked past him. "Next time let Vicky tell you why she's in trouble at home. She got yelled at for something her brothers or sisters did or didn't do, or because dinner was burnt, or the laundry didn't get done, or a dish was broken, or she didn't mop the floor."

"I thought Lincoln freed the slaves," Jack called after me.

"He did. He just didn't free the rest of the women or girls," I said over my shoulder. "I have a news flash for you, Jack. Most guys aren't like you and Dad. They can't pick up their socks or make their beds or put plates in the dishwasher."

"They can," Jack said, "but they don't."

"Good point." I kept walking and went into the living room to talk to my friend. It was my turn to let her snivel at me. She certainly listened when I whined at her.

* * * *

Tuesday, September 24th, 7:15 a.m.

Vicky was already in the Commons when I arrived. That was different. I headed for her and passed over the latte. "Hi. What are you doing here so early?"

"You mean on time?" Vicky smiled, but it didn't touch her eyes. "My mom and I had a screaming fight after I got off the phone with you. She issued another of her ultimatums and I told her where to shove it. So, she sent me down to sleep in the daylight basement."

"Are you okay?"

"I'm fine." A tear trickled down her cheek, and she wiped it away. "I hate having her mad at me, but I just couldn't stand being the family servant for another moment."

"But, the basement?" I shuddered, thinking of ours. "Isn't it creepy and dark with tons of bugs?"

Vicky shook her head. "No. Don't you remember? It's all set up like a studio apartment. There's a queen-size bed in the living room and an old entertainment center, plus a little computer room. It has a kitchen and a full bathroom."

"What did you do once you were there?" I asked.

"I took a hot shower, nuked a pizza, and did my homework," Vicky said. "The soda's kept in the garage so the kids can't drink it all in a day or two, so I could even have a couple colas. I went to bed early, and then I got up this morning. I had a chance to shower again. I dressed and left for school. If I end up living there full-time, hey, it's not all bad."

"It actually sounds pretty good," I said. "Won't your mom be looking for you?"

"With five kids to feed breakfast, dress and get off to school?" Vicky laughed, but she didn't sound happy. "She won't even miss me."

I got up. I walked around the table and hugged her. "I'm sorry you're hurt. Please don't be mad at me when I say that I think it's great that your mom has to do some of the stuff that you do all the time. She may be nicer to you now."

Chapter Twenty-Two

Tuesday, September 24th, 2:30 p.m.

During classes, my brain whirled around Vicky's problems. I didn't know how to get her mom to back off, but I also didn't think the basement was a permanent solution. Once her mom figured out that Vicky liked it down there, things would change. That afternoon, I hurried out to the field and saw the cross-country team clustered around Coach Norris.

I hurried over to stand by Gwen. "What's up?"

"New route today," Gwen whispered.

Coach Norris glanced around, then pinpointed me with a barely suppressed smile. "Steve says that the team has a new leader, and it's you, Robin."

"Me?" My jaw just about dropped on the grass. "Why me?"

"Because when Gwen and Porter run with you, they P.R.," Steve said. "Now, Olivia and her girls are next. It's only fair that the guys get the same chance to win."

"A team can't have two coaches," Lew told us. "I'm happy doing what Coach Norris wants and that includes the route we run."

"Okay." Steve glared at the other junior. "All the whiners can run the short route. Anybody who wants to be a winner follows Robin, and we're back in an hour and a half. Deal?"

"Sounds good to me," Olivia agreed. "Let's do it or we won't kick butt on Thursday."

"Well, stretch out," I said. "It's Tuesday and we're going up Golf Course Hill."

The team members moved into a semicircle, and Porter started a series of exercises. While people limbered up, I went over to Coach Norris. "I run six miles a day. I'm not trying to make trouble."

He grinned at me. "Hey, it takes work to build a winning team, and the most important part is attitude. Winners never quit and quitters never win. See you when you get back."

At four fifteen, I walked out of the school with Porter and Gwen. They had rides waiting for them, and it surprised me to see my dad's car. I went over and opened the passenger door. "Hi there. What's up?"

"Did you forget? We're going to see Mrs. Bartlett and investigate your horse." Dad waited for me to climb in and buckle up before he moved the car. "I'd really like some answers."

"Okay," I said. "Let's play detective."

I didn't add that I wished he'd just believe me when I told him about Caine Bartlett obviously abusing Twaziem. I didn't have any concrete proof beyond knowing him and his cousins, but it wasn't like they'd shoot videos of doing mean things to the horse and post them on the web for everyone to see.

It didn't take long to get to Mrs. Bartlett's home. Dad pulled into the drive and parked near the house. The row of kennels looked empty, but there was a guy cleaning them, throwing scraps of wood into the back of a pickup truck. My stomach tightened when he turned toward us. He was tall and skinny, with a long black ponytail threaded through the back of his ball cap. He started toward us.

"Do you know him?" Dad asked me.

"Yes. That's Caine Bartlett." I watched him approach. "Can we just go?"

Dad shook his head. "We won't find any answers by running away. Come on, Robbie."

"The guy's a jerk." I wasn't about to act scared, especially when I was, so I pushed open my door. "Hey, Caine. How are you? Is your grandma around?"

"At the grocery." Caine stopped and stared at us, a sneer twisting his mouth. "You took the only horse we had, so what else do you want?"

"To know more about him." Dad came around the car and stood next to me, sounding super friendly. "Did you folks have him for a long time?"

"Almost two years." Caine sauntered closer, leering at my chest. "Granny bought his mother and he was born here. Want to know what happened to her?"

"You killed her," I said in even tones, longing to smack him. "The only questions are how and did Twaz see it?"

"It wasn't me." He pointed to the woods at the back of the property. "It was Ash's turn to ride her. Ashley was riding her, galloping down one of the trails back there. The horse went down, broke her leg in a hole. My old man had to shoot her."

"But, Ashley was okay?"

"Oh sure. She walked away. That stupid colt screamed for days when his mother didn't come back." Caine shrugged. "It was like he actually knew who she was. Granny had a fit and kicked Wanda and Ashley off the property for months."

"Was the colt still nursing?" Dad asked, his voice low and grim.

Caine considered the question for a moment. "Yeah, he was. It was kind of weird since he had to be two months old. He used to freak whenever we took his mother out to ride her, but we didn't want the little snot following us. He'd run up and down the fence till she came back, whinnying the whole time."

"I see." Dad took a step closer to me. "And when did you start beating him?"

"I only threw a few rocks at him to shut him up." Caine smirked at us again. "Get serious. It's a horse. He doesn't have real feelings."

"Can we go now?" I asked. "If you stick around, he'll tell you what else he did and I'll puke."

"Sure." Dad patted my shoulder as if I were still five. "Get in the car, honey."

I did, but Dad didn't come right away. He stood and talked to Caine for another ten minutes. How could he stand it? I just wanted to cry for the little foal that lost his mom, who'd been knocked around almost from the day he was born. After what seemed like forever, Dad handed Caine a couple bills, then came around to get in the car.

"What did you pay him for?" I demanded as soon as he shut the door. "Horse abuse?"

"For his answers, Robbie," Dad said. "I know you don't like him. Neither do I, but now we know some of your horse's history. And I'm going to tell Jack to be a lot more careful. He has a certain resemblance to the Bartlett boy and Twaziem has plenty of reasons to pack a grudge."

I managed a nod while Dad started the car and backed out of the drive. Tears welled up, and I grabbed a tissue from the box on the console between our seats. "It's not fair. He was just a baby and they killed his mom in front of him."

Dad didn't answer for a moment. Then, he said, "You may want to rethink going out with Dr. Larry. You'll see sad things with him."

"Yes, but there's a big difference, Daddy." I blew my nose and took a deep breath. "The people who call the vet when their animals are sick honestly care what happens to the horse or the cow or whoever's ill. They don't deliberately try to cause harm, not when there will be a big bill to pay."

"I'm glad you can see that, Robbie."

"And I'll make sure that Twaziem doesn't hurt Jack," I went on. "I'll learn everything I can from Rocky and Sierra, so I can teach Twaz that all guys aren't mean."

At home, I changed my clothes and then headed for the barn with a brief pause in the back porch to grab my groom bucket and the garden to pull up some carrots. I'd halter up Twaziem and take him out to the indoor arena to brush him. If I kept him out there for the rest of the afternoon, it would be safe for Jack to clean the stall.

I grabbed the training halter off the hook by the door, and then went into the stall to catch Twaz. He dropped his head so I could slide on the noseband, then take the rope behind his ears and tie a knot in the loop. I gave him a carrot as a reward. "You're so good, and soon you'll know the difference between us and the Bartletts. I promise."

I attached the lead line to the loop by his chin. He walked beside me out of the stall, down the aisle to the arena, with just a pinned back glare for Nitro when the other horse stuck out his head. "Don't worry." I petted Twaziem's brown neck. "I won't let him hurt you."

In the arena, I laid the rope over his back. I gave him another carrot.

I grabbed my currycomb from the bucket and started to work on his left side. While I curried, I told him about my day. I didn't mention the visit to the Bartlett place. It still stressed and hurt me so I didn't want to put those emotions on him. I just talked about Vicky and the cross-country team and the way Lew puked halfway up Golf Course Hill.

"Hi, Freckle-face," Bill called from the hallway. "How's the Incredible Bulk? After the way he's been eating, he should start looking like a real horse."

"Stop being mean about my horse." I looked at Twaziem's ears. He hadn't pinned them back against his neck. He wasn't stamping his hooves. Instead, he'd turned his attention toward the gate where Bill stood and gave a low nicker. "You like him? Twaz, he's a jerk."

"Hey, I heard that." Bill leaned on the gate, grinning at me, mischief lighting his chocolate brown eyes. Then, he came into the ring and gave Twaziem a piece of apple. "Your horse has good taste. He could tell you that I'm a great guy."

"He doesn't lie." I couldn't help but smile back at Bill, especially when he stood there and fed quarters of a Red Delicious to my horse. "So, why are you here? Did you come with Jack?"

"Yes. I told Coach I'd help with chores so Jack doesn't overdo it. Coach was threatening your horse with violence if Jack can't run the ball on Friday night until I showed him the pic on my phone. This guy's suffered enough."

Twaziem nudged Bill for more apples, and he gave my horse the last one. "So, you're sixteen now."

"Yeah, and you're so bright. Did you just figure that out?"

"I can't help it, Freckle-face. I'm a guy, and everybody knows ball players aren't that smart."

"I don't know that. Jack gets better grades than I do, and he's done sports forever." I watched Bill scratch behind Twaz's ears. My horse leaned into the caress. Nice, I thought, but I didn't say so. "And stop calling me Freckle-face. I haven't had any since Felicia taught me to use makeup."

"You still have them," Bill told me, "even if they're invisible." He winked at me. "And you know what they say about freckles."

"No, what?"

"One freckle for each boyfriend you'll have."

I felt heat flood into my face. I was so dumb. Why hadn't I realized that he liked me? I mean, Bill really liked me. Why hadn't I seen him before? Really seen him? He was tall, red-haired and nice looking in faded blue jeans and a hooded Lincoln High sweatshirt. I stood like a rock and stared at him while he kept petting Twaziem. Dimly, I heard whistling and knew Jack had come into the barn.

"Bill, where are you? I thought you were going to start mucking."

"In here," I called out. "Take your friend away and tell him to quit picking on me."

Jack paused outside the gate. "Come on, you wolf. We have stalls to clean. Leave my little sister and her man-eating horse alone."

"But, I like picking on your sister," Bill said, giving Twaz one last scratch. "All I have is an older brother, and he always hassles me."

"Good for him." I hoped I sounded cool, nonchalant, not like I was weirded out because Bill looked at me in a new way. Or maybe it was just new to me. "And if you tell me that he still punches you, I'll laugh."

"No, you won't. Under that cynical attitude and smart mouth, you have a butter soft heart and you like me. You kicked my brother in the shins when you thought he made me cry."

"I was four." But, he was gone, so I turned back to Twaziem who was looking after him and flicking his ears. "Really. I was four and he played me." I gave my horse a carrot so he wouldn't miss Bill and the apples. "Okay, so he was barely six, but he was still a player. You should know that a guy who brings you apples the second time he sees you is up to no good."

Chapter Twenty-Three

Tuesday, September 24th, 5:45 p.m.

Twaziem's ribs still stuck out and so did his hips, but after ten days of solid eating, I could definitely see a difference. I knew Dr. Larry said Twaz had only gained thirty pounds but it looked like more to me. I finished brushing out his tail. Now, all that was left were those four hooves, and he didn't like holding up his legs for me to clean them. Luckily, Mom was in the barn untacking Singer from her trail ride, so I went and asked for help. Even if he'd been great with Bill, I didn't want to push my luck and have the guy bitten by my monster horse.

Mom came into the arena and gave Twaziem a carrot. Then, she ran a hand down his left front leg to check out the hoof. "He's going to need to see the shoer for a trim next week. Look how ragged the edges are."

I nodded. I'd seen the cracks, splits, and missing pieces before. "I've been putting hoof dressing on them, but he won't eat his grain if there's biotin or anything else in it."

"Let's try adding in some carrots and apples first," Mom said. "Maybe, we can disguise the supplements."

"Okay, it's worth a try." I petted Twaziem's neck, and then I passed the lead to Mom. I took my hoof pick. "When is the appointment with the shoer? Can I hold him for Beth?"

"During school breaks," Mom said. "She comes when you're at school, and you can't miss a day of class. Don't worry about your horse. I'll make sure Beth is gentle with him."

"She's gentle all the time." I finished scraping out the dirt, put down the foot and gave Twaz a piece of carrot. I moved to his left rear and ran my hand down from his hip to his ankle. While I cleaned the hoof, I asked, "What happens if he doesn't get this done all the time?"

"He can get thrush or grease heel or some other hoof infection," Mom said. "A horse is only as good as his feet. You can buy new tires for that car you want, but you can't buy new hooves or legs for Twaziem."

"Have I ever mentioned that I hate cleaning his feet?" I put down the hoof and stepped up to give him another piece of carrot. Third foot. Third carrot and finally I was finished. Yippee! It was over for another day.

While I fed Twaziem carrots, Mom hung around. "So, what did you find out about him when you and your dad went to see Mrs. Bartlett?"

I shuddered and kept my attention on the horse. "Could you talk to Dad about it? I don't want to think about all the mean things they did to Twaz when he was a baby."

"Sure." Mom put her arms around me and rocked me close to her. "Honey, you saved him. He's going to have a good life here. When you start to think about what he suffered, remember that, too. Okay?"

I buried my face against her shoulder so she couldn't see me cry. I felt Twaziem nuzzle my hair. Did he think it was hay, or was he just hunting for more carrots?

* * * *

Saturday, September 28th, 6:45 a.m.

The rest of the week zoomed by between school, cross-country practice, the meet on Thursday, which we won, Mom leaving with Singer on Friday and Jack's football game that night. Surprisingly, Vicky's dad showed up to take the kids, and she didn't have any trouble making the game. She was spending the night with Sierra and that meant no problems with her internship.

Saturday morning, I rolled out early. Jack and I did chores together, then I headed for the house to get ready to leave with Dani. Her parents would pick me up on the way to the fairgrounds in Monroe. They'd also drop me off tonight on the way home. It wasn't the first time I'd gone to the fair. I went every August with friends, and most of the local rodeos were held in the huge arena there.

"I don't even know what she's going to do today." I talked to Salt who sat on the vanity in the bathroom while I put on my makeup. He mewed back, and I knew he wanted breakfast. He really didn't care about anything but his cat meat. "I just hope I'm a big help to her."

Wearing jeans, a bright blue turtleneck under my western blouse, and my boots, I looked good, almost like one of the models in a horse magazine. I fed the kittens, then took the money Dad offered. "You're the best. Thanks."

"Call if you need a ride," Dad told me. "We'll be in Snohomish today, and it's not that far from Monroe."

"No worries," I said, taking the lunch bag he held out. "This is going to be fun. I'll tell you guys all about it tonight."

"Sounds good." Dad dropped a kiss on top of my hair. "I'm leaving all our cell numbers with Zeke so he can call if Twaziem has a problem, but since he'll spend the day eating, I think your horse will be fine by himself."

The doorbell rang and I hurried to answer it. Dani stood on the front porch.

"Hi," I said. "Let me grab my coat and I'm ready to go."

"We have ten minutes. Let's go look at your horse."

I hesitated. "He still doesn't look that great even if he's gained almost forty pounds."

"Stop worrying so much," Dani told me. "I'm not going to give you heartburn because you have a rescue horse. I'll bet he's a lot further along than you think."

"Okay. Well, let me introduce my dad to your folks," I said. "Mom's gone to an endurance ride in Eastern Washington."

Once the parents were talking to each other, Dani and I headed down to the indoor arena. I spotted Jack in with Nitro, grooming him before they left with Dad. I waved at him, but took her to see Twaziem. "Well, this is him." I held out a carrot. "Come on."

He glanced at us, then his attention returned to the bale of alfalfa-grass hay in his manger. "Everything comes second to food," I said.

"That's okay for now," Dani said. "Robin, he looks almost exactly like Lady. He's the same shade of bay. He even has ankle socks like she does, but she has a baby star in the middle of her forehead while he has a blaze. When you start showing him, he'll really catch the judge's eye."

"I've never been to a show before," I said. "I don't know if Twaz and I will be able to do it or not."

"Sure you can." Dani wiggled a carrot at Twaziem. "I'll help you and so will Rocky. She and Sierra are wonderful."

"It'll still take months before Twaz can be ridden." I glanced at my watch. "Come on. We need to go." I took her carrot and mine, then I broke them into pieces and put those in his grain bucket. He'd find them and eat them later. It'd be a good lesson for him since I wanted him to start eating supplements.

We arrived at the fairgrounds almost an hour before the show started. Dani's mom sounded like a general when she took charge. "Robin, you and my husband can groom Lady again for her first class. It's halter. She won't need a saddle. Remember to rub cornstarch into her white socks. And use hair spray on her mane so it stays in place."

"She needs to be shaved again." Dani pulled a garment bag and a suitcase from the back of the super cab. "Dad, you'd better do that. Robin won't know how. And Lady needs her hooves shined."

"We can handle it." Mr. Wilkerson smiled at me as the two blondes bustled away in the direction of the indoor arena and the bathroom. He was tall and sandy-haired. "Is this your first show?"

"Yes. My brother games. My dad ropes and my mom does endurance. We have a shower stall in our arena, but mostly we use brushes to groom our horses, and we only fly-wipe during the summer."

"Well, Lady is a pro." Mr. Wilkerson strolled toward the back of the trailer. "She behaves perfectly when we bathe, clip, or haul her. Sometimes I'm sure that we need to drop in coins to make her go like one of those rides at the grocery."

I couldn't help smiling as he opened the doors. He eased into the trailer, then backed out the mare. He passed me the lead. "Hold onto her for me."

I did and he climbed back inside only to return with a large tack trunk. "So, do you want to carry this crate? Or lead the horse?"

"I'll lead her," I said. "We know each other. I ride her son, Charming."

Lady was a reddish brown bay with a gold cast to her hide, just like Twaziem. Her mane and tail were long, lustrous, and black. She had four tiny white ankle socks. Of course, there were differences. She was twelve, not two. She was a mare, not a gelding, and she had to weigh at least seven hundred pounds more than my horse. Dani's mom might say she needed to be groomed, but Lady's coat gleamed. She must have had a bath last week.

She was as perfect as her name when we headed behind Mr. Wilkerson toward one of the huge barns. No matter who was on the road, she never spooked. She wasn't afraid of the horse trailers moving around the parking lot or the tractors hauling carts of shavings. Once a little kid raced by, a red balloon bouncing behind her on a string. Lady stopped and waited until the traffic died down, then walked beside me again.

Mr. Wilkerson stopped and talked to a barn official, then went down one of the wide aisles to an empty stall. "Well, what do you think of her?"

"She's amazing," I said. "I hope Twaziem acts like her someday."

"You'll have to share that with Rocky. She's the one who trained Lady. And Rocky can make that happen."

* * * *

Saturday, September 28th, 5:45 p.m.

As we headed home that night, memories jumbled my mind. I'd never known there was so much grooming that could be done with a horse. Lady looked like a beauty queen when she went into halter class. Her mane and tail floated in the breeze. Dani told me afterwards that the class was judged on cleanliness and manners. Well, Lady showed both. And she scored a first place.

Dani said it was because of the grooming that her dad and I did, but her mom said that Dani contributed, too. After all, Lady couldn't have gone in the ring without her. I still had trouble believing the manners that the horses exhibited. And the audience had been different too. There wasn't any whistling or yelling like I heard at rodeos or gaming events.

Even when the horses galloped in the show ring, they did it very slowly. The emphasis had been on control and discipline. If I closed my eyes, I could see the way Lady loped, as if she was recorded moving in slow motion. It was beautiful. Maybe one day Twaziem would do that same gait. It hadn't looked frightening. I might be able to ride it.

Dani poked me. "What did you think of your first show?"

"I loved watching the two of you gallop. It was like dancing in an old movie," I said. "They should have had music."

"Wait till Rocky teaches you to ride a slow lope," Dani said. "She plays waltzes until you learn to let the horse flow from one step to the next. It's always the slower, the better in traditional Western riding. Is that how your family's horses run?"

"No way," I said. "They go like they're exploding from a gate on a racetrack. Jack wants to get his time down to less than fifteen seconds when he barrel races or pole bends. And Buster goes from zero to zoom when he's after a calf for roping. Felicia does three day eventing. She and Vinnie can jump anything, and she really whines when she has to do a day of dressage and slow down. Endurance is another kind of racing."

"I guess what I was doing looked boring," Dani said.

"Are you kidding? I never ride with them, not since Nitro bolted across the highway with me. I love my family, but they're total speed demons and it freaks me out."

"Then it makes it even more amazing that you rescued Twaziem," Dani said. "I'd be so scared if a horse ran away with me that I'd never ride again."

Chapter Twenty-Four

Sunday, September 29th, 4:30 p.m.

Nobody showed up to run with me, and I was glad. I needed time to think and running always cleared my head. I jogged down the driveway, turned right and let everything that happened during the past week flow through my mind. Lunch with Harry when he came and joined me on his own, Vicky's problems with her family, the visit to Mrs. Bartlett's, leading the cross-country team—the list went on and on and on.

When I returned home, I didn't have any solutions, but I felt more at peace with myself and the world. I could handle whatever life threw at me. I always managed somehow. Even if I didn't know what to do about Bill or how to teach Twaziem how to trust guys, an answer would come. I changed to my boots and went down to the barn to help with night chores. I took my horse out to the closest paddock to graze so we could do his stall.

Jack was already mucking when I returned, so I cleaned out the manger. Twaz didn't need another bale of grass hay. He had about six flakes left, so I added four more. "Dr. Larry says to cut back now and start feeding him more like the other horses."

"Works for me," Jack said, pitching manure into the wheelbarrow. "How did your internship go?"

"All right. I learned to stock the truck with medical supplies, and we only had two emergency calls. One was for a colicked horse up past Arlington, and the second was for a colt that gashed his leg on a barbed wire fence. Both horses are going to be fine. Dr. Larry says next time I'll get to stitch."

Jack stopped scooping. "Really? He didn't let me sew anything until I'd been riding along for a year."

I pulled out the water tub to dump and scrub it. "I'm not looking forward to it. What if I mess up and the horse tears out the sutures?"

"Then, you go back with him and redo it," Jack said. "That happened at Rocky's. Sierra's stepdad decided he knew more than the vet, and Dr. Larry's associate hadn't specifically said to keep the horse in a stall while his leg healed. So, we sewed it up again and Dr. L. ripped into Sierra. She told him it was a good lecture and for him to repeat it to her folks."

I laughed, leaning on the tub. "I can just hear her. She doesn't take crap from anybody. Today, we bandaged the colt after we sewed him up. Then he couldn't chew on the stitches when he got bored. Dr. Larry said he couldn't wear a cone like what you put on a dog, so his owners just have to pay attention."

"That's part of having animals." Jack picked up the last forkful of wet shavings. "You could have Mom teach you to crewel. She uses a lot of the same stitches that Dr. Larry does. Of course, he's sewing up skin and she sews on cloth when she makes those decorator wall-hangings."

"And I wouldn't have to worry about hurting anything. Thanks, Jack."

He moved on to the next stall. I pulled the tub to the yard and dumped the extra water on the grass. I glanced at the pasture and saw Twaziem stop grazing. He threw his head up, whinnied, and trotted toward the white board fence. I heard an answering neigh and spotted Mom riding Singer across the back pasture from Linda's place.

Twaziem ran up and down along the fence, but he didn't seem too agitated. It was more like he just wanted to greet the other horse. I went to meet Mom. "Hi. How was it?"

"Good." Mom swung out of the saddle and parked her horse near the paddock gate so she could nuzzle Twaziem. "Help me untack her, and then she can go in with him for a little bit while we do her stall."

"It's all done. I did it last night during chores."

Mom hugged me. "Wonderful. Have I ever told you that you're my favorite?"

I laughed. She got that from some sitcom on TV, and I didn't believe her for more than a heartbeat. "You told Felicia that when she did your laundry and Jack when he changed the oil in your truck."

"Well, to be honest, you're all my favorites." She stepped to Singer's left side and began undoing the latigo. "Tell me about the horse show. Did you like it? Was it fun? What did you learn to do? How was your first day with Dr. Larry?"

Before I started chattering, I eyed her. When was the last time I'd asked her about what she and Singer did on a race? Never, I thought. I was a kid and her world revolved around me. Instead, I said, "You first. How was the race? What was the terrain like? Did you see any rattlesnakes?"

* * * *

Monday, September 30th, 7:10 a.m.

It was back to the usual routine the next day. I sat in the Commons with my mocha and a latte for Vicky, and she was late. I sighed and shook my head. The more things changed, the more they stayed the same. I just hoped she made it before the bell rang and she was dead meat in Weaver's class. Porter and Gwen showed up next, and Vicky hustled across the room just as the warning bell rang.

I passed her the latte. "Chug it," I said. "Weaver will make you toss it if you try to take it in her class. What happened?"

"Oh, the usual," Vicky said, peeling off the cap. "Dad returned the kids with backpacks of dirty clothes. Mom didn't wash them, and I about had to take them to day care naked. I ran into Safeway and grabbed a big box of disposable diapers on the way for the baby."

"Good for you," Porter said.

Vicky took a big swallow of coffee and shook her head. "Not really. I caught hell for destroying the planet from the day care bitch because it takes a million years for the diapers to die in a landfill. I told her they weren't my kids, and if she wanted to wash the bag full of crappy diapers, I'd bring it tomorrow. And right now, I had to get to school."

Gwen laughed so hard that I had to grab her so she didn't fall on the floor. "Won't she be calling your mom?" I asked.

"Yeah, probably. And with any luck at all, I'll be sent to the dungeon." Vicky drained her coffee. "Come on. If we don't get to Weaver's in two minutes, we'll all be in the office for tardy slips."

She and Porter hurried down the hall ahead of us, and Gwen walked quickly beside me. "So, what's the dungeon?"

"The daylight apartment in the basement," I said. "Vicky's dad redid it as a studio so he could get away from the kids every once in a while. And when her mom gets pissed, Vick is sent there as a punishment."

"Well, she'd better not let her mom know that she likes being thrown in that particular briar patch," Gwen said, as we slid into English class, "or she'll be locked out of it."

At lunch, Vicky was the first to arrive at my table. "I had a question that I'm supposed to ask you, but there wasn't time before school."

"What is it?" I looked around for Harry, then spotted him in the line at the sub-station talking to Dani while they waited for their sandwiches. "Do you want me to babysit for you again?"

"Not yet," Vicky said. "Are you trying to give my mom heart failure? No, it's about this Friday's game. Jack wants you to go with us for something to eat after the game."

"Jack and I live in the same house. Why didn't he ask me?"

"Because fixing up his little sister on a date with his buddy just feels creepy." Vicky opened her carton of milk. "And Bill will be coming along. So, do you want to join us or not?"

I unwrapped my sandwich, trying to figure out how I felt. It had really surprised me when Bill showed up to feed Twaziem apples last week. I hadn't known that he liked me, and I wasn't sure how I felt about him.

"It's not that hard of a question, Robin. Do you want to come or not?"

"I don't know," I said. "I've never thought of Bill that way."

"What way?" Vicky asked. "Sure, he acts like a comedian, but he's okay. And you two actually have a lot in common. You try to hide who you are behind a mask, too."

"I know that." I looked across the cafeteria, wondering what was taking Harry and Dani so long. Then, I saw it—saw them choose a table and sit down together. "Oh, no."

Vicky followed my gaze. "It doesn't mean anything. Dani changes boys like she does earrings. You have to let Harry learn that on his own. And the best way for him to realize you're a girl is for him to see you with a different guy. Yes or no for Friday?"

I blinked hard. I wouldn't cry. Not here and not now. "I don't want to hurt Bill's feelings."

"How could you?" Vicky asked. "You don't even know him like a real guy yet, just as a friend of your older brother's. Come with us. You might decide you prefer him. He actually sees you as a person and that makes him much more appealing to me."

I bit hard into my ham sandwich and chewed. "You only want me going out with someone that you and Jack like. Okay, I'll do it, but only once. If I don't like Bill that way, then I'll let him down easy. No hard feelings either way."

"All right! Way to go!" Vicky grinned at me. "And think positive. Dani won't be out with Harry on Friday night. She'll probably be babysitting for me since my dad won't show up two weekends in a row."

Vicky had a point, I thought, as I led the team up Golf Course Hill that afternoon. Her dad probably would bail this time around. I should be mad at Dani for taking Harry, but it wasn't totally her fault. She didn't know how I felt about him, but he did. Only a dimwit wouldn't figure out a girl liked him when she showed up to eat lunch with him every day since school started, and Harry wasn't stupid. He knew how I felt, but he didn't care.

My eyes burned with unshed tears. I jogged at the crosswalk while I waited for the light to change. Then I led the way across the street and started down the winding road through the development.

Lew puffed up beside me. "How far are we going?"

"At least six miles," I said. "I don't want to run again when I get home tonight."

"Works for me," Gwen said from my other side. "It was great winning last week. We're kicking butt this time, too."

Lew dropped back behind us. If he'd had more air, I knew he'd be whining at Steve and the other guys. I shook my head. Lew should just be happy that he hadn't puked on the way up the steep part of the last hill.

* * * *

Monday, September 30th, 7:30 p.m.

I'd barely finished rinsing the plates and loading the dishwasher that night when the phone rang. I went to answer the kitchen extension and heard my sister's cheery greeting.

"Hey, how are you?" I asked. "How's school?"

I perched on a bar stool and listened while she shared everything that was going on in Pullman. Finally, she paused for breath, and I said, "Jack will want to know how Vinnie's doing, so how is he?"

More chatter, this time about the gelding, and how hard the dressage classes were at the barn near the university, but they'd mastered something she called a 'counter canter,' and she was really proud of her horse.

"How is your boy?" Felicia asked. "Has he colicked again?"

"No. It's only happened twice. Dr. Larry said to turn him out on grass a couple hours a day because that's a natural laxative, and it seems to be helping." I glanced around the empty room and lowered my voice. "Felicia, can I talk to you?"

"I thought that's what we were doing." She giggled. "Why, what's up?"

"Bill wants to ask me out and—"

A big squeal in my ear and I held away the phone, waiting until she stopped screaming. "Will you listen to me? I like Harry but he seems to like another girl."

"Then, he's a jerk," Felicia told me. "Bill's sweet. He may not be the guy that you'll be with forever, Robin, but you're in high school. You need to date different guys and learn who and what kind of person you want to be with. Bill likes you the way you are, and believe me, that's really special. And a person can never have too many friends."

"He brought Twaz apples," I said, "and it's weird because Twaziem hates most guys, but he likes Bill."

"Well, trust your horse because he trusts you to take care of him."

Chapter Twenty-Five

Wednesday, October 2nd, 5:10 p.m.

We stopped at the feed store on the way home from my lesson and bought a tube of dewormer for Twaziem. Rocky had advised us to only give him enough for a six hundred pound horse, and Dr. Larry concurred when I called him for his opinion. If Twaz had too much wormer, he could colic again, and twice was definitely enough. Nobody wanted to spend the night walking him, and I certainly didn't want to clean out a blockage of dead worms. Yuck!

He was good when I haltered him and took him to the indoor arena. The carrots helped. Mom dialed in the correct amount of wormer, stuck the tip of the tube in his mouth, and hit the plunger. All done. He was pasted, and I held up his head so he couldn't spit like a llama. I didn't want the meds flying everywhere.

"What are you doing to him?" A guy asked from the far doorway.

I glanced over my shoulder and saw the Animal Control cop. He so needed to get a life, or was he trying for overtime? "Deworming him. If I had known you were coming today, I'd have the paperwork ready. I'll go up and get his log sheet. He's gained eighty pounds since we got him almost three weeks ago."

"We should see a real difference now that we've wormed him," Mom said. "I expect him to put on fifty pounds in the next week to ten days."

"Awesome," I said. "Rocky says he can start training next month."

Shannon Kennedy

"Is that the owner of Shamrock Stables?" Officer Yardley made a note in his file.

"Yes." I rubbed the blaze on Twaziem's face, and he pricked up his ears as though I was his best friend. He kept rolling his tongue like he still tasted wormer. "We won't be riding him until next summer, but he has a lot of ground school to do before then."

"Okay, then." More notes and the cop looked at us. "There's really nothing more I can do until he gains more weight, and that's going to take time. I'll be back to visit him in four weeks."

I blinked and almost felt guilty for being rude to him. Almost, but not quite, because I hadn't liked his threats to take away Twaz right after we rescued him. "All right. I'll get copies of his feed and activity logs for you. Do you want me to mail them to you each week? Or do you want to pick up the ones for October when you come in November?"

Officer Yardley nodded. "That makes sense. I'll pick them up then. Since you're one of Rocky's students, I know you'll keep an accurate record of everything you do with him."

"Let me put him away, then I'll walk up to the house," I said. When I led Twaziem into the hallway, I spotted Bill finishing his stall. "Guess what? Officer Yardley is done with Twaz for the next month."

"All right!" Bill high-fived me. Then when Twaziem nickered at him, Bill dug into his pocket for apples. "Hey, buddy. You're out on parole. Is that cool or what?"

I laughed and watched as the two guys communed over chunks of Red Delicious. "So, what are we doing on Friday night after the game?"

"Dinner, bowling and the midnight matinee if that works for you," Bill said. "It's the same thing Jack and I have done for the last two seasons. A word of advice. Don't share Vicky's popcorn. She loads it up with so much salt that I almost choke."

"That's why I always get my own," I told him.

It actually did sound like fun, and I wouldn't have to worry about being careful of what I said if I was with Bill. I could just be me. And if he didn't like it, too bad.

* * * *

146

No Horse Wanted

The meet this week was in Snohomish at a combination park and campground. We'd raced there last year, and I really liked the trails. I spotted Phillip and the Mount Pilchuck team stretching. I nudged Porter. "I bet they think they'll win because they train here a lot."

"In their dreams." Olivia rocked back on one heel, then the other. "We are so going to State this year and they're not."

I laughed. "I hope you're right."

"I know I am. How's your horse?"

"He's doing really well," I said. "We wormed him yesterday, and he'll start piling the weight on now. He's already gained almost a hundred pounds."

"I'm glad you're doing it slow and steady," Olivia said. "Then, he'll keep the weight on."

"Got that right." I finished stretching and we headed for the starting line. I smiled at Cedar. "I know you'll P.R. today."

"Then, you're ahead of me."

"You just need faith." I glanced at the grandstand and waved when I saw my mom and dad. They were sitting next to an older woman with a totally bad wig. "Hey, I'll be right back. That's Mrs. Bartlett, the lady I got my horse from. I want to tell her how wonderful he's doing."

I ran across the track and up the steps. "Hi, Mrs. Bartlett."

"Hi, Robin." She smiled at me. "Your folks say that Twaziem is doing very well."

I nodded and fished out my phone to show her his picture. "Here. Take a look. We wormed him yesterday. He's gained a ton of weight. You have to come visit him."

"Really?" Tears sparkled in her eyes. "I'd love that."

"Okay." I looked over my shoulder to be sure the race wasn't starting yet. I eyed my folks. "What about after the meet? Could she come then?"

"If that works for her, she certainly can," Dad said. "You'd better go, honey. We'll figure out the logistics."

"All right." I handed him my phone. "See you after my race."

I turned and ran back down the stairs, pausing to grin at Jack and

147

Bill. "You guys are only allowed to root for Lincoln High."

"We knew that," Bill said. "Same rule tomorrow night."

"You got it."

With all our training, we took the lead early and we kept it. The trail was clearly marked through groves of cedars. We raced up the hills, down them, around curves and then along the lakeshore. It was a beautiful day for a run. The sun shone and the breeze kept us cool. It wasn't hot either. I could have run for another three miles, but I saw the finish line up ahead. I came in first with Olivia right behind me. Then, it was Porter and Gwen, followed by Cedar.

Lincoln High won the meet. Coach Norris was totally revved because so many of us had P.R.'d. He told us how wonderful we were all the way back to the school. Next week, we'd be in Everett, and he knew we'd remain undefeated. We were destined to be division champs this year and go to the state competitions.

Mom picked me up at the school. "Mrs. Bartlett is with your dad. She was thrilled that you asked her to come see Twaziem, and they went straight from the meet. I told your dad that we could order in pizza later."

"Sounds great." I shut my door and buckled up. "After we saw Caine at her house and he told us all the mean things they'd done to Twaziem, well, I wanted her to know that he's okay. She tried to protect him, but she had to stand up to her grandkids and that's really tough."

"Yes, it is." Mom shifted in her seat, then leaned across to hug me. "I may not say it often enough, but I'm proud of you, Robin. You're a good person."

"Does this mean I get my car?"

She kissed my forehead. "Only if we win the lottery, so you'd better give me a dollar so I can buy you a ticket."

Mrs. Bartlett was in the barn when I arrived. She stood outside Twaziem's stall, feeding him one carrot after another. He nosed her for more, but when he saw me, he whinnied.

I offered him a carrot. "He's looking good, isn't he?"

"He looks amazing," Mrs. Bartlett said. "I'm glad your mom let you have him. When are you going to start riding him?"

"Not until next summer," I said. "He's only two, and I don't want the trainer or anybody on him till he turns three. Of course, Dr. Larry has to agree."

"Dr. Larry?"

"Our veterinarian. He's seen Twaz three times, once for a checkup and twice when he had colic." I rubbed Twaz's blaze. "He had a tough time adjusting to regular meals. It upset his digestive system, but he's doing better now."

I didn't tell her about my car or selling Twaziem to be able to buy my Mustang. I didn't want to upset her or him. And it wasn't as if he would go to just anyone. The next home had to be at least as good as ours. He needed regular meals, a clean stall, and lots of love. We stood and fed Twaziem treats and talked about him. Mrs. Bartlett was smiling when she left and that made me happy. I didn't know how much longer she had to live, but she didn't have to worry about Twaz anymore, and it should make things easier for her.

After the pizza, I followed Dad into his study. "Hey, am I going to get my Mustang? Have you and Mom decided whether we can do the installment plan?"

"I don't like installments, Robbie. You end up paying a lot more over the life of a contract than you do if you just pay cash." Dad opened his file cabinet and pulled out a folder. "Take a good look at this printout. This is what you'd end up paying for the car if we accepted Brenna's deal. It's really not do-able, honey."

* * * *

Friday, October 4th, 7:15 a.m.

I was alone at my table in the Commons when Vicky showed up. She grinned at me. "Hey, Jack and Bill said the cross-country team kicked butt yesterday."

"Yeah. We did okay." I swirled the straw in my mocha.

"And you're sulking because…?"

"My dad figured out that I'd be paying way too much for the Mustang, and he already told Brenna that it's not going to happen. He suggested she find another buyer."

"How much is too much?"

"Almost twenty-five thousand," I said, "and that doesn't include gas, repairs, insurance, licensing, or taxes."

"Wow, that's a lot of money, Robin. Does it ever occur to you that your folks might have a point? It's not like you have a 'real' job, so how could you help pay for the car?"

"I hate it when you're right about stuff like this, Vick."

"I know." She actually sounded sympathetic as she drank her latte. "And I hate it when you tell me that my mom's mean because she treats me like a slave."

I guessed that was what made us such good friends for so long. We could be honest with each other and not freak out or bear grudges when we shared our truths.

"But, I really want a Mustang." I propped my chin on my fists, feeling like a whiny little kid. "And I want to be mad at my parents, but I can't. They're great people, and they're not trying to piss me off. They just think the car is too expensive."

"You'll get one someday. I know it."

I eyed her suspiciously. "Are you playing me?"

"No," Vicky said. "You always get what you want, so I know that one day I'll see you wheeling around in town in a gorgeous classic Mustang. And you'd better stop to pick me up."

"Only if you've left the kids at home."

Chapter Twenty-Six

Friday, October 4ᵗʰ, 2:20 p.m.

No cross-country practice today, so I'd go for a run when I got home, but that meant I had time to walk to Dad's office. I checked out my wonderful Presidential blue Mustang in the lot. No, it wasn't mine, and it didn't look like it ever would be unless I could figure out how to get a job to pay for it. And I was sixteen. How would I possibly make it happen?

I glanced toward the office trailer, but it was difficult to see inside from here so I walked across the pavement toward the door. I heard something drop in the service area, so I went to the mechanic's shop first and spotted Brenna with her head under the hood of the puke green loss leader. "Hi. What's going on?"

"A tune-up," Brenna said, flicking me a quick glance. "I've been rebuilding the engine. Want to help me make it run?"

I blinked. "Sure, but aren't you mad at me?"

"For what?" Brenna stepped back to open a little box in her hand. "Being sixteen? Wanting something beautiful? If I didn't love these cars, do you think I'd have taken over the lot when my grandfather retired?"

She had a point. I shrugged out of my backpack and put it in the corner. "I am going to buy a Mustang from you someday. And I will be back to help you sell these cars to the perfect owners as soon as you hire me."

"Okay." She laughed. "Then, we have a deal. Now, tell me about your friend, the one that Harry's been seeing."

"I really like Harry," I said, "but I can't make him want me the way I want him."

"No, you can't," Brenna agreed, passing me the tiny boxes of spark plugs. "And you're smart to learn that at sixteen. I didn't learn it till Afghanistan when I met this dangerous, deadly, devastating Army Ranger and he became everything I ever wanted."

"What happened?" I ripped open the end of the little carton. She'd been in a combat zone so the question seemed obvious to me. I handed over the spark plug to her. "Did he die?"

"No. We connected, and when I got home I discovered he had a fiancée. For him, I was *Ms. Right There*. I didn't know I was just a stopgap until he came home to *Ms. Right*. It felt like my heart would fall out of my chest at his feet. He'd stomp it into dust, or crush it in his hand the way that witch does on TV." Brenna checked the gap on the spark plug before she slid it into place, finger tightening it first. "And I was ten years older than you are. I should have been smarter."

"I think you're plenty smart," I told her. "I couldn't run a place like this. My grandma says that 'love makes fools of us all,' and neither of us are stupid."

"Well, then let's go with what your grandmother says and believe we've both learned and grown a lot." Brenna forced a smile. "Now, what about the girl?"

"She's nice," I said. "Dani looks like a model, but she's smart and good with animals and keeps her promises. She tries to make other people feel good, too."

As I talked to Brenna and we worked on the car together, I realized that I was telling the truth. I still liked Dani, and maybe I hadn't really seen who and what Harry was as a person. I kept seeing him as blond and beautiful, but he was more than a pretty face. He was a human being, and he undoubtedly had baggage of his own. He must. He lived with his older sister, not his parents. Did Dani see the person when I hadn't?

* * * *

No Horse Wanted

Friday, October 4th, 10:10 p.m.

Bill and Jack were riding high when they came out of the locker room to meet me and Vicky. They should be. Lincoln High had wiped up the field with Lake Gurlock, thirty-two to nothing. Jack made one touchdown and Bill scored two.

"Dinner first." Jack hugged Vicky and kept his arm around her waist. "Where do you want to eat?"

I smiled at Bill, feeling suddenly shy. "What do you guys like? You won tonight."

"Italian? Chinese? Mexican?" Bill grinned at me. "What sounds good?"

We discussed restaurants while we headed toward the parking lot and my dad's car. We opted for a pizza place up in Stewart Falls that Vicky raved about. I hadn't been there before, but Parthenon Pizza was totally cute in a checkered tablecloth, big candles in wine bottles kind of way. And the pizza was amazing, thick layers of cheese over meat, olives, and peppers on a homemade crust. We took the leftovers with us, squabbling about who would get to keep them.

Bowling was a blast too, girls against the guys, and we won. Jack said that meant we had to buy the popcorn, but Vicky told him that was against the rules. Losers paid, and we would choose the movie. It was 'chick flick' time, and he could just suck it up. Lots of whining ensued as he drove to the theater for the midnight show, and I never laughed so much in my life.

We got back to our house a little before three in the morning. Luckily, Bill and Vicky were staying over, so it meant there wouldn't be a hassle about curfews from their folks. I froze when Jack pulled in the drive. I'd expected a few lights on in the house, but not the ones in the indoor arena. Oh no! Not again. I pushed open my door and was running for the barn before my brother parked the car.

I passed Dr. Larry's truck and raced in the side door of the building. Mom walked Twaziem around the ring.

"What happened?" I demanded. "Is he all right?"

"Colic." Mom kept leading Twaz. "It's a reaction from the wormer, so it's good that we used a mild one and under-dosed him, rather than going by his actual weight."

I nodded and went to my horse. He nudged his blazed head into my side, and I hugged him. "Poor baby."

"Poor us," Dad told me. "Zeke thought he saw someone around the barn and came to check things out. He found Twaziem in distress so he started walking him. We took over when we got home from the game.'"

"Why didn't you call us? We'd have come straight here," I said. "Bill and Vick wouldn't have minded."

"That's why," Mom said. "You and Jack are uber-responsible kids. So are your friends. Every once in a while, you need to act like teenagers, and we need to remember to let you. If we desperately needed you, we'd have called."

"And this way you missed cleaning out the gobs of dead worms that caused the impaction," Dr. Larry added. "Next time, Robin."

I rubbed Twaziem's neck. "Is 'gobs' a medical description?"

"Considering what was inside him, I'd call it accurate." Dr. Larry stretched and yawned. "I'm headed home. Call me in the morning, and let me know how he's doing. I'll swing by to get you on Sunday, Robin, and check on him then."

"Okay." I took the lead line from Mom. "I have him now. I'll walk him. Has he pooped yet?"

"No. He doesn't have much in the way of gut sounds either, so keep him moving."

Mom and Dad headed out of the arena with the vet, just as Bill came inside. Jack and Vicky were right behind him. I glanced at the three of them. "What a way to end a great night. Sorry, guys."

"Not your fault." Bill came to walk beside me. "We came up with a plan. You and I will take the shift now and Vick and Jack will take over at seven. Is that all right?"

I stopped and looked up at him. "Are you sure about this? It doesn't sound like a fun time to me."

He winked, then reached out to tug my braid. "Any time I spend with you is fun."

"A-h-h, aren't you sweet?" I laughed and all my worry about him evaporated. "You know exactly the right thing to say." Twaziem nudged him, and I cracked up again. "Oops, you're in trouble. You don't have any apples for him."

"Wouldn't matter if I did." Bill massaged one of Twaz's ears. "He can't have them until he passes gas or manure."

"Wow, we have fascinating discussions. Horsy poop."

I started walking Twaziem again and Bill paced me. Jack and Vicky vanished out the barn door in the direction of the house. So, it wasn't super romantic, I thought. Still, there was something special about a guy who stuck with you when your horse was sick, and who arranged to walk most the night so you could save a life together. Next time Bill teased me, I'd remember his good points.

During the next four hours, I learned more about Bill. He liked sports, which I already knew since he and Jack were on a lot of the same teams. However, he also read a lot. He could quote speeches, poems and what he called ballads, an old kind of story song. He claimed if I came up with a topic, he could deliver an oration on the subject.

"No way," I said. "You can't possibly do that."

"Sure I can. Pick a subject, any subject, and I'll show you."

"You're lying."

Twaziem snorted agreement and tossed his head. He hadn't bitten or kicked at Bill once tonight, even if there weren't any apples.

"Come on." Bill took my left hand in his. "You know you want to test me."

"Okay." I remembered the lecture in my history class that day. "Something about the Revolutionary War, and it can't be King George's quote about nothing happening on July 4th."

"All right." Bill thought for a moment, then began, "They tell us, sir, that we are weak; unable to cope with so formidable an adversary. But when shall we be stronger? Will it be the next week, or the next year? Will it be when we are totally disarmed, and when a British guard shall be stationed in every house? Shall we gather strength by irresolution and inaction? Shall we acquire the means of effectual resistance by lying supinely on our backs and hugging the delusive phantom of hope, until our enemies shall have bound us hand and foot?"

"Oh my Gawd." I stopped walking and stared at him. "Who said that?"

Bill grinned. "Patrick Henry. It's part of his speech to the Virginia

155

Convention in March of 1775. Want to hear more?"

"You're amazing. I'd never remember all that."

"You would if it interested you," Bill said. "I'll bet you can tell me every detail about the engine in that Mustang you want."

"You're right. Do you want to know the specs?"

Before Bill answered, Twaziem tugged on the rope, and I gave him a quick glance. Was he trying to lie down? Did he want to roll? I couldn't let him. He'd twist a gut and rupture something. As I watched, he lifted his tail. He cut loose with a long fart, then proceeded to take a giant dump.

Bill and I both laughed. Then, he took a step closer and rested his hands on my shoulders. "If I kiss you, will you turn your man-eating horse on me?"

I caught my breath. "No, but I can't guarantee he won't bite you."

"I'll take the risk."

He bent his head and brushed his lips over mine. A whisper soft, sweet kiss. It ended far too soon when Twaz bumped us with his head. He was on a mission for apples.

I touched Bill's cheek. "Next time without an audience?"

"Yes, but now we know he really likes me."

The truth slipped out before I could stop it. "So do I."

Chapter Twenty-Seven

Saturday, October 5th, 1:05 p.m.

I was still stumbling around the house in my pj's and bathrobe when Vicky popped into the kitchen. "Hey, Sierra's here to visit Twaziem. Do you want to get dressed and come to the barn?"

I yawned and stared longingly at the coffeepot, which took forever to brew. "Sure. I'll be right there. Why did Sierra come?"

"So Rocky can give me credit for internship hours today." Vicky came across the room and took down two of the plastic cups we took to the barn from the shelf. "I love her. She says as soon as I turn eighteen, I can move in with her to finish high school. And I'll only be a slave to the horses, not my parents, or their kids."

"And you're getting credit for walking my horse all morning until he is a hundred-percent better. She's fabulous." I added cream and sugar, then poured in strong coffee from the glass pot and took a big swallow. "I'll hit the shower and be right there."

"We're grooming him and clipping him if that's okay." Vicky filled her two cups. "Sierra says he needs a bridle path, his fuzzy ears trimmed, fetlocks…You know, the whole works so he looks like a real horse."

"Okay, but if Dani shows up, don't let her polish his hooves."

"Are you still friends with her?" Vicky eyed me with concern. "I know that it bugged you when she and Harry clicked."

"That was all in my head, not his or hers," I said. "And it's better to have somebody who actually sees me and likes me, anyway. Didn't you tell me that?"

"Yeah, but I'm glad you were listening."

A half hour later, I made it to the barn. Sierra ran the electric clippers while Vicky held my horse. Twaziem didn't like the sound, but they weren't actually cutting any hair. He was just supposed to grow accustomed to the noise. I took my bucket of carrots and went over to join them. I offered a long, skinny carrot, and Twaz took it. Crunch. Munch. Now his brain was on me and treats. He really didn't care what Sierra did.

She started behind his ears, trimming a section of mane so his halter could lie on the one inch gap in his black hair. Then, she gently folded his right ear and cut away the excess fuzz. Two carrots later, she was finished with the left ear. "Want me to do his whiskers?"

"Yes, but leave the ones around his eyes. I'll get them with the scissors." I broke up a carrot into pieces. "You do what you can, and then I'll give him treats."

"Works for me." She stepped up, letting the clippers buzz until he relaxed. "He's being really good. A lot of the colts on the farm totally freak the first time we do this."

"The carrots help," I said. "Dani showed me the trick you taught her of using bribery to get results. Since he was starved, food has a constant appeal."

Sierra nodded. Tall, red-haired, and skinny, she looked like a giant-sized version of her mom, Rocky. But like her mother said, Sierra didn't have patience for stupid people—stupid horses, yes. She never got angry with a four-legged critter, even when she said she'd found another two-legged one that was a complete waste of time, space and oxygen.

She slid the clippers around his muzzle, along his mouth and between his nostrils until he was smoothly shaven and most of the billy whiskers were gone. When I ran my hand over his face, I still felt the occasional bump of stubby hairs. He wasn't as smooth as Lady had been at the show, but I didn't plan to use a disposable safety razor on him. I gave him three pieces of carrot as a reward before Sierra began trimming his chin and jaw.

"Next time, you'll be able to do this," she told me. "Think of it as part of your ground school class, only this time we're using your horse, not Charming."

"Twaz is looking pretty good," I said. "He got his hooves trimmed last week. He's had his first bath, lots of grooming, and now he's been clipped. All he needs is to gain about six hundred pounds."

"Well, that will take time," Sierra said. "Don't count on him being up to weight for at least another six months."

"We're not going to wait that long to start training him, are we?" I asked.

"No way. There's a lot he can learn in the meantime," Sierra said. "And you don't want him to just stand around and eat. He'll lose muscle tone and get ornery. He needs to work so he learns to respect you, or he'll think he's large and in charge."

That made sense, and I was glad to hear it. I didn't want him staying in his stall and eating his head off when I meant to find him a home. A real home, not just the one he had here, but the kind of home a horse deserved, with people who honestly loved and cared for him. He'd have better luck if he knew what was expected of him. I'd learned that when I adopted and tamed feral kittens. If they'd cuddle with their new owners, they received more love.

The gate opened and Dani came across the ring. "Hi. Your mom said I'd find you down here with Twaziem, Robin, and it was okay if I came to hang out with you guys."

Vicky laughed. "We're trimming Twaz, but you're not allowed to put nail polish on his hooves."

"And to think I have a bottle of pink rose in my purse," Dani teased. She wore blue jeans and a Shamrock Stable sweatshirt, so she'd obviously come from the stable. "I think I freaked out your mom last night, Vicky. She was stunned when she met my *au pair*. Didn't you tell her that we were coming to take care of the kids and the house?"

"She doesn't listen," Vicky told us, keeping the tension on the lead line so Twaziem held still for his haircut. "I explained that I need to be with the squad at the games, or we'd never get to the regional competitions, and all she talked about was how much she needed me to babysit the brats."

"They're really not brats." Dani joined us and petted Twaziem before she gave him one of my carrots. "They helped clean up their toys,

159

dusted the house, put away laundry, and tidied their rooms too."

"Whoa. How did you manage that?" I asked. "Trade them in for pod people?"

"I just threatened to call you." Dani grinned and poked me in the ribs. "The mean sitter who puts them to bed right after supper. I told them if they didn't want to go to bed early like babies, they had to show me they were big kids and could stay up till ten o'clock."

"And that worked?" Vicky asked.

"Yes. When your mom got home from work, my *au pair* gave her a stack of resumes from her friends who need positions. She could hire one of them to pick up the slack at your house. The nanny would do household tasks around college classes."

"How would she pay one?" Vicky heaved a long sigh. "She's always griping that my dad barely pays the child support and we're hardly getting by. That's why she pulls me out of school to take care of the kids."

"Most of the ones that my *au pair* knows are college students." Dani picked up a brush and began to groom Twaziem. "They would work to get a place to live like the downstairs apartment and a flexible schedule so they could attend their classes. It's worth considering, and your mom didn't reject the idea. She asked me why we were rallying around to babysit for free, and I told her that it was a school project. We want Lincoln High represented at the regional cheerleading trials. Without you, we don't have a chance of winning."

"That's the same thing I told her." I gave Twaziem another carrot. "I swear it went in one ear, out the other and didn't even pause in the middle."

"Yeah, but my mom says the brain learns through repetition," Sierra said. "If she hears the same thing from enough different people, maybe Vicky's mom will actually listen." She dropped to one knee and ran the clippers along Twaziem's lower right front leg. "So, do you need a sitter next week or do you have it covered, Dani?"

"She would, but my mom does better when we switch things up," Vicky said. "You want to take it on Friday? My dad's supposed to take the kids on weekends, but he doesn't always show up, and I won't know until five o'clock if he's coming or not."

"Call me and I'll be there by six." Sierra moved to the right rear leg. "I thought he was your stepdad, Vick."

"He is, but since I barely remember my biological dad, I figure I'll keep calling him my dad and maybe he'll figure out that I'm not a servant," Vicky said, "or else he'll start paying me to take care of the kids."

"Good thinking." I broke up more carrots and gave Twaziem another piece. So far he was amazing me. He didn't try to kick Sierra, and she was running the clippers down his cannon bone, along the fetlock joint to his ankle and then around the coronet band. "I swear he's a rocket scientist."

"No, he's just like a lot of guys," Dani teased. "He loves having all this feminine attention."

We all cracked up, and Twaziem flicked his neatly trimmed ears. Then he nuzzled Vicky. She didn't have any treats, but I did, so he happily crunched more carrots. I glanced at Dani who was brushing his right side now, carefully staying out of Sierra's way. "Are you coming to the football game next week?"

She nodded. "Afraid so. Harry asked me to come watch him play even after I told him that football wasn't my thing."

"You can sit with me," I said. "Vick will be down in front cheering on the players."

"And I'll be using your technique on her brothers and sisters," Sierra said.

Dani glanced at me warily. "I didn't know you had a thing for Harry. Are you really okay with me dating him?"

I still felt a bit of a twinge when I thought about Harry, but I wasn't sharing that with any of my friends. I'd been awfully shallow when I didn't think of him as a human being, and I didn't want Vicky or Sierra knowing I could actually be a stereotypical blonde.

I shrugged. "It was more my thing than his. Go for it, Dani."

Chapter Twenty-Eight

Sunday, October 6th, 5:15 p.m.

When I returned from my afternoon run, I showered and changed to a T-shirt and jeans, then went down to the barn to help with chores. Twaziem and Singer stood in the middle of the paddock, grooming each other with their teeth. Like I hadn't thoroughly brushed Twaz before I turned him out, I thought. Everybody's a critic.

I walked into the barn and found Bill mucking my horse's stall. I lingered in the doorway. "Isn't Jack among the living yet? Or is he still having problems with his leg?"

"No. I just came to hang out, so I figured I'd help." Bill finished raking the bedding until the floor was level. He leaned the plastic fork against the wall and came toward me. He stopped in front of me. "You could move, so I can grab the bale of shavings."

"I could, but we don't have an audience."

A slow smile crept across his lips and landed in his eyes. "You're right."

He bent his head and kissed me. Long, slow and oh so sweet. My legs felt as if they'd barely hold me up, so I hung onto his shoulders. My pulse thudded and I could have stayed there in his arms forever. Dimly, I heard music.

Bill lifted his head and stepped back. "What a time for Jack to show up."

"You're telling me." I took a step sideways so I could pretend I wanted to check out Twaziem's water tub. The song I heard came from my brother who whistled pretty much the whole time he was in the barn. At least we had an early warning system. I definitely didn't want to be teased about the first guy I dated.

Bill shook out half the shavings in the plastic-wrapped bale. "Homecoming is in two weeks. Will you go with me to the dance?"

"Yes." I untied the baling twine that kept the blue garbage can against the wall so Twaz couldn't flood his stall. "I'll even come cheer you on at the game that Friday, but you guys better kick Mount Pilchuck's butt."

He laughed. "Count on it. What about this Friday, too? Will you be at the game?"

"I wouldn't miss it."

That earned me a steady look before he began smoothing out the pine chips. Heat trickled into my face as I remembered that Harry was on the football team too, and I'd pretty well made a fool of myself chasing him since school started.

"I'm coming to see you play," I said, "unless you've changed your mind. In that case, I'll come watch Jack and boo every time you're on the field."

Bill laughed. "I almost forgot how honest you are, Freckle-face."

I shrugged. "My sister thinks you're sweet, but I told her that you're not."

"Thanks a lot."

"And even if you don't make fun of me when I do stupid stuff, you're still not sweet," I said. "So, I'm not perfect. I make mistakes. You should know that by now, but if you don't, get used to it."

He raked out the last of the bedding. "If you were perfect, I'd have to be too. I'm not either."

"Well, I like you anyway," I said. "And perfection is hard to live up to, especially when we're both human beings."

* * * *

Friday, October 18th, 2:15 p.m.

The next two weeks flew. I was so busy with cross-country practice, riding lessons, working with Dr. Larry, spending time with Twaziem and going out with Bill twice that 'I didn't know if I was coming or going,' as Grandma said. We'd won our next two cross-country meets. Lew even P.R.'d at the last one. When I saw Phillip during one of our practices, he warned me that the Bartlett cousins were seriously pissed. I'd told him that he should suggest they turn their anger to running, and then their school might beat us. He'd just laughed.

We were on assembly schedule this Friday. No surprise there since this was the biggest game of the season with our archrival, Mount Pilchuck High. Lots of yelling, clapping and stomping later, the principal dismissed us to head for the buses. I met Jack and Bill out front. Bill had his car, so he could drive me home. We stalled around waiting for Vicky. She was coming to our house, and then we'd all leave for the game from there.

She hurried out of the school, backpack on her shoulder and school duffel in her hand. "Let's get out of here."

"What's going on?" Jack asked.

"My mom has to go to work, and my dad says he doesn't know when he can get the kids."

"But it's the Homecoming game," I protested. "They have to understand that."

Tears rolled down Vicky's cheeks. "They don't care. They want a sitter, and my mom sent a message to my last class for me to take the bus home. I called her from the office and reminded her about Homecoming. She said that my brothers and sisters are more important than football."

I pulled out my cell and called my mom to bring her up to speed. Once I finished telling her about the situation, she stepped up. She promised to babysit so Mrs. Miller would be able to go to the casino and work. I spotted Jack on his cell. His call ended about the same time mine did. "Did you catch Dad?"

"Yes, and he's contacting Vicky's father. Dad and Mom will meet us at the game. We need to do the chores because they can't pick up the slack at Vick's house and ours too."

"That makes sense. We'll meet you guys there. With all four of us working, we'll be done in plenty of time." Bill took my hand. "Let's move it."

164

Vicky stared at me, wiping away her tears. "Next time I'm a bitch, call me on it. You've been the best friend ever, Robin. Nobody else would have helped me stay on the cheer squad."

"Hey, we all helped." I squirmed inside. "You're making it sound like I'm nice, and I'm not. I was really rude to your mom. And I only got Dani to babysit because she's my Mini-Me and can be as snarky as I am."

"Life is good." Jack hugged Vicky super quick. "Let's go. You'll never get Robin to admit she can do the right thing occasionally."

"Most of the time." Vicky walked away with him, explaining why he should be kinder to me.

"Jack's pretty decent as brothers go." I walked beside Bill to his car on the other side of the parking lot. "I hope he doesn't think I gripe about him."

"No, he knows better than that," Bill said. "Vicky just needed to vent after you two helped her again. I really hope her parents get their acts together."

"Do you think that's even possible? They dump on her all the time."

"That's why I'm hoping," Bill said. "Vicky's already talking about moving in with Rocky and Sierra on her eighteenth birthday, but that's not her only choice. Once she's a legal adult, Vicky can go where she wants. And don't tell her that she can opt for emancipation now that she's sixteen. If she blows off her family in the next couple of months, it could take years for the breach to mend. I don't think her folks really want to lose her forever."

I waited while he unlocked my door. "You really believe her parents honestly love her?"

"Of course they do," Bill said. "If they didn't, why would they pay for her tuition here? Why would her mom have encouraged her to go out for cheer since middle school? If her folks hadn't bought her uniforms this year, how could she be on the squad? Why would her dad paint all her campaign signs when she ran for Sophomore Class President and come to all those assemblies last spring to listen to her speeches?"

"Then, why are they being so mean now?" I asked, sliding into the passenger seat.

"Because they're hurting," Bill said. "When most people hurt, they do mean things."

"Okay, time-out." I made a T with my hands. "If you tell me the Bartlett brats tortured Twaz because they're in pain, you're walking to my house."

He laughed. "It's my car, Freckle-face." He leaned in and kissed me. "No, they're beyond pain. They're just evil. Buckle up!"

Wow, he made me think. He was so smart. No wonder I liked him. He accepted me for who and what I was, but he didn't just look at the surface of people or events. He saw things for what they were. Next time I got ticked at Vick's parents, I'd try to give them the benefit of Bill's wisdom.

Maybe I'd use it on my own folks. Then again, perhaps I already had. I wasn't angry with them about not buying the Mustang. I understood why they turned me down. It wasn't that they wanted to destroy my happiness. It was just too much money, and having big payments hanging over me when I didn't have a good job really didn't make a lot of sense.

Dani, Porter, Gwen, and I were up in the grandstand when my parents arrived at the game. We had great seats and Gwen shifted our coats. I stood and waved. "Up here!"

Dad heard my shout. He and Mom wove their way to us through the crowded bleachers where other parents, students, and families waited for the big game to start. "Thanks for saving us seats, Robbie."

"No worries. I'm just glad you guys made it before we got mugged." I moved closer to Gwen. "Did Vick's dad get there?"

"No." Mom smiled and pressed next to me. "Your dad and I packed up the kids and their stuff and took them to the tire store he manages."

"No way." Porter leaned forward, looking around Gwen and me. "What did he say?"

"What could he say?" Mom asked. "He was too busy to come get them. We explained that normally we would make arrangements to stay with the kids, but not at Homecoming. It's unfair to expect Vicky to stop being a cheerleader because her folks divorced. He and her mom should be making arrangements to come see her perform with the squad at football games, not abandon her at a crucial time of her life. If she wasn't such a smart girl, she could turn her life into a total train wreck."

"It's also unfair for him to keep making her friends babysit for free so she can fulfill her dreams," Dad said. "It's past time for him to quit punishing the girl."

"Now, John. You know he didn't think of it like that. He was shocked when you told him that you believe he hates his oldest daughter."

Dad's jaw jutted forward, and he took on his most stubborn look. "I call it like I see it."

"Must be a guy thing," I teased. "Great job, Dad."

Mom and I shared an amused look. Maybe he'd made a difference. We wouldn't know until next week. We'd have to talk about it later. No time for it now. The teams raced onto the field.

* * * *

Saturday, October 19th, 12:20 p.m.

"Wasn't that a great game?" Porter glanced over her shoulder at me while the technician worked on her nails. "I couldn't believe the run Jack made, eighty-three yards."

"It was something," I agreed. "I liked the three turnovers with Bill better."

"You would." Vicky sipped hot tea. She always sounded like a giant frog after an exciting game, but she didn't mind. She shook her head at the bottle of red polish Gwen held up. "No. Our colors are blue and gold. Where's your school spirit?"

I laughed. Trust Vick to think of that. I glanced at the rack filled with containers of fingernail polishes on the other side of the salon. We'd joined up to come to the Everett Mall to primp for the dance tonight. Once we finished with our manicures and pedicures, we'd have lunch at our favorite Chinese place. Then, we'd have our hair done at the studio on the other side of the mall. I wondered what traditions the guys had today. They probably weren't anything like ours. I bet Bill would tell me if I asked. And I might later tonight.

I arrived home early enough to help with the chores before I hit the shower and dressed for the dance. I wore a scarf over my hair and gloves to keep my nails nice. I wouldn't win any prizes as a fashion diva, but I wanted to look awesome tonight. Between Dad being gone to the store to collect the supplies for what he called a date night with Mom, and Jack off to get his tux, I was the first one to go to the barn. I headed straight for Twaziem's stall. I had carrots for him, but I'd taken them from the fridge, not the garden. I'd make up the difference tomorrow.

He stood in the center of his stall. His head drooped down, almost to his knees. Snot streamed from his nostrils and mouth. "Oh my Gawd! What happened? What did you do?"

Chapter Twenty-Nine

Saturday, October 19th, 4:45 p.m.

Mom arrived at the barn in less than five minutes. She took one look at Twaziem and announced. "He has choke."

"What? How could he be choking?"

"Choke," Mom repeated. "Something is lodged in his esophagus. Call Dr. Larry while I start massaging him." She came into the stall and stepped up next to Twaz. While I pushed buttons on my cell phone, she began rubbing my horse's chin, then his jaw, working her way up between his cheeks to his throatlatch and back down again.

I explained the symptoms to the receptionist, and she promised to send Dr. Larry immediately. She told me to keep massaging the throat to help clear the blockage until the veterinarian arrived. "We are," I said, "and we will."

"What could he have choked on?" I asked Mom as soon as I ended the call. "Not his hay or his grain. He hasn't had any problems before."

"He's still wormy and debilitated," Mom said. "It could be anything he's eaten from hay or grain to carrots to his manure. Why don't you clean his stall while I massage, and then when my hands get tired, we'll switch."

I nodded. "Okay."

I fetched the wheelbarrow and tools as well as a partial bale of shavings. It didn't take long to pick the stall and dress it with new bedding. Despite Mom's massage, Twaziem didn't look better. White mucus with bits of grain still flowed from his nose and mouth. "Are you sure you're doing it right?"

She nodded. "Yes, honey. You probably don't remember, but this used to happen to Cobbie when he got rolled oats instead of wet cob. After the first couple of times, I didn't bother with Dr. Larry. I just massaged Cobbie's throat until the blockage cleared. I don't want to take any chances with Twaziem. He's such a baby."

"What is wet cob?" I asked.

"The kind of grain we feed," Mom said. "It's corn, oats and barley mixed together with molasses to dampen it. The feed store also has dry cob, the kind without molasses. Our horses get enough work that they need the extra energy." She stepped back and flexed her hands. "Your turn."

I put the tools outside the stall. "What do I do?"

"Come on over and I'll show you."

I placed my hand on Twaziem's throatlatch, but there wasn't a bump or anything pushing against my fingers. "What should I be feeling?"

"It's a bit swollen already," Mom said. "You want to rub softly there and stroke down the underside of his neck. Think of it as if you have something stuck in your own throat. You're trying to clear the blockage. While you do that, I'll get a grooming kit and brush him. It's psychological first aid. He'll feel better if we both fuss over him."

That made sense. For the next hour, we took turns massaging Twaziem's throat, but it didn't help. He still had white snot streaming from his nose and mouth when Dr. Larry came in the barn. He smiled at both of us before he eyed Twaziem. "I'm going to have to be put on retainer with this fellow. Let's see what I can do to make him more comfortable. How long have you been massaging his throat?"

I looked at my watch. "I found him an hour and a half ago. Probably about an hour and fifteen minutes."

"Any change in the amount of saliva?" Dr. Larry asked.

I shook my head. "No. What are we going to do?"

"Let's rule out some causes first, Robin. Any chance that he got to rat poison or other toxic substances? Some can cause excess saliva."

"No way," I said. "We don't have any rats, and we don't use poison because the cats could get to it."

"I'm still going to examine him and look for physical trauma," Dr. Larry said. "We'll need a halter and lead since he may not stand still for this."

"Okay." I went and got the training halter. When I returned, I found the veterinarian with his hand inside Twaziem's mouth. "What are you doing?"

"Checking his teeth. There aren't any sharp points on any of the molars. He should have been able to chew his lunch, not choke on it. He doesn't have a broken jaw, and there aren't any other signs of trauma."

Mom and Dr. Larry shared a look before she said, "You're going to have to flush the blockage, aren't you?"

"Afraid so." Dr. Larry turned toward me. "I'm going to run a surgical tube through his nostril and down his throat to move the obstruction toward his stomach. I won't use a twitch to immobilize him. Instead, I'm going to give him a light dose of a local anesthetic to ease his stress. While it takes effect, can you get me some warm water to flush the blockage away?"

"All right." I took a bucket and headed for the shower stall. Suddenly, it occurred to me that Bill would be showing up anytime to take me to Homecoming, and I couldn't leave Twaziem. While I waited for the water to warm, I pulled out my phone and texted Bill. I hated breaking our date, but this stupid horse came first. He was making it easier and easier for me to sell him to get a car next summer. I swear Twaz lived to wreck my life.

Twaziem had started to relax when I returned, his eyes half-closed as he drowsed and drooled on Dr. Larry's gold coveralls. I put down the bucket of water. "How is he?"

"I think he's ready," Dr. Larry said. "I know you've never held a horse while the vet does this before, Robin, but I'll need you to do what I say, when I say it. Deal?"

"Of course she can do it," Mom said. "The two of you need to be careful, honey. If anything goes wrong, it'll damage Twaziem's nasal passages, cause a nose-bleed, or injure his lungs."

I eyed her and the vet. "Do we have to do it this way?"

"Yes, because nothing else has worked." Dr. Larry pulled a long three-eighths inch tube out of his pocket and squirted surgical lubricant into his hand to smooth over the plastic. Then, he stepped up to my horse and eased the rounded tip of the tube into Twaz's nostril. "Okay, son. Here we go."

He slid the tube slowly up through the right nostril, never forcing the plastic line. I shifted my hold on the Twaziem's head to help him partially flex it so he could swallow. Dr. Larry didn't try to push the tubing into the stomach. He stopped when it was at the esophagus.

"Hold the line for me, Maura," Dr. Larry told Mom. "Don't push on it or pull it out."

She nodded agreement. "You're the boss."

Dr. Larry hooked up a plunger to the tube, then began to force water through the plastic. Running water through the tube seemed to do the trick. The flow of mucus from the nose and mouth eased as the lump of feed was flushed down toward Twaziem's stomach. He heaved a huge sigh of relief when Dr. Larry removed the plastic line.

Mom rubbed Twaz's face. "You'll be fine now, fella. Promise."

Dr. Larry turned to me. "Clear that hay out of his manger, and he'll need fresh water in his bucket. You may want to add a bit of apple juice to it so he takes on extra fluids."

"Anything else?" I asked.

"I'll be leaving him electrolytes and pain relievers with instructions for you to follow. No hay until Tuesday while his throat heals. We don't want him to choke again. The next time could be fatal. And when he goes back on hay, I'll want it dampened for him so he eats more slowly. Hold off on that second dose of wormer for another week until he recovers from this episode." Dr. Larry glanced at Mom. "Do you folks have any straight alfalfa?"

"No, but I'll send John to the feed store to get him some," Mom said. "What do you think about pellets if we really soak them down? I hate to have him miss any meals."

"I understand," Dr. Larry said. "We still don't know what choked him, and we don't want it to happen again. So, let's be careful. Watch the pellets and his grain so they don't clump and block his throat."

I finished cleaning out his manger and taking the hay to Nitro. Twaziem gave me the evil eye like I was trying to starve him, but then he sighed again and started to doze off. I checked his water tub. It was still clean. I headed for the feed room to grab a small bottle of apple juice from the barn fridge.

I'd just poured it into the water tub when Dad hustled in the barn, Bill and Jack right behind him. "I saw Larry's truck," Dad said. "What happened?"

"Choke," Mom said. "But, he's going to be okay."

"What is that?" Bill looked like a total hunk in his black tux, white shirt, gold cummerbund, and gold tie. No wonder he asked me what color my dress was. When I told him it was a metallic short waffle knit, he seemed baffled. I added that when my dad and Jack saw it, they'd totally freak about the way it fit, and Bill was happy. We'd have been awesome together. I listened while Mom explained with a few facts thrown in by Dr. Larry.

"So, what's going on?" Dr. Larry asked. "Do you always wear a tux to the barn?"

"Only on special occasions like Homecoming." Bill smiled at me. "I'm sure I can borrow some jeans and a sweatshirt from Jack, and we can stay with Twaziem tonight. Otherwise, you'll worry about him."

A tear slid down my cheek, and I wiped it away. "You don't have to do that. This is your last year to go because you're a senior."

"It won't be any fun without you."

"And she's going to your celebration," Dr. Larry said, surprising both of us. "Take my word for it. All your horse will want to do tonight is sleep, Robin. It will stress him out more if you're hanging out in his stall for the next few hours. It's enough if you check in on him when you get home."

"Are you sure?" I asked.

"Hey, I'm the doctor, and that's why I get the big money." He winked at me. "Besides, I'll be back tomorrow to take you with me on rounds, so we'll make this guy our first patient. Deal?"

"And your mother and I will pop down to see him too," Dad said. "Now, we're taking over on chores. You and Jack need to head for the house and get ready to go. We'll be up in a bit to take photos for the family album."

I lingered by Twaziem to pet his neck and breathe in his warm horsy odor. When I got home, I'd bring down my sleeping bag and stay with him just to be on the safe side. He sleepily nuzzled me, and I rubbed the blaze on his face. "No carrots for you till Tuesday when your throat's better. I'll see you later."

Chapter Thirty

Sunday, October 20th, 3:05 a.m.

The dance lasted till a little after one in the morning. When I called home for the fifth time, Dad had just come back from the barn. He said that Twaziem was sound asleep. If I stopped phoning, then my parents might be able to go to bed too. Bill and I went out for breakfast with the rest of our crowd. But, when they headed off for late night bowling, we decided to go to my house and the stable, with a brief stop by his place so he could change clothes. He looked concerned when he came back to the car where I waited.

"What's up?" I asked.

"I've misplaced my phone," Bill said. "I thought I must have left it at home, but it's not in my room or the car."

"Where was the last place you saw it?" I adjusted my seat belt. "Retrace your steps, and then you'll be able to find it."

"Good idea."

At my house, Bill headed down to the barn to check on Twaziem while I went in to trade my dress for jeans and a sweatshirt. Then, I grabbed a bag of chips and two colas as well as my sleeping bag. I left a note so my folks would know we were down with the horses and went to meet Bill.

* * * *

Monday, October 21st, 5:10 p.m.

As soon as Dad and I turned into the drive, I saw the county cop car. "Give me a break. Why is he here? He said he'd be back in a month, and it's only been a couple weeks."

"Well, let's go find out what's up." Dad turned off the motor. "I'm sure there's a good reason."

"I so don't need this when Twaziem is off hay until tomorrow. He's going to lose weight and Officer Yardley will notice."

"Robbie, let's go talk first. You can panic afterwards."

"Okay. Okay." I climbed out of the car and hurried in the direction of the barn. When I arrived, I saw the cop standing outside Twaziem's stall talking to Mom. "What's going on?"

"Nothing much." Officer Yardley smiled at me. "He's gained weight, Robin. He's looking pretty good."

"So, why are you here?" I asked. "I still have two more weeks to get more pounds on him and make him look like a horse."

"My boss sent me. Somebody posted a video of Twaziem on the Internet, and it went viral. He had patches of moving lice. I explained that you'd treated the horse for external and internal parasites." Officer Yardley shook his head. "But my boss is catching it from his boss, and he's hearing about it from the county council members. I'm back to make sure that Twaziem is continuing to improve."

I caught my breath, remembering the first day that Twaz arrived. He'd been covered with lice and Jack wouldn't let us put him in the barn until we deloused him. And Bill had wanted to use his phone to take pictures. I wasn't saying any of that to the cop, but I was going to kill Bill as soon as I saw him. He hadn't put the video up. I knew that. Still, he'd taken the pictures, and somehow he passed them on to whoever did post them.

"He was a mess when we got him," I said. "And he'd obviously had lice for quite a while or they wouldn't have been so gross. Did you ever go after the Bartlett beasts? Dad and I went to see Mrs. B and talk to her about Twaz. Her grandson bragged about killing Twaz's mom in front of him when he was only a couple months old."

Okay, that was a slight exaggeration. Caine put the blame on

Ashley, but hey, I was a teenage girl and I was allowed to make the story more dramatic. "I wonder if they'd have filmed him when he had lice."

"Only one way to find out." Officer Yardley made a couple more notes. "I'm sorry folks, but I'll have to come see him every three or four days until the heat dies down."

"Well, Robbie will run off her log sheets for you," Dad told him. "And when you talk to the veterinarian, you'll find out that Twaziem colicked after he was wormed."

"You have to expect those kinds of reactions dealing with an overload of worms," Officer Yardley said, closing his metal notebook. "His system needs to adjust to regular care."

"And he had choke over the weekend," Mom added. "That's why he doesn't have a lot of hay right now. We've changed his feed."

"Dr. Larry advised it," I said. "He was here to see Twaz yesterday."

"And he'll continue to see him quite frequently throughout the next year. Rescue horses need that too." Officer Yardley smiled at us. "I'll be in touch with him and the farrier. Yes, Robin, I will follow up on the history of the horse too. He's doing well here, but if he'd had good care his entire life, then you wouldn't need to do so much of it."

"Yeah, but if they'd taken care of him, I wouldn't have him." I stepped up to rub Twaziem's blaze when he nickered at me. "No carrots until tomorrow, buddy."

Once my folks escorted the cop from the barn, I pulled out my cell and called Bill. He picked up right away, and I asked. "Where did you find your phone?"

"At the tux shop. I must have put it down while I was renting my suit. Why? What's going on?"

I leaned against Twaziem's stall. "Remember the first day he got here?"

"Sure, he was a mess."

"My mom told you not to video him. Did you do it anyway?"

Utter silence and I knew for sure. Fury boiled up inside me. "You took a video of Twaz's lice and somebody got it off your phone, then posted it on the Internet. The Animal Control guy was just here, and we're back on probation again. Thanks a lot! I so don't need to deal with that cop."

Shannon Kennedy

The silence grew until it deafened me.

Finally, Bill said, "I'm sorry, Robin. I didn't post a video. I have no idea who did. What can I do?"

"Oh, I think dropping dead works." And I ended the call.

* * * *

Tuesday, October 22ⁿᵈ, 7:10 a.m.

I felt like the center of attention while I waited for Vicky in the Commons. It wasn't in a good way, either. No, I wasn't a cross-country star today who was leading her team to an undefeated season. People were poking each other and whispering about me. I wanted to jump up and scream that I saved Twaziem. I didn't torture him.

Vicky came across the room and hugged me before she sat down. "Jack told me about the video. I checked it out, and it looks really bad, Robin. What are you going to do?"

"There's nothing I can do," I said. "I contacted the site and asked them to take it down, but they haven't yet."

"They won't when it's getting so many hits," Vicky said. "I wish he looked better. If he had gained all the weight that he will in the next ten months, you could put up a new video showing that."

"He is clean," I pointed out. "He doesn't have any lice now."

"Yeah, but even stupid people will see his ribs and hips," Vicky said. "At least Twaziem is back on hay this morning."

"That's true." I stirred my mocha, wishing I could come up with a brilliant idea. "I fought with Bill because he was dumb enough to take that video of the lice and then let somebody get it off his phone."

"I know. Jack told me. Bill feels really bad about it, Robin."

"He should. He's too freaking stupid to live."

"Who is?" Dani dropped into the seat next to me. "What happened? How did that video get on the Internet?"

Between sips of her latte, Vicky brought her up to speed. Dani listened, then said, "Lady looks almost exactly like Twaziem. We could do a video of her and put it up, pretend it's him."

"It won't work," I said. "He has a blaze and she has a star and snip.

178

And they're two different breeds. They're almost the same color, but they're two different body types. I appreciate the thought. I just have to think of something else."

"Yeah. It's too bad you don't know who did it because then we could so get them." She waved at Harry as he came in the cafeteria, and he headed toward us. "You do know that he's a total geek, don't you?"

"Harry is?" I stared at her.

"I'm what?" Harry dropped into the chair on the other side of Dani. "So, who hates you bad enough to put up that video, Robin?"

"We don't know, but you need to take it down," Dani told him. "And then you need to create a different video using the pictures people have taken of Twaziem since he was rescued and post that. You'll use music and add in voice-overs from the vet, the shoer, and the trainer."

"And I suppose you want me to play detective and get the guy who did the dirty deed too, all while I wear a superhero cape." Harry looked interested, not put off by the idea. "I can do that, but you have to do something for me, Robin."

"What? My folks won't let me have that blue Mustang."

"Brenna wants me to take over more of the mechanical work and that means we need somebody to detail the cars. Will you stop in and see her about it? It's not that many hours, about twenty a week, but we do pay ten bucks an hour."

"Sounds good," I said. "I'll swing by after practice today." The first bell rang, and we got up to head for English class. Olivia met us on the way. "So, when are we kicking Caine's butt?"

"What?" I stared at her. "Why would I?"

"The word around Mount Pilchuck is that he put up a nasty video about you to make trouble so we'd choose somebody else to lead the cross-country team."

"How did you hear about that?" Vicky asked. "I know people who go there, but we hardly talk anymore."

"From Cedar's cousins," Olivia said. "Her family had a barbeque last night, and they bragged to her that we'd lose this week. When she went on the Internet, she found out it was all about your horse. She told me this morning that Caine did it to sabotage our team, and she thought we should keep you as our leader."

179

"I hadn't planned to quit," I said. "Coach tells us, winners never quit and quitters never win. We are so winning the meet this Thursday. Like my grandma says, 'We'll teach them to suck eggs,' and Caine will be sorry he ever messed with me."

Olivia grinned at me. "I knew you'd nail him and we're helping."

"Why?" Vicky asked.

"Because we are a team," Olivia said, "and when you go after one of us, all of us get you."

"Well, we're not on cross-country," Dani told her, "but Harry and I are helping."

I lifted my chin, determined to act strong even when all I wanted to do was break down and bawl. I had wonderful friends, and from now on, I'd remember to appreciate them. In class, I sat down and pulled out my comp book before I looked at the writing prompt on the board.

Were you ever accused of something that you didn't do? How did it make you feel and what did you do about it?

Chapter Thirty-One

Friday, October 25th, 4:45 p.m.

While I groomed Twaziem, I told him all about the week. We'd kicked butt at the meet yesterday. Lincoln High remained undefeated. Harry got together with his geek squad friends, and they'd taken down the video. He tried to explain the details to me, but I didn't get it. I truly didn't speak the guy's language. Luckily, Dani did. The two of them had already started compiling pics and interviews for the new video they were doing of Twaziem. Dani would visit next week to take more photos of my horse. I'd stopped in at the car lot, and Brenna hired me to wash cars, starting tomorrow afternoon.

"I guess I'll have to start cutting up apples for you," I told Twaziem. "I'm still pissed at Bill for being a screw-up."

"Must be nice to be perfect." Jack lined up his stall mucking tools in the aisle. "If you put him out, I'll do his stall. Are you coming to the game tonight, Princess Robin?"

"Yes, but only to cheer you on, not your 'too stupid to live' buddy."

"Don't do me any favors." Jack passed me the training halter and lead. "I told Bill he should hold out for a human being instead of waiting for you to grow up."

I tossed my head. "Shove it. You, your horse, and the little blue dog that follows behind."

* * * *

181

Shannon Kennedy

Sunday, October 27ᵗʰ, 5:10 p.m.

Another day working with the vet, another colic. I was amazed at how often horses had trouble with their feed, but like Dr. Larry said, there were so many causes, ranging from bad hay to stress. This time a horse up in Darrington had been overworked at a Saturday show, then had trouble with his feed the next day. I waved goodbye to the vet and headed for the house.

Carrots first and I'd go to the barn, hoping that Jack was done being angry at me. I knew he loved me, and if Bill had done anything that really hurt me, my brother would totally be on my side. Right now, Jack felt I was unfair to his friend, and he didn't hesitate to tell me so. As soon as I opened the front door, I heard my dad yelling for help.

I raced down the hall to the kitchen. "What is it? What's wrong?"

Dad propped up Jack, guiding him into the room from the back porch. A torn shirt flapped from his shoulders. Bloody U-shaped prints on his side, his chest. One arm hung limp. More blood and manure splattered his jeans.

"What happened?" I barely managed a whisper.

Jack managed to wink at me, a bruise around his left eye. He wiped at the blood on his lip. "Don't worry. I'm fine."

Dad glared at me. "Get my coat and keys. I'm taking Jack to the hospital. Tomorrow, that killer goes to the slaughter house."

"What killer?" Dread filled me. "What happened?"

"Twaziem cornered Jack and almost killed him. I'm done with that horse." Rage filled Dad's face, tightening his jaw. "He's out of here first thing in the morning. I'm not giving that monster another chance at your brother."

"It's not his fault." More blood ran down Jack's chin.

I remembered what I'd heard about internal injuries in health class and ran for the phone to call 9-1-1. Jack needed an ambulance. When I glanced at him again, he drooped in Dad's arms.

I gave our address to the operator and told her that my brother had lost consciousness. Why did I even try to save Twaz? I should have let Mr. Johnson take him to the slaughter house in the first place. It would have saved us from all this grief. "I'm sorry, Dad."

"Not as sorry as that crazy horse is going to be."

After they left for the hospital, I wandered from room to room. I saw the kittens playing in the living room drapes, but I couldn't pick them up for a quick cuddle. Mom was off at one of her craft fairs and wouldn't be back for ages. I knew if both my parents agreed that Twaziem was a threat, the guy was a goner. It wasn't fair. I'd spent so much time on him. And maybe I didn't gush over the horse, but it didn't mean I didn't care about him.

I grabbed my coat and a handful of carrots, and stopped in the back porch for my boots. I would go visit him and see if I could discover why he went berserk. There had to be a reason. Nobody freaked without one. In the barn, I flipped the light switch. I walked down the aisle, checking the horses. All of them munched hay.

What was that about? Normally, Twaziem would be in a paddock while his stall was cleaned and return in time for supper. The wheelbarrow stood in front of his door. I eyed it suspiciously. Why was my horse inside if Jack was mucking? Or had my perfect brother made a mistake?

I slid open the stall door to look inside. A bale of shavings sat in the opposite corner from the water tub. Twaziem turned his head when he heard me and nickered. "Good boy," I managed to say around the lump in my throat. "You're a good boy, Twaz."

What had Jack been thinking? The rake and flat shovel leaned against the wall, but the pitchfork lay on the floor. It was pure luck that Twaziem hadn't stepped on the plastic tines and broken them or stabbed himself with the fork. Okay, so it couldn't kill him the way an old-fashioned metal one could, but it was still dangerous.

I walked over to it, bent, and snaked the fork over to me. Then, I walked around Twaz and collected the other tools. Last of all, I brought the bale of shavings up to the front of the stall. "Okay, booger-butt, I'll clean the horsy rooms before I do the rest of the chores, but you have got to get over yourself. Stop picking on Jack. It's not his fault he looks like Caine, and my brother would never hurt you."

Twaziem snorted at the sound of my voice. He didn't budge from where he stood in front of the manger. Nothing ever seemed to distract him from a meal, but my brother had.

"Robin, what are you doing?" Mom stood at the stall door. "Your dad called from the hospital and said that he left you at home. He's totally lost it."

"Well, his perfect Jack screwed up," I said, scooping poop, "and my stupid horse hurt him."

Twaziem stomped his front feet, and I paused to pet him. "Of course, that didn't give you the right to kick him."

"Nobody except you says your brother is perfect." Mom sighed and walked in to check the water tub. "And your dad always freaks when one of you kids gets hurt. He wanted to shoot Vinnie the last time Felicia fell during a jumping lesson."

"I don't want Twaziem to go to slaughter," I said, beginning to feel a bit better. It sounded like she was on my side. "Maybe I don't get mushy all the time, but it doesn't mean I want him dead."

"Honey, I'd never send a horse there. I'd just have Dr. Larry put Twaziem down at home, and we'd bury him here like we did Cobbie." Mom left the stall to go after the hose. "I don't think your horse needs to worry about a long trip to Canada from Stanwood. Did your brother try to clean around him?"

"Yes. At least I think so. I found the tools in the stall along with Twaz. He must have been frightened and attacked Jack before—"

"Your brother got him." Mom sighed and shook her head as she filled the water tub. "Sweetie, I don't think we can wait to train him. We're going to have to arrange for Rocky to start working with him now before this bad behavior escalates anymore."

I cleaned up the last of the wet spot, then took the tools to the hallway so I could put down fresh shavings. "Will you talk to Dad?"

"Yes. He's already calming down and starting to think. At the hospital, Jack kept telling your father that the accident was his entire fault." Mom finished watering. "Come on, Robin. We have a lot of chores to do. And since your horse made the problem, you'll have to do the barns full-time until Jack recovers."

"I'm going to be totally overloaded until Christmas." I moaned. "Cross-country practice, two more meets, my first job, my internship, and I'll bet you still expect me to do homework for all my classes."

Mom laughed and patted my back. "Let's go, drama diva. I'll help you."

* * * *

Monday, October 28th, 7:20 a.m.

This time I was the one who was almost late for school. Morning chores took forever even when Mom milked the cow. Vicky flagged me down in the Commons, holding out a huge mocha. "My turn to buy. Your turn to chug it."

I managed to smile at her. "I'm amazed you're speaking to me after what Twaz did to Jack."

"Oh, I'm talking to you," Vicky said. "I'm just not speaking to him. He got all pissy with me when I told him that he got what he deserved for being so stupid."

I finished gulping my coffee on our way to English class. I'd barely sat down when Dani plopped into the chair beside me. "Is this afternoon still a good time for Harry and me to come shoot some video of your horse?"

"Yes," I said, "but Harry needs to be careful. Jack went in to clean Twaz's stall last night. He was kicked, struck, and bitten before he managed to get away. Coach will probably be looking for me since there's no way that Jack will be able to play this week. He has cracked ribs, a wrenched shoulder and a twisted ankle, plus a ton of bruises."

"And he's really whiny." Vicky leaned around me. "Jake should never have trusted a horse that Caine abused, but my silly boyfriend said he was in a hurry to get chores done. Now, he's out of the barn until he's back to a hundred-percent."

"And I'm in it," I said. "It takes forever for me to do chores by myself. The only comfort is that Mom says Jack's on housework for the duration of his injuries. You should have heard him snivel when she said it only took one hand to run the vacuum cleaner."

"I'll bet he loves that," Dani teased.

"Hardly." Vicky began to giggle. "I'll have to call and sympathize with him. Now, he'll know what my nights are like."

"Barely," I said, starting to smile. "We don't have any little kids."

The last bell rang and the three of us dove for comp books. Mondays always meant an extra-long write, and Mrs. Weaver had been on an anti-bullying kick for the past week. Gawd knew how awful the prompt would be!

* * * *

Monday, October 28th, 2:20 p.m.

Gwen led the stretching exercises for the team today, and then we took off for our run through Marysville. The pressure was on, so nobody complained when she headed for Golf Course Hill. If we won the next two meets, we'd be the undefeated champions in our division. I was really looking forward to rubbing our victories in the faces of the Mount Pilchuck team. We knew we had to be going to the state competitions. None of the other schools came close to what we'd done this year. And Olivia was already talking about kicking butt next spring in track.

When practice ended, it was time to go to the Mustang Corral. I'd be washing cars for the next hour and a half. Then, Dad would pick me up, and we'd go home so I could do the chores. Jack had skipped school today, but he'd be back tomorrow. I figured it was up to my folks to keep him out of the barn and away from the critters. Mom had already started making a list of housework. Jack complained, but I knew he'd turn out to be as good at house cleaning as he was at stall mucking.

I'd just soaked the candy-apple red Mustang when I saw a guy in a fancy blue uniform walking toward me. As he came closer, I realized he was a soldier. The combat boots and tan beret were a definite giveaway. He had a ton of medals on his jacket. I turned the nozzle on the end of my hose to cut off the spray. "Can I help you? Are you thinking about buying a car?"

"Actually, I'm looking for someone." He smiled at me. "Is this Brenna Thornton's place?"

"Yes, it is." I didn't smile back. "Are you the guy who broke her heart for a joke in Afghanistan?"

He eyed me and the hose. "That's not the way I'd phrase it."

"But, you're not me," I said, "and a player doesn't deserve any respect from me."

I lifted my hose, cranked the end, and watched him run for the office trailer. He didn't know the cross-country creed of, "When you go after one of us, all of us get you." It was only fair to give him a couple steps so he'd think he'd make it. And then I cut loose with the spray.

Chapter Thirty-Two

Monday, October 28ᵗʰ, 5:05 p.m.

I'd finished the last of the red Mustangs and moved onto the black one when Brenna came out of the office trailer. I flicked a quick glance at her and kept soaping the hood. "So do I still have a job? Or are you firing my butt for watering down the jerk?"

A smile trickled across her lips, up to her eyes and then she burst out laughing. "Honey, you have a job for life if you want it." She grabbed me in a hug. "Nobody has ever stood up for me the way you did. I admire your guts."

"Hey, I admire yours. I couldn't go to war."

"Sweetheart, I think you just did." Brenna stepped back and grinned at me. "You deserve to know that he came to see me because he broke things off with the fiancée as soon as he got home. He just wouldn't do it from a war zone when she was waiting for him. I don't know what comes next—"

"What took him so long to get here?" I asked. "Haven't you been home for months?"

"He's a career soldier, and it took a while for him to get leave." She shrugged. "So, we wait and see. He has a lot to do to convince me he can be trusted."

At least she was thinking. She wasn't just falling at his feet. I glanced at my watch. "Okay if I finish this car and head out today? I have to do chores. My horse attacked Jack over the weekend, and he can't do barns for a while."

"That's fine. When is your next meet?"

"Oh, I forgot," I said. "It's been moved to Wednesday because everybody complains so much when we have one on Halloween. I don't mind washing cars on Thursday if that's all right."

"It's fine. I'll see you then." With a wave, she headed back to the office.

When Dad and I arrived home, Rocky's pickup was in the drive. I changed and headed to the barn. Rocky was feeding carrots to Twaziem when I arrived. She'd already groomed him and had started teaching him to work on a longe line. She waved to me, and I walked over to her to stand in the middle of her circle.

"What's up?" I asked.

"Some things you need to know about him." She flipped the end of the rope at him and Twaz eyed her warily before he took a step. "Never use a whip on him, not even a long one to get him going. He sees it as a threat and wants to attack."

I nodded, turning with her. "Okay, I hadn't thought about it, but I won't take chances with a whip. How do I deal with his gender bias?"

"Start by teaching him that all guys aren't the same," Rocky said. "Dani and I did a little bit earlier this afternoon. She and her boyfriend groomed Twaziem while I held him. He's coming back tomorrow. Are there any other guys this horse likes?"

"Bill, but I haven't seen him since I got angry at him last week."

"You may want to consider apologizing to him if he can help with training."

"He totally pissed me off when he let a guy steal a video off his phone."

Rocky just gave me her 'drop dead' stare before she said, "With a crappy attitude like that, Robin, it's a good thing you don't work in law enforcement. Why aren't you blaming your horse for almost dying of starvation?"

"It's not his fault that he didn't get fed." I stopped to think. Okay, she had a point. "I have to go muck stalls, and maybe I was too hard on Bill."

"Then, I'll let you figure out how to make amends." She gave a little wave of her hand. "Go shovel poop. It'll be good for you."

After I finished the rest of the chores, I came back to the arena.

189

Rocky had me longe Twaziem for a few minutes before I led him to his stall for supper. "How often are you going to come train him?"

"Either Sierra or I will be here every day to work with him. Groom him at least an hour a day and clean his feet several times during the process. Many young horses hate having their hooves done, and you don't want to have new problems start."

"I hate picking hooves," I said, "and today I had to do everybody else's feet."

"Poor baby." Rocky didn't sound like she meant it. She patted my shoulder as if I were my horse. "Actually, you've done a good job training Twaziem so far. I'll need you to keep helping me and Sierra. He trusts you, and it'll be easier for him if you spend time with us."

I nodded. "Okay. I think I'll probably keep him longer than I originally planned. He needs to bond with people, and so far I'm one of the few that he actually likes."

"What are your plans for him?" Rocky asked. "You'll be riding him next summer."

"I'd like to show him the way that Dani shows Lady."

"Then, we'll concentrate on training him for western pleasure."

I was in the middle of my algebra assignment that night when Jack limped into my room. "What?"

"Vicky's on the landline. We're done talking, and she wants to connect with you." He gave me an older brother look. "This is the last time I'm going to ask you to stop being mean to Bill. He's taking it hard. I had to tell him that punching out Caine wasn't an answer, and that's pretty touchy-feely for me."

"Yeah, well, Rocky jumped on my case about it today too." I got up and headed for the door, stopping to give him a baby hug on the way. I didn't want to hurt his ribs. "I guess I wanted to be mad at someone about that video, and Bill was handy. I sure couldn't go kick Caine's butt."

"Life will kick him in the teeth for us." Jack hugged me back. "Glad you're not mad at me anymore."

"Likewise." Mom was in her craft room and Dad was in his study, so I nabbed the living room extension to talk to Vicky. "Hey, what's up? Jack and I aren't fighting anymore. Are you okay?"

"Oh, I'm fine. I finished whining at him about my family, and he sniveled at me about having to help cook supper and then do dishes. So, we decided it's your turn to listen."

"Yeah, well how do I tell Bill I'm sorry I was a jerk?" I asked.

"I don't know. Send him flowers?"

We both laughed, but actually it wasn't a bad idea. I could have them delivered to him at school. We threw around a few other ideas, like a card or candy or just walking up and saying what I had to say.

After a few minutes, Vicky cut to the subject on her mind. "Anyway, I was talking to my mom about helping you out in the barns because I'd be off the cheer squad if you hadn't stepped up to help me. She says the only days I could come would be Fridays and Saturdays since that's when my dad has the kids and I don't. Will it be any help?"

"It'd be a lot of help," I said. "Friday, we could take you to the game after chores, and if you spent the night here, then we could go straight to Shamrock Stable. When I finish my lesson, I go to work down at the Mustang Corral."

"How do you like it? Washing cars seems like a stupid job to me."

"I love it." I giggled. Then I told her all about cutting loose with the hose on Brenna's heartthrob. We talked for another half-hour before I went back to my algebra and knocked the problems into submission. I didn't have a hose, but then again, I didn't need one.

Afterwards, I went online and found a cool arrangement of ten long-stemmed blue iris and ten yellow roses. School colors. Awesome! They'd be perfect to send to Bill. I didn't talk to Dad about it. He was such a guy, and he wouldn't believe I wanted to give flowers to Bill. I headed for Mom's sewing room. She listened to everything. She totally understood how I felt. And she loaned me her credit card. Yippee! I'd have to pay her back from my first check at the Mustang Corral. That was cool. Now, the flower arrangement would truly be from me.

* * * *

Wednesday, October 30th, 3:30 p.m.

The meet was back in Snohomish this week. I spotted my parents and Jack in the grandstand with Mrs. Bartlett. Leaving Harry to run the lot, Brenna had shown up with her guy who wore camouflage, another beret, and more combat boots. They sat next to the rest of my personal cheering squad. I popped up to show Mrs. B. the latest pics of Twaziem. Rocky had saddled and bridled him for the first time yesterday, so he looked almost like a horse.

"Is it my imagination or is he a bit thin?" Sergeant Dawson gave me a wary look. "Just a question, not an accusation."

"Don't worry," I told him. "They don't allow me to have a hose at the meets. And he's gained a lot of weight in the last six weeks. The vet says he's put on almost two hundred pounds."

"Do I want to know what you did with a hose, Robbie?" Dad asked.

"I handled it since it happened at the Corral," Brenna told him, "And now Kyle knows to stay out of the way when we're washing cars."

"What she said." Kyle Dawson glanced past me. "Some old guy's waving at you, Robin. Is that important?"

"Yes." I looked over my shoulder. "It's my coach. Got to go. Mrs. B., you need to come see Twaz more often. He misses you."

She straightened her wig. "I will. Go win, honey."

"Are you sure about that? Your grandkids are running, too."

"You work a lot harder at things than they do, so go show them what happens when people do their best."

Good advice. I hurried down the steps and ran over to join my team. Olivia high-fived me. "We're ready to rock and roll today. Isn't that the Bartlett beasts' grandma?"

"Yeah, but she's a nice lady," I said. "And we choose our friends, not our relatives."

Coach Norris came up and gave the usual pep talk. "I know you think it's going to be easy because we're down to the end of the season and you've won all the other meets. People are going to try harder so you need to do the same. Remember—"

"Winners never quit," I started up and the rest of the team joined in, "and quitters never win!"

The long distance runners headed over to line up. Once again, we took the lead and held it. The trail was a bit cooler today. We'd had a few rains, although none of the regular storms had hit yet. Once that happened, we ran through the mud and creeks. A breeze ruffled the trees. Gold, red, and green leaves from the alders and maples scattered across the paths. We hit the groves of cedars, up and down the hills, around curves and then along the lakeshore.

The rest of my team was with me as we came down the last slope and hit the track again, running full out for the finish line. I was the first through the tunnel, followed by the rest of the Lincoln High team. I heard Jack yelling. He sounded really loud. When I looked up, I saw Bill next to him. I waved at them and kept going.

Bill wound his way through the audience and came toward me, a huge grin on his face. I was so forgiven. I ran into his arms. He scooped me up and kissed me. He wasn't mad at me anymore, and I wasn't mad at him either.

When he lifted his head, he said. "So next time you make a mistake, do I have to send flowers if I yell at you?"

"Possibly," I said, "but only if you yell at me for something that's truly not my fault."

"Okay. It's a deal." And he kissed me again.

Chapter Thirty-Three

Thursday, October 31ˢᵗ, 4:05 p.m.

I'd finished up early with the cars. I was too old to go trick or treating, but Porter was having a Halloween party at her house. I needed to do chores so I would be ready when Bill arrived. When I made the barn, Rocky was busy with Twaziem. She'd already groomed, bridled, and saddled him. Now, she was teaching him to ground drive. He didn't much like the idea so Harry was leading him. Surprisingly, my horse didn't try to chew on him.

"Why isn't he going after Harry?" I asked Dani, who was filming the class.

"Horses can see some colors," Dani said, "and he has blond hair, not black. Plus he looks thinner than Jack."

"I never thought of that."

"You might ask Jack what aftershave he uses," Dani went on. "Because they're prey animals, horses have a keen sense of smell. If Jack used the same kind of cologne as Caine, then Twaziem would associate the two of them as threats."

Those were all good points. I went off to clean stalls, wondering if I could convince my brother to wear a hat when he worked around Twaziem. If my horse didn't see black hair, perhaps he wouldn't hate Jack so much. I'd ask him to wear the same lime aftershave that Bill did and bring Twaz apples. Every little thing would help.

After I cleaned, fed, watered, and groomed the other horses, I returned to the ring. Rocky was teaching Twaziem to stop and stand square on all four feet so his weight was evenly distributed. She would lead him forward, stop, make him balance, back up, balance, jog forward, and then repeat the same pattern again.

"It's like what you do in halter class," I told Dani.

"How do you think that Lady learned it? We do this for hours to get ready for shows."

Rocky waved at me and I went to her. "Hi. What do you want me to do?"

"The same thing I was," she said. "You need to review basics with him. Keep him at a walk as much as possible. You probably take in a lot of calories when you run."

"Of course, I do. I have to or I'd pass out."

"The same goes for your horse. Hard work makes him lose weight."

"And we want him to put on the pounds," I said, "not take them off. I got it, Rocky."

I clicked to Twaziem, and we headed off to do the same pattern he'd already learned. We had a half hour more to work before I finished chores. Then, I'd go up to the house, shower, and get into my dance-hall costume for Porter's party.

* * * *

Thursday, November 7th, 3:45 p.m.

The next week rushed by. Between a haze of classes, barn work, training Twaziem, riding lessons, cross-country practices, visits from the Animal Control guy, and my internship hours with Dr. Larry no wonder sometimes I felt like I didn't have time to breathe.

The last meet was back at the park outside of Arlington where the first one took place. It'd rained a few times, and Coach Norris told us they'd changed our route to bypass the wasp nest. All we had to do was win this time and we'd be school champions. He promised us that we could hang a banner in the school gym. Mom was already designing it. Talk about having faith in us.

We lined up with the other long distance runners. Ashley Bartlett scowled at me and Wanda flipped me off. Those two so needed to get a life. I wondered where Caine was hiding. I hadn't seen him anywhere today. The starter fired his pistol and we were off, Lincoln High taking the lead as usual.

The trail wound up hill and down, twisting through the maple trees. I heard the gurgle of the creek up ahead. It was higher than last time, but I didn't have to run through it yet. I leaped over it and kept going. Out of the corner of my eye, I saw Porter right behind me. We were making great time. A log up ahead and a couple evergreen branches lay across the path. Were they the same ones we'd seen last time? We raced through a grove of pine trees.

This time, the trail led along the river. I heard a dog bark a few times, then yelp. What was going on? There shouldn't be any hikers out, not during a cross-country meet. Gwen caught up with me. She pointed and I saw Caine on the bank. He held a big white feed sack, the kind that held horse grain. A gold and white collie mix leapt around him, barking at him.

Oh my Gawd. Not again!

We ran toward him. He waited until we were closer. He swung the bag over his head. The dog went nuts. He hurled the sack right into the river. The collie broke for the bank. She dove into the water.

She. I knew it was a she. And she'd had pups. Her nipples hung down below her belly. They were still nursing.

"You son of a..." I gave him a hard shove. He landed on his butt in the path.

Then, I was past him and running for the water. It had barely rained, I told myself again and again. The water wasn't high. If I got them now, they wouldn't drown. I wouldn't let them die. I splashed into the river. The rocks slipped beneath my shoes.

"What are you doing?" Olivia screamed from the trail.

"Puppies. He threw them." I saw the bag floating ahead of me. "Send Cedar and Kanisha. They have to win."

"Okay."

I grabbed for the bag. Missed it. The mom dog snarled at me. I gave her a quick pet while I splashed toward the bag. "Come on. Let's get your babies."

I heard high pitched yelps and puppy barks now. I snagged the feed sack this time. It was heavier than it looked. Of course. It was waterlogged, or rather the pups were. I pulled it toward the bank.

Steve and Lew waded toward me. As soon as I was close enough, Lew grabbed the bag. He carried it to the bank. "If a single pup dies, I'm kicking the hell out of Caine. He's just sicko."

"We don't have time for that," Steve said. "It'll be better if the girls beat his cousins to the finish line."

"Gwen went too," Olivia said as we climbed ashore. "Hustle up. We can still get there and win."

Lew and Steve ripped into the bag. They began pulling out puppies. Porter took the first one, a black and white furball. Olivia caught the second, a little gold one. They couldn't have weighed five pounds each. The next three were even smaller. The mother danced around us, sniffing each one and us, of course. She must have realized we were helping since she didn't try to nip us.

Wet, yes. Dead, no! Thank heaven, the rainy season hadn't started. Thank Gawd, the river hadn't risen to its normal winter height, or they'd be goners. I took the next pup and snugged it close. I heard runners coming. We were losing our lead.

"Let's go. We have to win today if we want that banner my mom's making."

Still holding the pup, I turned and ran for the trail. After less than a moment, Olivia and Porter followed me. Steve whistled to the mother dog, and then he and Lew were with us. We had a race to finish. There were people ahead of us, but they wouldn't be for long. I increased my pace.

I ran six miles a day, every day. And my team ran with me, so we were beyond ready for this course. I saw Wanda ahead of me, but Caine's trick wouldn't do her any good. I booked past her, then I was by Ashley and still going. When I hit the track, there were only three girls in front of me, and they wore Lincoln High blue and gold.

Cedar was first, Kanisha second and Gwen third, but I came in fourth. They cleared the finish line funnel for us, then whirled back to meet us. "Did you save them?" Gwen demanded.

"All of them." I headed for the grass where Coach Norris waited.

"Go grab the towels."

"Why?" Kanisha asked. "We're in shape. We never use them."

Cedar elbowed her. "For the pups, you idiot. We have to dry them off before they catch cold. And I'm so telling my cousins what Caine did. He's evil. They'll kick his butt all over the rez."

The two of them headed to our bags of stuff and spoke to Coach Norris. He hurried to us. "What did you ladies find?"

"Puppies," Gwen said. "Caine threw them in the river."

"What?" He looked at me, then at the other girls and the collie dog that followed us to an open spot. "Robin, I know you have issues with the boy, but that's a serious accusation."

"And she's not making it," Gwen said. "We are."

"Got that right." Kanisha handed out towels, then dropped to her knees to rub on the adult collie. "You don't have to do anything, Coach. We'll handle it."

He looked at us again, then at Olivia and Porter as they came toward us. "I'm talking to the race officials. I can't believe you were able to save them and still come in first."

"Hey, our leader runs us at least six miles a day," Lew said. "We could have saved more dogs, but we don't want to do that again."

Coach Norris walked away. I rubbed my puppy dry, then put him down by his mother to nurse. "I wonder if they have burgers at that concession stand."

Steve handed me the gold and white female pup he'd carried. "Finish drying her and I'll go see."

"What are we doing with them?" Olivia asked me.

"I'm taking them home," I said. "We haven't had a dog in ages. They can move into the back porch."

Porter hugged her puppy tightly. His dry fur fluffed up and he licked her chin. "I want this one. Will you save him for me while I talk my folks into it?"

"You bet."

* * * *

No Horse Wanted

Thursday, November 7th, 5:45 p.m.

"I don't believe this." Smiling, Dad watched the dog family settle into the corner of the back porch. "Only you could go to a cross-country meet and bring home six dogs, Robbie."

"Blame Mom," I said. "She's the one who stopped to buy puppy kibble."

Dad wrapped his arm around my shoulders. "I can't send you girls anywhere. You know that when you tell Felicia about them, she'll want one of the babies."

"She'd have to move out of the dorm if she intends to take it to Pullman," I said. "Jack and I will look after it for her at home. Then, Lassie won't freak over losing her babies."

"Lassie?" Dad eyed me and then looked at the momma dog again, content with her family. "I can see that. She does look like the dog in the movie."

"I couldn't believe it when Officer Yardley showed up and took our statements, then sent the cops out to arrest Caine for animal cruelty," I said. "That was incredible."

My phone vibrated and I dug it out of my pocket. "It's Bill. I've got to tell him that Caine is going to jail. And after that, I'm going to the barn."

"Why?" Dad asked. "It's almost dinnertime, and I've already fed all the other animals."

"Because I have to give Twaziem carrots and tell him that he's safe." I answered my cell and told Bill all about the events at the meet.

"But, where did the dog come from?" Bill wanted to know. "Will her owners be looking for her?"

"No, she's a stray. Officer Yardley got the truth out of Wanda when he threatened to arrest her as an accessory. She said the dog was just hanging around, looking for handouts, and that was how Caine trapped her."

While I was talking, Lassie looked up from her puppies and barked. I heard the knock on the back door a moment later and went to answer it.

Bill stood there. He tucked his phone into his pocket. "Hi."

"Hey." I ended the call on mine. "I was on my way down to give

Twaz some carrots and share the good news. Want to come?"

"Always."

He took my hand and we headed for the arena together. Everything had changed in the last two months for the better. I could live with that. And it was all due to Twaziem, the horse I hadn't known I wanted.

THE END

Coming Soon...
"No Time for Horses"
Book Two of the Shamrock Stable Series

Sixteen-year-old Vicky Miller feels overloaded since her parents filed for divorce. Her mother got the house and a new job. Her step-dad has the new car and a new girlfriend. Vicky has the five kids, her younger half-brothers and sisters who range from 18 months to 10 years old to look after, and her own life now comes second to their needs and wants.

It's been six months of house-cleaning, baby-sitting, cooking, non-stop laundry and Vicky is through waiting for her life to improve. She has plans for her sophomore year at Lincoln High and they don't include being an unpaid servant. If it takes a constant battle to attend her riding classes and complete her internship at Shamrock Stable, she's ready to fight for her goal to be the best natural horse trainer around.

Her parents may not have time for her to be with horses, but she has dreams no one can steal. Why should she give them away? But, will keeping them mean she loses her family

Shannon Kennedy

About the Author

Shannon lives and works at her family business, Horse Country Farm, just outside of Granite Falls in Washington State. Teaching kids to ride and know about horses since 1967, she finds in many cases, she's taught three generations of families. Her life experiences span adventures from dealing cards in a casino, attending graduate school to get her Masters in Teaching degree, being a substitute teacher, and serving in the Army Reserve—all leading to her second career as a published author. Visit her at her website, www.shannonkennedybooks.com to learn about her books.

CPSIA information can be obtained
at www.ICGtesting.com
Printed in the USA
LVHW110922171218
600723LV00002B/386/P

9 781612 357669